THE SAINT VERSUS SCOTLAND YARD

FOREWORD BY MATT LYNN

THE ADVENTURES OF THE SAINT

Enter the Saint (1930), *The Saint Closes the Case* (1930),
The Avenging Saint (1930), *Featuring the Saint* (1931),
Alias the Saint (1931), *The Saint Meets His Match* (1931),
The Saint Versus Scotland Yard (1932), *The Saint's Getaway* (1932),
The Saint and Mr Teal (1933), *The Brighter Buccaneer* (1933),
The Saint in London (1934), *The Saint Intervenes* (1934),
The Saint Goes On (1934), *The Saint in New York* (1935),
Saint Overboard (1936), *The Saint in Action* (1937),
The Saint Bids Diamonds (1937), *The Saint Plays with Fire* (1938),
Follow the Saint (1938), *The Happy Highwayman* (1939),
The Saint in Miami (1940), *The Saint Goes West* (1942),
The Saint Steps In (1943), *The Saint on Guard* (1944),
The Saint Sees It Through (1946), *Call for the Saint* (1948),
Saint Errant (1948), *The Saint in Europe* (1953),
The Saint on the Spanish Main (1955), *The Saint Around the World* (1956),
Thanks to the Saint (1957), *Señor Saint* (1958), *Saint to the Rescue* (1959),
Trust the Saint (1962), *The Saint in the Sun* (1963),
Vendetta for the Saint (1964), *The Saint on TV* (1968),
The Saint Returns (1968), *The Saint and the Fiction Makers* (1968),
The Saint Abroad (1969), *The Saint in Pursuit* (1970),
The Saint and the People Importers (1971), *Catch the Saint* (1975),
The Saint and the Hapsburg Necklace (1976), *Send for the Saint* (1977),
The Saint in Trouble (1978), *The Saint and the Templar Treasure* (1978),
Count On the Saint (1980), *Salvage for the Saint* (1983)

THE SAINT
VERSUS
SCOTLAND
YARD

LESLIE CHARTERIS

SERIES EDITOR: IAN DICKERSON

Text copyright © 2014 Interfund (London) Ltd.
Foreword © 2014 Matt Lynn
Preface from early editions of *The Saint Versus Scotland Yard*
Introduction to "The Million Pound Day" from *The First Saint Omnibus* (October, 1939)
Publication History and Author Biography © 2014 Ian Dickerson
All rights reserved.

Published by Thomas & Mercer, Seattle

www.apub.com

ISBN-13: 9781477842676
ISBN-10: 1477842675

Cover design by David Drummond, www.salamanderhill.com

Printed in the United States of America.

To Pauline
For Happy Days

PUBLISHER'S NOTE

The text of this book has been preserved from the original edition and includes vocabulary, grammar, style, and punctuation that might differ from modern publishing practices. Every care has been taken to preserve the author's tone and meaning, allowing only minimal changes to punctuation and wording to ensure a fluent experience for modern readers.

FOREWORD TO THE

NEW EDITION

You can debate endlessly what makes the Saint such an enduring character. Partly it is the energy and wit of Leslie Charteris's writing: the stories take off at a hundred miles an hour and speed up after that. Partly because in their mixture of gadgets and exotic locations, the stories introduced a new world to readers still stuck in an old one. But for me, it is because Simon Templar was essentially a cowboy—someone who was outside the law and outside the usual confines of society, and yet who was still a hero, righting wrongs, even if it was on his own terms.

The Saint Versus Scotland Yard is one of the books in which that comes through most clearly. And nowhere more so than in the novella "The Inland Revenue."

Every writer has had his or her brushes with the Revenue. It is in the nature of the work. You get paid irregularly, often with quite large sums (followed disappointingly by very small ones), and often from a whole host of different countries, each with their own tax codes. Writers by their nature are not very good at keeping records, or bothering themselves with the details of their tax returns. Whether Leslie Charteris ever spent one of those tedious days sorting through his paperwork with a pedantic tax inspector, I don't know. I imagine he did, and whilst trying to remember whether that two hundred pounds was from Australia or Spain in 1929 or 1930, he hatched the plot for the novella "The Inland Revenue."

It is classic Saint. It turns out that Templar has written a novel, and now the Revenue is chasing him for the taxes owed on it. He doesn't have the cash. Of course, the Saint can't actually defeat Her Majesty's Revenue and Customs: that would be beyond even his powers. Instead, he hatches a cunning plan to lay his hands on the money by capturing a notorious blackmailer. It is an audacious tale, brilliantly told.

The two other stories are just as good. In "The Million Pound Day" Templar uncovers a plot to undermine a new Italian currency (a plot device that a writer might well be able to resurrect if the euro collapses). And in "The Melancholy Journey of Mr Teal" Templar sets himself the goal of amassing one hundred thousand dollars in his bank account, enough, he reckons, for him to retire (things clearly cost less in 1932 when the book was published). Both of them are a master class in concise, impactful storytelling.

Charteris was an amazingly consistent writer. He knocked out dozens of books, and there is hardly a dud among them. But these stories from his 1930s heyday are among the best, perfect for new and old fans alike.

—*Matt Lynn*

THE SAINT VERSUS SCOTLAND YARD

PREFACE:

BETWEEN OURSELVES,

BY LESLIE CHARTERIS

Now that the last line of this, the eighth book about the Saint, has been written and blotted and passed on to its fate, I begin to wonder whether anyone has realised why I should have carried on with him so long.

Eight books, comprising some twenty adventures of the same character, is a pretty impressive sequence. I am not sure if it has yet broken the record for fictional biographies, but I'm quite sure that it's going to. For there is going to be more.

And why?

Because, in spite of the wrath of *The Gotherington Gazette and Argus*, and the patronising paragraphs of *The Tarsus (Tennessee) Tribune*, I sincerely believe that those eight books were well worth writing, and that the next eight will be even better.

Personally, I like the Saint—but maybe I'm prejudiced.

He is my protest against the miserable half-heartedness of these days. To him you may say—as has always been said to me—"One day you will settle down. One day you'll lose this youthful impetuosity and impatience, and settle down to a normal life. It is one of the things that happen." But he will not believe you. Because it will not be true.

This rubbing off of corners, this settling down, this normal life! You have tried so hard to make Youth believe you, with your specious arguments about civilisation, your weight of pot-bellied disapproval, your cheap and facile sneers!

> *You have taken the wine and the laughter,*
> *The pride and the grace of days.*

You tried to make me believe you when I was younger, but I knew better. And so you shall not shake the faith of anyone who reads a line of mine.

You are surprised? You are slightly shocked that any writer of mere "thrillers" should have the impertinence to take himself seriously?

I am sorry for you.

But you may still read of the Saint. He will at least entertain you. For his philosophy—and mine—is happy. You will be bored with no dreary introspections about death and doom, as in the works of your dyspeptic little Russians. You will not find him gloating interminably over the pimples on his immortal soul, as do the characters of your septic little scribblers in Bloomsbury.

Of course, if you will only admit into the sacred realms of "literature" those adventure stories in which the fighting is done with swords and the travelling on horseback, I can only amuse your idle moments. But even that is worthwhile. I shall be a breath of fresh air to you, and it will do you a lot of good.

Or are you of our own mettle?

Then come with us. And if your faith is weakening, if you have begun to believe the lies or fear the mockery of the fools who have never been young, the Saint and I will inspire you.

We will go out and find more and more adventures. We will swagger and swashbuckle and laugh at the half-hearted. We will boast and sing and throw our weight about. We will put the paltry little things to derision, and dare to be angry about the things that are truly evil. And we shall refuse to grow old.

Being wise, we shall not rail against the days into which we have been born. We shall see stumbling blocks, but we shall find them dragons meet for our steel. And we shall not mourn the trappings and accoutrements of fancy dress. What have they to do with us? Men wore cloaks and ruffles because they were the fashionable things to wear, but it was the way they wore them. Men rode horses because they had nothing else to ride, but it was the way they rode. Men fought with swords because they knew no better weapons, but it was the way they fought. So it shall be with us.

We shall learn that romance lies not in the things we do, but in the way we do them. We shall discover that catching a bus can be no less of an adventure than capturing a galleon, and that if a man loves a lady he need not weep because the pillion of his motor-cycle is not the saddlebow of an Arab steed. We shall find that love and hate can still be more than empty words. We shall speak with fire in our eyes and in our voices, and which of us will care whether we are discussing the destiny of nations or the destination of the Ashes? For we shall know that nothing else counts beside the vision.

Hasta la vista, companeros valientes! Y vayan con Dios!

THE INLAND REVENUE

CHAPTER 1

Before the world at large had heard even one lonely rumour about the gentleman who called himself, among other things, the Scorpion, there were men who knew him in secret. They knew him only as the Scorpion, and by no other name, and where he came from and where he lived were facts that certain of them would have given much to learn.

It is merely a matter of history that one of these men had an unassailable legal right to the name of Montgomery Bird, which everyone will agree was a very jolly sort of name for a bloke to have.

Mr Montgomery Bird was a slim and very dapper little man, and although it is true he wore striped spats there were even more unpleasant things about him which were not so noticeable but which it is the chronicler's painful duty to record. He was, for instance, the sole proprietor of a night club officially entitled the Eyrie, but better and perhaps more appropriately known as the Bird's Nest, which was a very low night club. And in this club, on a certain evening, he interviewed the Scorpion.

That Simon Templar happened to be present was almost accidental.

Simon Templar, in fact, having for some time past cherished a purely business-like interest in the affairs of Mr Montgomery Bird, had decided that the time was ripe for that interest to bear its fruit.

The means by which he became a member of the Eyrie are not known. Simon Templar had his own private ways of doing these things. It is enough that he was able to enter the premises unchallenged. He was saluted by the doorkeeper, climbed the steep stairs to the converted loft in which the Eyrie had its being, collected and returned the welcoming smile of the girl at the reception desk, delivered his hat into the keeping of a liveried flunkey, and passed on unquestioned. Outside the glass doors that separated the supper-room from the lounge he paused for a moment, lighting a cigarette, while his eyes wandered lazily over the crowd. He already knew that Mr Bird was in the habit of spending the evening among his guests, and he just wanted to make sure about that particular evening. He made sure, but his subsequent and consequent movements were forced to diverge slightly from schedule, as will be seen.

Mr Bird had met the Scorpion before. When a waiter came through and informed him that a gentleman who would give no name was asking to speak to him, Mr Bird showed no surprise. He went out to the reception desk, nodded curtly to the visitor, signed him under the name of J. N. Jones, and led the way into his private office without comment.

He walked to his desk, and there he stopped and turned.

"What is it now?" he asked shortly, and the visitor shrugged his broad shoulders.

"Must I explain?"

Mr Bird sat down in his swivel chair, rested his right ankle on his left knee, and leaned back. The fingers of one carefully manicured hand played a restless tattoo on the desk.

"You had a hundred pounds only last week," he said.

"And since then you have probably made at least three hundred," replied the visitor calmly.

He sat on the arm of another chair, and his right hand remained in the pocket of his overcoat. Mr Bird, gazing at the pocket, raised one cynical eyebrow.

"You look after yourself well."

"An elementary precaution."

"Or an elementary bluff."

The visitor shook his head.

"You might test it—if you are tired of life."

Mr Bird smiled, stroking his small moustache.

"With that—and your false beard and smoked glasses—you're an excellent imitation of a blackguard," he said.

"The point is not up for discussion," said the visitor smoothly. "Let us confine ourselves to the object of my presence here. Must I repeat that I know you to be a trader in illicit drugs? In this very room, probably, there is enough material evidence to send you to penal servitude for five years. The police, unaided, might search for it in vain. The secret of your ingenious little hiding-place under the floor in that corner might defy their best efforts. They do not know that it will only open when the door of this room is locked and the third and fifth sections of the wainscoting on that wall are slid upwards. But suppose they were anonymously informed—"

"And then found nothing there," said Montgomery Bird, with equal suavity.

"There would still be other suggestions that I could make," said the visitor.

He stood up abruptly.

"I hope you understand me," he said. "Your offences are no concern of mine, but they would be a great concern of yours if you were placed in the dock to answer for them. They are also too profitable for you to be ready to abandon them—yet. You will therefore pay me one hundred pounds a week for as long as I choose to demand it. Is that sufficiently plain?"

"You—"

Montgomery Bird came out of his chair with a rush.

The bearded man was not disturbed. Only his right hand, in his overcoat pocket, moved slightly.

"My—er—elementary bluff is still waiting your investigation," he said dispassionately, and the other stopped dead.

With his head thrust a little forward, he stared into the tinted lenses that masked the big man's eyes.

"One day I'll get you—you—swine."

"And until that day, you will continue to pay me one hundred pounds a week, my dear Mr Bird," came the gentle response. "Your next contribution is already due. If it is not troubling you too much—"

He did not bother to complete the sentence. He simply waited.

Bird went back to the desk and opened a drawer. He took out an envelope and threw it on the blotter.

"Thank you," said the visitor.

His fingers had just touched the envelope when the shrill scream of a bell froze him into immobility. It was not an ordinary bell. It had a vociferous viciousness about it that stung the eardrums—something like the magnified buzzing of an infuriated wasp.

"What is that?"

"My private alarm."

Bird glanced at the illuminated clock on the mantelpiece, and the visitor, following the glance, saw that the dial had turned red.

"A police raid?"

"Yes."

The big man picked up the envelope and thrust it into his pocket.

"You will get me out of here," he said.

Only a keen ear would have noticed the least fraying of the edges of his measured accents, but Montgomery Bird noticed it, and looked at him curiously.

"If I didn't—"

"You would be foolish—very foolish," said the visitor quietly.

Bird moved back, with murderous eyes. Set in one wall was a large mirror; he put his hands to the frame of it and pushed it bodily sideways in invisible grooves, revealing a dark rectangular opening.

And it was at that moment that Simon Templar, for his own inscrutable reasons, tired of his voluntary exile.

"Stand clear of the lift gates, please," he murmured.

To the two men, wheeling round at the sound of his voice like a pair of marionettes whose control wires have got mixed up with a dynamo, it seemed as if he had appeared out of the fourth dimension. Just for an instant. And then they saw the open door of the capacious cupboard behind him.

"Pass right down the car, gents," he murmured, encouragingly.

He crossed the room. He appeared to cross it slowly, but that, again, was an illusion. He had reached the two men before either of them could move. His left hand shot out and fastened on the lapels of the bearded man's coat—and the bearded man vanished. It was the most startling thing that Mr Montgomery Bird had ever seen, but the Saint did not seem to be aware that he was multiplying miracles with an easy grace that would have made a Grand Lama look like a third-rate three-card man. He calmly pulled the sliding mirror back into place, and turned round again.

"No—not you, Montgomery," he drawled. "We may want you again this evening. Back-pedal, comrade."

His arm telescoped languidly outwards, and the hand at the end of it seized the retreating Mr Bird by one ear, fetching him up with a jerk that made him squeak in muted anguish.

Simon steered him firmly but rapidly towards the open cupboard.

"You can cool off in there," he said, and the next sensations that impinged upon Montgomery Bird's delirious consciousness consisted of a lot of darkness and the sound of a key turning in the cupboard lock.

The Saint straightened his coat and returned to the centre of the room.

He sat down in Mr Bird's chair, put his feet on Mr Bird's desk, lighted one of Mr Bird's cigars, and gazed at the ceiling with an expression of indescribable beatitude on his face, and it was thus that Chief Inspector Claud Eustace Teal found him.

Some seconds passed before the detective recovered the use of his voice, but when he had done this, he made up for lost time.

"What," he snarled, "the blankety blank blanking blank-blanked blank—"

"Hush," said the Saint.

"Why?" snarled Teal, not unreasonably.

Simon held up his hand.

"Listen."

There was a moment's silence, and then Teal's glare re-calorified.

"What am I supposed to be listening to?" he demanded violently, and the Saint beamed at him.

"Down in the forest something stirred—it was only the note of a bird," he explained sweetly.

The detective centralised his jaw with a visible effort.

"Is Montgomery Bird another of your fancy names?" he inquired, with a certain lusciousness. "Because, if it is—"

"Yes, old dear?"

"If it is," said Chief Inspector Teal grimly, "you're going to see the inside of a prison at last."

Simon regarded him imperturbably.

"On what charge?"

"You're going to get as long as I can get you for allowing drinks to be sold in your club after hours—"

"And then—?"

The detective's eyes narrowed.

"What do you mean?"

Simon flourished Mr Bird's cigar airily.

"I always understood that the police were pretty bone-headed," he remarked genially, "but I never knew before that they'd been reduced to employing Chief Inspectors for ordinary drinking raids."

Teal said nothing.

"On the other hand, a dope raid is quite a different matter," said the Saint.

He smiled at the detective's sudden stillness, and stood up, knocking an inch of ash from his cigar.

"I must be toddling along," he murmured. "If you really want to find some dope, and you've any time to spare after you've finished cleaning up the bar, you ought to try locking the door of this room and pulling up bits of wainscoting. The third and fifth sections—I can't tell you which wall. Oh, and if you want Montgomery, he's simmering down in the Frigidaire . . . See you again soon."

He patted the crown of Mr Teal's bowler hat affectionately, and was gone before the detective had completely grasped what was happening.

The Saint could make those well-oiled exits when he chose, and he chose to make one then, for he was a fundamentally tactful man. Also, he had in one pocket an envelope purporting to contain one hundred pounds, and in another pocket the entire contents of Mr Montgomery Bird's official safe, and at such times the Saint did not care to be detained.

CHAPTER 2

Simon Templar pushed back his plate.

"Today," he announced, "I have reaped the first-fruits of virtue."

He raised the letter he had received, and adjusted an imaginary pair of pince-nez. Patricia waited expectantly. The Saint read:

Dear Mr Templar,

Having come across a copy of your book "The Pirate" and having nothing to do I sat down to read it. Well, the impression it gave me was that you are a writer with no sense of proportion. The reader's sympathy owing to the faulty setting of the first chapter naturally goes all the way with Kerrigan, even though he is a crook. It is not surprising that this book has not gone to a second edition. You do not evidently understand the mentality of an English reading public. If instead of Mario you had selected for your hero an Englishman or an American, you would have written a fairly readable and a passable tale—but a lousy Dago who

*works himself out of impossible difficulties and situations is
too much. It is not convincing. It does not appeal. In a word
it is puerile.*

*I fancy you yourself must have a fair amount of Dago blood
in you—*

He stopped, and Patricia Holm looked at him puzzledly.
"Well?" she prompted.

"There is no more," explained the Saint. "No address—no
signature—no closing peroration—nothing. Apparently words failed
him. At that point he probably uttered a short sharp yelp of intolerable
agony, and began to chew pieces out of the furniture. We may never
know his fate. Possibly, in some distant asylum—"

He elaborated on his theory.

During a brief spell of virtue some time before, the Saint had
beguiled himself with the writing of a novel. Moreover, he had actually
succeeded in finding a home for it, and the adventures of Mario, a
super-brigand of South America, could be purchased at any bookstall
for three half-crowns. And the letter that he had just read was part of
his reward.

Another part of the reward had commenced six months previously.

"Nor is this all," said the Saint, taking another document from
the table. "The following *billet-doux* appears to close some entertaining
correspondence:

*Previous applications for payment of the under-mentioned
instalment for the year 1931–1932, due from you on the
1st day January, 1932, having been made to you without
effect, Personal Demand is now made for payment, and I
Hereby Give You Final Notice that if the amount be not*

11

paid or remitted to me at the above address within Seven Days from this date, steps will be taken for recovery by Distraint, with costs.

Lionel Delborn, Collector.

In spite of the gloomy prognostications of the anonymous critic, *The Pirate* had not passed utterly unnoticed in the spate of sensational fiction. The Intelligence Department ("A beautiful name for them," said the Saint) of the Inland Revenue had observed its appearance, had consulted their records, and had discovered that the author, the notorious Simon Templar, was not registered as a contributor towards the expensive extravagances whereby a modern boobocracy does its share in encouraging the survival of the fattest. The Saint's views about his liabilities in this cause were not invited: he simply received an assessment which presumed his income to be six thousand pounds per annum, and he was invited to appeal against it if he thought fit. The Saint thought fit, and declared that the assessment was bad in law, erroneous in principle, excessive in amount, and malicious in intent. The discussion that followed was lengthy and diverting; the Saint, conducting his own case with remarkable forensic ability and eloquence, pleaded that he was a charitable institution and therefore not taxable.

"If," said the Saint, in his persuasive way, "you will look up the delightful words of Lord Macnaghten, in *Income Tax Commissioners v. Pemsel*, 1891, A.C. at p. 583, you will find that charitable purposes are there defined in four principal divisions, of which the fourth is *'trusts for purposes beneficial to the community, not falling under any of the preceding heads.'* I am simply and comprehensively beneficial to the community, which the face of the third Commissioner from the left definitely is not."

We find from the published record of the proceedings that he was overruled, and the epistle he had just quoted was final and conclusive proof of the fact.

"And that," said the Saint, gazing at the formidable red lettering gloomily, "is what I get for a lifetime of philanthropy and self-denial."

"I suppose you'll have to pay," said Patricia.

"*Someone* will," said the Saint significantly.

He propped the printed buff envelope that had accompanied the Final Demand against the coffee-pot, and his eyes rested on it for a space with a gentle thoughtfulness—amazingly clear, devil-may-care blue eyes with a growing glimmer of mischief lurking somewhere behind the lazily drooping lids.

And slowly the old Saintly smile came to his lips as he contemplated the address.

"Someone will have to pay," repeated the Saint thoughtfully, and Patricia Holm sighed, for she knew the signs.

And suddenly the Saint stood up, with his swift soft laugh, and took the Final Demand and the envelope over to the fireplace. On the wall close by hung a plain block calendar, and on the mantelpiece lay an old Corsican stiletto. "*Che la mia ferita sia mortale,*" said the inscription on the blade.

The Saint rapidly flicked over the pages of the calendar and tore out the sheet which showed in solid red figures the day on which Mr Lionel Delborn's patience would expire. He placed the sheet on top of the other papers, and with one quick thrust he drove the stiletto through the collection and speared it deep into the panelled overmantel.

"Lest we forget," he said, and turned with another laugh to smile seraphically into Patricia's outraged face. "I just wasn't born to be respectable, lass, and that's all there is to it. And the time has come for us to remember the old days."

As a matter of fact, he had made that decision two full weeks before, and Patricia had known it, but not until then had he made his open declaration of war.

At eight o'clock that evening he was sallying forth in quest of an evening's innocent amusement, and a car that had been standing in the darkness at the end of the cul-de-sac of Upper Berkeley Mews suddenly switched on its headlights and roared towards him. The Saint leapt back and fell on his face in the doorway, and he heard the *plop* of a silenced gun and the thud of a bullet burying itself in the woodwork above his head. He slid out into the mews again as the car went past, and fired twice as it swung into Berkeley Square, but he could not tell whether he did any damage.

He returned to brush his clothes, and then continued calmly on his way, and when he met Patricia later he did not think it necessary to mention the incident that had delayed him. But it was the third time since the episode chez Bird that the Scorpion had tried to kill him, and no one knew better than Simon Templar that it would not be the last attempt.

CHAPTER 3

For some days past, the well-peeled eye might at intervals have observed a cadaverous and lantern-jawed individual protruding about six and a half feet upwards from the cobbled paving of Upper Berkeley Mews. Simon Templar, having that sort of eye, had in fact noticed the apparition on its first and in all its subsequent visits, and anyone less well-informed than himself might pardonably have suspected some connection between the lanky boulevardier and the recent disturbances of the peace. Simon Templar, however, was not deceived.

"That," he said once, in answer to Patricia's question, "is Mr Harold Garrot, better known as Long Harry. He is a moderately proficient burglar, and we have met before, but not professionally. He is trying to make up his mind to come and tell me something, and one of these days he will take the plunge."

The Saint's deductions were vindicated twenty-four hours after the last firework display.

Simon was alone. The continued political activities of a certain newspaper proprietor had driven him to verse, and he was covering a sheet of foolscap with the beginning of a minor epic expressing his own views on the subject:

Charles Charleston Charlemagne St Charles
Was wont to utter fearful snarls
When by professors he was pressed
To note how England had progressed
Since the galumptious, gory days
Immortalised in Shakespeare's plays.
For him, no Transatlantic flights,
Ford motor-cars, electric lights,
Or radios at less than cost
Could compensate for what he lost
By chancing to coagulate
About five hundred years too late.
Born in the only days for him
He would have swung a sword with vim,
Grown ginger whiskers on his face,
And mastered, with a knobbly mace,
Men who wore hauberks on their chests
Instead of little woolen vests.
And drank strong wine among his peers
Instead of pale synthetic beers.

At this point, the trend of his inspiration led the Saint on a brief excursion to the barrel in one corner of the room. He replenished his tankard, drank deeply, and continued:

Had he not reason to be glum
When born in nineteen umpty-um?

And there, for the moment, he stuck, and he was cogitating the possible developments of the next stanza when he was interrupted by the *zing!* of the front door bell.

As he stepped out into the hall, he glanced up through the fanlight above the door at the mirror that was cunningly fixed to the underneath of the hanging lantern outside. He recognised the caller at once, and opened the door without hesitation.

"Come in, Harry," invited the Saint cordially, and led the way back to the sitting-room. "I was busy with a work of art that is going to make Milton look like a distant relative of the gargle, but I can spare you a few minutes."

Long Harry glanced at the sheet half-covered with the Saint's neat handwriting.

"Poetry, Mr Templar? We used to learn poetry at school," he said reminiscently.

Simon looked at him thoughtfully for two or three seconds, and then he beamed.

"Harry, you hit the nail on the head. For that suggestion, I pray that your shadow may always be jointed at the elbows. Excuse me one moment."

He plumped himself back in his chair and wrote at speed. Then he cleared his throat, and read aloud:

> *Eton and Oxford failed to floor*
> *The spirit of the warrior;*
> *Though ragged and bullied, teased and hissed,*
> *Charles stayed a Medievalist;*
> *And even when his worldly Pa*
> *(Regarding him with nausea)*
> *Condemned him to the dismal cares*
> *Of sordid trade in stocks and shares,*

Charles, in top-hat and Jaeger drawers,
Clung like a limpet to his Cause,
Believing, in a kind of trance,
That one day he would have his Chance.

He laid the sheet down reverently.

"A mere pastime for me, but I believe Milton used to sweat blood over it," he remarked complacently. "Soda or water, Harry?"

"Neat, please, Mr Templar."

Simon brought over the glass of Highland cream, and Long Harry sipped it, and crossed and uncrossed his legs awkwardly.

"I hope you don't mind my coming to see you, sir," he ventured at last.

"Not at all," responded the Saint heartily. "Always glad to see any Eton boys here. What's the trouble?"

Long Harry fidgeted, twiddling his fingers and corrugating his brow. He was the typical "old lag," or habitual criminal, which is to say that outside of business hours he was a perfectly ordinary man of slightly less than average intelligence and rather more than average cunning. On this occasion he was plainly and ordinarily ill at ease, and the Saint surmised that he had only begun to solve his worries when he mustered up the courage to give that single, brief, and symptomatic ring at the front door bell.

Simon lighted a cigarette and waited impassively, and presently his patience reaped its harvest.

"I wondered—I thought maybe I could tell you something that might interest you, Mr Templar."

"Sure." The Saint allowed a thin jet of smoke to trickle through his lips, and continued to wait.

"It's about . . . it's about the Scorpion, Mr Templar."

Instantaneously the Saint's eyes narrowed, the merest fraction of a millimetre, and the inhalation that he drew from his cigarette was long and deep and slow. And then the stare that he swivelled round in the direction of Long Harry was wide blue innocence itself.

"What Scorpion?" he inquired blandly.

Long Harry frowned.

"I thought you'd've known about the Scorpion, of course, Mr Templar, you being—"

"Yeah?"

Simon drawled out the prompting diphthong in a honeyed slither up a gently persuasive G-string, and Long Harry shuffled his feet uncomfortably.

"Well, you remember what you used to be, Mr Templar. There wasn't much you didn't know in those days."

"Oh, yes—once upon a time. But now—"

"Last time we met, sir—"

The Saint's features relaxed, and he smiled.

"Forget it, Harold," he advised quietly. "I'm now a respectable citizen. I was a respectable citizen the last time we met, and I haven't changed. You may tell me anything you like, Harry —as one respectable citizen to another—but I'd recommend you to forget the interview as you step over the front door mat. I shall do the same—it's safer."

Long Harry nodded.

"If you forget it, sir, it'll be safer for me," he said seriously.

"I have a hopeless memory," said the Saint carefully. "I've already forgotten your name. In another minute, I shan't be sure that you're here at all. Now shoot the dope, son."

"You've got nothing against me, sir?"

"Nothing. You're a professional burglar, housebreaker, and petty larcenist, but that's no concern of mine. Teal can attend to your little mistakes."

"And you'll forget what I'm going to say—soon as ever I've said it?"

"You heard me."

"Well, Mr Templar—" Long Harry cleared his throat, took another pull at his drink, and blinked nervously for some seconds. "I've worked for the Scorpion, Mr Templar," he said suddenly.

Simon Templar never moved a muscle.

"Yes?"

"Only once, sir—so far." Once having left the diving-board, Long Harry floundered on recklessly. "And there won't be a second time— not if I can help it. He's dangerous. You ain't never safe with him. I know. Sent me a message he did, through the post. Knew where I was staying, though I'd only been there two days, an' everything about me. There was five one-pound notes in the letter, and he said if I met a car that'd be waiting at the second milestone north of Hatfield at nine o'clock last Thursday night there'd be another fifty for me to earn."

"What sort of car was it?"

"I never had a chance to notice it properly, Mr Templar. It was a big, dark car, I think. It hadn't any lights. I was going to tell you—I was a bit suspicious at first. I thought it must be a plant, but it was that talk of fifty quid that tempted me. The car was waiting for me when I got there. I went up and looked in the window, and there was a man there at the wheel. Don't ask me what he looked like—he kept his head down, and I never saw more than the top of his hat. 'Those are your instructions,' he says, pushing an envelope at me, he says, 'and there's half your money. I'll meet you here at the same time tomorrow.' And then he drove off. I struck a match, and found he'd given me the top halves of fifty pound notes."

"And then?"

"Then—I went an' did the job, Mr Templar."

"What job?"

"I was to go to a house at St Albans and get some papers. There was a map, an' a plan, an' all about the locks an' everything. I had my tools—I forgot to tell you the first letter said I was to bring them—and it was as easy as the orders said it would be. Friday night, I met the car as arranged, and handed over the papers, and he gave me the other halves of the notes."

Simon extended a lean brown hand.

"The orders?" he inquired briefly.

He took the cheap yellow envelope, and glanced through the contents. There was, as Long Harry had said, a neatly-drawn map and plan, and the other information, in a studiously characterless copperplate writing, covered two more closely written sheets.

"You've no idea whose house it was you entered?"

"None at all, sir."

"Did you look at these papers?"

"Yes." Long Harry raised his eyes and looked at the Saint sombrely. "That's the one reason why I came to you, sir."

"What were they?"

"They were love-letters, sir. There was an address—64 Half Moon Street. And they were signed—'Mark.'"

Simon passed a hand over his sleekly perfect hair.

"Oh yes?" he murmured.

"You saw the Sunday papers, sir?"

"I did."

Long Harry emptied his glass, and put it down with clumsy fingers.

"Sir Mark Deverest shot 'imself at 64 'Alf Moon Street, on Saturday night," he said huskily.

When he was agitated, he occasionally lost an aspirate, and it was an index of his perturbation that he actually dropped two in that one sentence.

"That's the Scorpion's graft, Mr Templar—blackmail. I never touched black in my life, but I'd heard that was his game. An' when he sent for me, I forgot it. Even when I was looking through those letters, it never seemed to come into my head why he wanted them. But I see it all now. He wanted 'em to put the black on Deverest, an' Deverest shot himself instead of paying up. And—I 'elped to murder 'im, Mr Templar. Murder, that's what it was. Nothing less. An' I 'elped!" Long Harry's voice fell to a throaty whisper, and his dull eyes shifted over the clear-etched contours of the Saint's tanned face in a kind of panic of anxiety. "I never knew what I was doing, Mr Templar, sir—strike me dead if I did—"

Simon reached forward and crushed out his cigarette in an ashtray.

"Is that all you came to tell me?" he asked dispassionately, and Long Harry gulped.

"I thought you'd be laying for the Scorpion, sir, knowing you always used to be—"

"Yeah?"

Again that mellifluous dissyllable, in a voice that you could have carved up with a wafer of butter.

"Well, sir, what I mean is, if you were the Saint, sir, and if you hadn't forgotten that you might ever have been him, you might—"

"Be hunting scorpions?"

"That's the way I thought it out, sir."

"And?"

"I was hanging around last night, Mr Templar, trying to make up my mind to come and see you, and I saw the shooting."

"And?"

"That car—it was just like the car that met me out beyond Hatfield, sir."

"And?"

"I thought p'raps it was the same car."

"And?"

Simon prompted him for the fourth time from the corner table where he was replenishing Long Harry's glass. His back was turned, but there was an inconspicuous little mirror just above the level of the eyes—the room was covered from every angle by those inconspicuous little mirrors. And he saw the twitching of Long Harry's mouth.

"I came because I thought you might be able to stop the Scorpion getting me, Mr Templar," said Long Harry, in one jerk.

"Ah!" The Saint swung round. "That's more like it! So you're on the list, are you?"

"I think so." Long Harry nodded. "There was a shot aimed at me last night, too, but I suppose you wouldn't've noticed it."

Simon Templar lighted another cigarette.

"I see. The Scorpion spotted you hanging around here, and tried to bump you off. That's natural. But, Harry, you never even started hanging around here until you got the idea you might like to tell me the story of your life—and still you haven't told me where that idea came from. Sing on, Harry—I'm listening, and I'm certainly patient."

Long Harry absorbed a gill of Maison Dewar in comparative silence, and wiped his lips on the back of his hand.

"I had another letter on Monday morning, telling me to be at the same place at midnight tomorrow."

"And?"

"Monday afternoon I was talking to some friends. I didn't tell 'em anything, but I sort of steered the conversation around, not bringing myself in personal. You remember Wilbey?"

"Found full of bullets on the Portsmouth Road three months ago? Yes—I remember."

"I heard—it's just a story, but I heard the last job he did was for the Scorpion. He talked about it. The bloke shot himself that time, too.

An' I began thinking. It may surprise you, Mr Templar, but sometimes I'm very si-chick."

"You worked it out that as long as the victims paid up, everything was all right. But if they did anything desperate, there was always a chance of trouble, and the Scorpion wouldn't want anyone who could talk running about without a muzzle. That right?"

Long Harry nodded, and his prominent Adam's apple flickered once up and down.

"Yes, I think if I keep that appointment tomorrow I'll be—what's that American word?—on the spot. Even if I don't go—" The man broke off with a shrug that made a feeble attempt at bravado. "I couldn't take that story of mine to the police, Mr Templar, as you'll understand, and I wondered—"

Simon Templar settled a little deeper into his chair and sent a couple of perfect smoke-rings chasing each other up towards the ceiling.

He understood Long Harry's thought processes quite clearly. Long Harry was a commonplace and more or less peaceful yegg, and violence was not among the most prominent interests of his life. Long Harry, as the Saint knew, had never even carried so much as a life-preserver . . . The situation was obvious.

But how the situation was to be turned to account—that required a second or two's meditation. Perhaps two seconds. And then the little matter of spoon-feeding that squirming young pup of a plan up to a full-sized man-eating carnivore hopping around on its own pads . . . maybe five seconds more. And then—

"We deduce," said the Saint dreamily, "that our friend had arranged for you to die tomorrow, but when he found you on the outskirts of the scenery last night, he thought he might save himself a journey."

"That's the way I see it, Mr Templar."

"From the evidence before us, we deduce that he isn't the greatest snap shot in the world. And so—"

"Yes, Mr Templar?"

"It looks to me, Harry," said the Saint pleasantly, "as if you'll have to die tomorrow after all."

CHAPTER 4

Simon was lingering over a cigarette and his last breakfast cup of coffee when Mr Teal dropped in at half-past eleven next morning.

"Have you breakfasted?" asked the Saint hospitably. "I can easily hash you up an egg or something—"

"Thanks," said Teal, "I had breakfast at eight."

"A positively obscene hour," said the Saint.

He went to an inlaid smoking-cabinet, and solemnly transported a new and virginal packet of spearmint into the detective's vicinity.

"Make yourself at home, Claud Eustace. And why are we thus honoured?"

There was a gleaming automatic, freshly cleaned and oiled, beside the breakfast-tray, and Teal's sleepy eyes fell on it as he undressed some Wrigley. He made no comment at that point, and continued his somnambulation round the room. Before the papers pinned to the overmantel, he paused.

"You going to contribute your just share towards the expenses of the nation?" he inquired.

"Someone is going to," answered the Saint calmly.

"Who?"

"Talking of scorpions, Teal—"

The detective revolved slowly, and his baby eyes suddenly drooped as if in intolerable ennui.

"What scorpions?" he demanded, and the Saint laughed.

"Pass it up, Teal, old stoat. That one's my copyright."

Teal frowned heavily.

"Does this mean the old game again, Saint?"

"Teal! Why bring that up?"

The detective gravitated into a pew.

"What have you got to say about scorpions?"

"They have stings in their tails."

Teal's chewing continued with rhythmic monotonousness.

"When did you become interested in the Scorpion?" he questioned casually.

"I've been interested for some time," murmured the Saint. "Just recently, though, the interest's become a shade too mutual to be healthy. Did you know the Scorpion was an amateur!" he added abruptly.

"Why do you think that?"

"I don't think it—I know it. The Scorpion is raw. That's one reason why I shall have to tread on him. I object to being shot up by amateurs—I feel it's liable to lower my stock. And as for being finally killed by an amateur . . . Teal, put it to yourself!"

"How do you know this?"

The Saint renewed his cigarette at leisure.

"Deduction. The Sherlock Holmes stuff again. I'll teach you the trick one day, but I can give you this result out flat. Do you want chapter and verse?"

"I'd be interested."

"O.K." The Saint leaned back. "A man came and gave me some news about the Scorpion last night, after hanging around for three days—and he's still alive. I was talking to him on the phone only half an hour ago. If the Scorpion had been a real professional, that man would never even have seen me—let alone have been alive to ring me up this morning. That's one point."

"What's the next?"

"You remember the Portsmouth Road murder?"

"Yes."

"Wilbey had worked for the Scorpion, and he was a possible danger. If you'll consult your records, you'll find that Wilbey was acquitted on a charge of felonious loitering six days before he died. It was exactly the same with the bird who came to see me last night. He had also worked for the Scorpion, and he was discharged at Bow Street only two days before the Scorpion sent for him. Does that spell anything to you?"

Teal crinkled his forehead.

"Not yet, but I'm trying."

"Let me save you the trouble."

"No—just a minute. The Scorpion was in court when the charges were dismissed—"

"Exactly. And he followed them home. It's obvious. If you or I wanted someone to do a specialised bit of crime—say burglary, for instance—in thirty hours we could lay our hands on thirty men we could commission. But the genuine aged-in-the-wood amateur hasn't got those advantages, however clever he may be. He simply hasn't got the connections. You can't apply for cracksmen to the ordinary labour exchange, or advertise for them in *The Times*, and if you're a respectable amateur you haven't any among your intimate friends. What's the only way you can get hold of them?"

Teal nodded slowly.

"It's an idea," he admitted. "I don't mind telling you we've looked over all the regulars long ago. The Scorpion doesn't come into the catalogue. There isn't a nose on the pay-roll who can get a whiff of him. He's something right outside our register of established clients."

The name of the Scorpion had first been mentioned nine months before, when a prominent Midland cotton-broker had put his head in a gas-oven and forgotten to turn off the gas. In a letter that was read at the inquest occurred the words: *"I have been bled for years, and now I can endure no more. When the Scorpion stings, there is no antidote but death."*

And in the brief report of the proceedings:

THE CORONER: Have you any idea what the deceased meant by that reference to a scorpion?

WITNESS: No.

THE CORONER: Is there any professional blackmailer known to the police by that name?—I have never heard it before.

And thereafter, for the general run of respectable citizens from whom the Saint expressly dissociated Teal and himself, the rest had been a suavely expanding blank . . .

But through that vast yet nebulous area popularly called "the underworld" began to voyage vague rumours, growing more and more wild and fantastic as they passed from mouth to mouth, but still coming at last to the respective ears of Scotland Yard with enough credible vitality to be interesting. Kate Allfield, "the Mug," entered a railway carriage in which a Member of Parliament was travelling alone on a flying visit to his constituency: he stopped the train at Newbury and gave her in charge, and when her counter-charge of assault broke down under ruthless cross-examination she "confessed" that she had acted on the instigation of an unknown accomplice. Kate had tried many ways of making easy money, and the fact that the case in question was a new one in her history meant little. But round the underworld travelled two words of comment and explanation, and those two words said simply "The Scorpion."

"Basher" Tope—thief, motor-bandit, brute, and worse—was sent for. He boasted in his cups of how he was going to solve the mystery of the Scorpion, and went alone to his appointment. What happened there he never told; he was absent from his usual haunts for three weeks, and when he was seen again he had a pink scar on his temple and a surly disinclination to discuss the matter. Since he had earned his nickname, questions were not showered upon him, but once again the word went round . . .

And so it was with half a dozen subsequent incidents, and the legend of the Scorpion grew up and was passed from hand to hand in queer places, unmarked by sensation-hunting journalists, a mystery for police and criminals alike. Jack Wilbey, ladder larcenist, died and won his niche in the structure, but the newspapers noted his death only as another unsolved crime on which to peg their perennial criticisms of police efficiency, and only those who had heard other chapters of the story linked up that murder with the suicide of a certain wealthy peer. Even Chief Inspector Teal, whose finger was on the pulse of every unlawful activity in the Metropolis, had not visualized such a connecting link as the Saint had just forged before his eyes, and he pondered over it in a ruminative silence before he resumed his interrogation.

"How much else do you know?" he asked at length, with the mere ghost of a quickening of interest in his perpetually weary voice.

The Saint picked up a sheet of paper.

"Listen," he said.

His faith was true: though once misled

By an appeal that he had read
To honour with his patronage
Crusades for better Auction Bridge
He was not long deceived; he found
No other paladins around
Prepared to perish, sword in hand,
While storming in one reckless band
Those strongholds of Beelzebub
The portals of the Portland Club.
His chance came later; one fine day
Another paper blew his way:
Charles wrote; Charles had an interview;
And Charles, an uncrowned jousting Blue,
Still spellbound by the word Crusade,
Espoused the cause of Empire Trade.

"What on earth's that?" demanded the startled detective.

"A little masterpiece of mine," said the Saint modestly. "There's rather an uncertain rhyme in it, if you noticed. Do you think the Poet Laureate would pass patronage and Bridge? I'd like your opinion."

Teal's eyelids lowered again.

"Have you stopped talking?" he sighed.

"Very nearly, Teal," said the Saint, putting the paper down again. "In case that miracle of tact was too subtle for you, let me explain that I was changing the subject."

"I see."

"Do you?"

Teal glanced at the automatic on the table and then again at the papers on the wall, and sighed a second time.

"I think so. You're going to ask the Scorpion to pay your income tax."

"I am."

"How?"

The Saint laughed. He pointed to the desecrated overmantel.

"One thousand three hundred and thirty-seven pounds, nineteen and five-pence," he said. "That's my sentence for being a useful wage-earning citizen instead of a prolific parasite, according to the laws of this spavined country. Am I supposed to pay you and do your work as well? If so, I shall emigrate on the next boat and become a naturalised Venezuelan."

"I wish you would," said Teal, from his heart.

He picked up his hat.

"Do you know the Scorpion?" he asked suddenly.

Simon shook his head.

"Not yet. But I'm going to. His donation is not yet assessed, but I can tell you where one thousand three hundred and thirty-eight pounds of it are going to travel. And that is towards the offices of Mr Lionel Delborn, collector of extortions—may his teeth fall out and his legs putrefy! I'll stand the odd seven-pence out of my own pocket."

"And what do you think you're going to do with the man himself?"

The Saint smiled.

"That's a little difficult to say," he murmured. "Accidents sort of—er—happen, don't they? I mean, I don't want you to start getting back any of your naughty old ideas about me, but—"

Teal nodded; then he met the Saint's mocking eyes seriously.

"They'd have the coat on my back if it ever got round," he said, "but between you and me and these four walls, I'll make a deal—if you'll make one too."

Simon settled on the edge of the table, his cigarette slanting quizzically upwards between his lips, and one whimsically sardonic eyebrow arched.

"What is it?"

"Save the Scorpion for me, and I won't ask how you paid your income tax."

For a few moments the Saint's noncommittal gaze rested on the detective's round red face; then it wandered back to the impaled memorandum above the mantelpiece. And then the Saint looked Teal in the eyes and smiled again.

"O.K.," he drawled. "That's O.K. with me, Claud."

"It's a deal?"

"It is. There's a murder charge against the Scorpion, and I don't see why the hangman shouldn't earn his fiver. I guess it's time you had a break, Claud Eustace. Yes—you can have the Scorpion. Any advance on four-pence?"

Teal nodded, and held out his hand.

"Four-pence half-penny—I'll buy you a glass of beer at any pub inside the three-mile radius on the day you bring him in," he said.

CHAPTER 5

Patricia Holm came in shortly after four-thirty. Simon Templar had lunched at what he always referred to as "the pub round the corner"—the Berkeley—and had ambled elegantly about the purlieus of Piccadilly for an hour thereafter, for he had scarcely learned to walk two consecutive steps when his dear old grandmother had taken him on her knee and enjoined him to "eat, drink, and be merry, for tomorrow is Shrove Tuesday."

He was writing when she arrived, but he put down his pen and surveyed her solemnly.

"Oh, there you are," he remarked. "I thought you were dead, but Teal said he thought you might only have taken a trip to Vladivostok."

"I've been helping Eileen Wiltham—her wedding's only five days away. Haven't you any more interest in her?"

"None," said the Saint callously. "The thought of the approaching crime makes my mind feel unbinged—unhinged. I've already refused three times to assist Charles to select pyjamas for the bridal chamber. I told him that when he'd been married as often as I have—"

"That'll do," said Patricia.

"It will, very nearly," said the Saint.

He cast an eye over the mail that she had brought in with her from the letter-box.

"Those two envelopes with half-penny stamps you may exterminate forthwith. On the third, in spite of the deceptive three-half-penny *Briefmarke*, I recognise the clerkly hand of Anderson and Sheppard. Add it to the holocaust. Item four"—he picked up a small brown-paper package and weighed it calculatingly in his hand—"is much too light to contain high explosive. It's probably the new gold-mounted sock-suspenders I ordered from Asprey's. Open it, darling, and tell me what you think of them. And I will read you some more of the Hideous History of Charles."

He took up his manuscript.

With what a zest did he prepare
For the first meeting (open-air)!
With what a glee he fastened on
His bevor and his morion,
His greaves, his ventail, every tace,
His pauldrons and his rerebrace!
He sallied forth with martial eye,
Prepared to do, prepared to die,
But not prepared—by Bayard! not
For the reception that he got.
Over that chapter of the tale
It would be kind to draw a veil:
Let it suffice that in disdain,
Some hecklers threw him in a drain,
And plodding home—

"Excuse me," said the Saint.

His right hand moved like lightning, and the detonation of his heavy automatic in the confined space was like a vindictive thunderclap. It left the girl with a strange hot sting of powder on her wrist and a dull buzzing in her ears. And through the buzzing drifted the Saint's unruffled accents:

And plodding home, all soaked inside,
He caught pneumonia—and died.

Patricia looked at him, white-faced.

"What was it?" she asked, with the faintest tremor in her voice.

"Just an odd spot of scorpion," answered Simon Templar gently. "An unpleasant specimen of the breed—the last time I saw one like that was up in the hills north of Puruk-jahu. Looks like a pal of mine has been doing some quick travelling, or . . . Yes." The Saint grinned. "Get on the phone to the Zoo, old dear, and tell 'em they can have their property back if they care to send round and scrape it off the carpet. I don't think we shall want it any more, shall we?"

Patricia shuddered.

She had stripped away the brown paper and found a little cardboard box such as cheap jewellery is sometimes packed in. When she raised the lid, the tiny blue-green horror, like a miniature deformed lobster, had been lying there in a nest of cotton-wool; while she stared at it, it had rustled on to her and . . .

"It—wasn't very big," she said, in a tone that tried to match the Saint's for lightness.

"Scorpions run to all sizes," said the Saint cheerfully, "and as often as not their poisonousness is in inverse ratio to their size in boots. Mostly, they're very minor troubles—I've been stung myself, and all I got was a sore and swollen arm. But the late lamented was a member of the one and only sure-certain and no-hokum family of homicides in the species. Pity I bumped it off so quickly—it might have been really valuable stuffed."

Patricia's finger-tips slid mechanically around the rough edges of the hole that the nickel-cased .45 bullet had smashed through the polished mahogany table before ruining the carpet and losing itself somewhere in the floor. Then she looked steadily at the Saint.

"Why should anyone send you a scorpion?" she asked.

Simon Templar shrugged.

"It was the immortal Paragot who said, 'In this country the unexpected always happens, which paralyses the brain.' And if a real man-sized Scorpion can't be expected to send his young brothers to visit his friends as a token of esteem, what can he be expected to do?"

"Is that all?"

"All what?"

"All you propose to tell me."

The Saint regarded her for a moment. He saw the tall slim lines of reposeful strength in her body, the fine moulding of the chin, the eyes as blue and level as his own. And slowly he screwed the cap on his fountain pen, and he stood up and came round the table.

"I'll tell you as much more as you want to know," he said.

"Just like in the mad old days?"

"They had their moments, hadn't they?"

She nodded.

"Sometimes I wish we were back in them," she said wistfully. "I didn't fall in love with you in a pair of Anderson and Sheppard trousers—"

"They were!" cried the Saint indignantly. "I distinctly remember—"

Patricia laughed suddenly. Her hands fell on his shoulders.

"Give me a cigarette, boy," she said, "and tell me what's been happening."

And he did so—though what he had to tell was little enough. And Chief Inspector Teal himself knew no more. The Scorpion had grown up in darkness, had struck from the darkness, and crawled back deeper into the dark. Those who could have spoken dared not speak, and those who might have spoken died too soon . . .

But as he told his tale, the Saint saw the light of all the mad old days awakening again in Patricia's eyes, and it was in a full and complete understanding of that light that he came to the one thing that Chief Inspector Teal would have given his ears to know.

"Tonight, at nine—"

"You'll be there?"

"I shall," said the Saint, with the slightest tightening of his lips. "Shot up by a bloody amateur! Good God! Suppose he'd hit me! Pat, believe Papa—when I pass out, there's going to be a first-class professional, hall-marked on every link, at the thick end of the gun."

Patricia, in the deep armchair, settled her sweet golden head among the cushions.

"What time do we start?" she asked calmly.

For a second, glancing at him sidelong. She saw the old stubborn hardening of the line of his jaw. It happened instinctively, almost without his knowing it, and then suddenly he swung off the arm of the chair in the breath of an even older Saintly laughter.

"Why not?" he said. "It's impossible—preposterous— unthinkable—but why not? The old gang have gone—Dicky, Archie, Roger—gone and got spliced on to women and come over all bowler-hat. There's only you left. It'd make the vicar's wife let out one piercing squawk and swallow her knitting-needles, but who cares? If you'd really like to have another sniff at the old brew—"

"Give me the chance!"

Simon grinned.

"And you'd flop after it like a homesick walrus down a water-chute, wouldn't you?"

"Faster," she said.

"And so you shall," said the Saint. "The little date I've got for tonight will be all the merrier for an extra soul on the side of Saintliness and soft drinks. And if things don't turn out exactly according to schedule, there may be an encore for your especial entertainment. Pat, I have a feeling that this is going to be our week!"

CHAPTER 6

It was one of the Saint's most charming characteristics that he never hurried and never worried. He insisted on spending an idle hour in the cocktail bar of the May Fair Hotel, and seven-thirty had struck before he collected his car, inserted Patricia, and turned the Hirondel's long silver nose northwards at an unwontedly moderate speed. They dined at Hatfield, after parking the Hirondel in the hotel garage, and after dinner the Saint commanded coffee and liqueurs and proceeded to incinerate two enormous cigars of a plutocratically delicate bouquet. He had calculated exactly how long it would take to walk out to location, and he declined to start one moment before his time-table demanded it.

"I am a doomed man," he said sombrely, "and I have my privileges. If necessary, the Scorpion will wait for me."

Actually he had no intention of being late, for the plan of campaign that he had spent the nicotinised interval after dinner adapting to Patricia's presence required them to be at the rendezvous a shade in advance of the rest of the party.

But this the Scorpion did not know.

He drove up slowly, with his headlights dimmed, scanning the dark shadows at the side of the road. Exactly beside the point where his shaded lights picked up the grey-white blur of the appointed milestone, he saw the tiny red glow of a cigarette-end, and applied his brakes gently. The cigarette-end dropped and vanished under an invisible heel, and out of the gloom a tall dark shape stretched slowly upwards.

The Scorpion's right hand felt the cold bulk of the automatic pistol in his pocket as his other hand lowered the nearside window. He leaned over towards the opening.

"Garrot?"

The question came in a whisper to the man at the side of the road, and he stepped slowly forward and answered in a throaty undertone.

"Yes, sir?"

The Scorpion's head was bent low, so that the man outside the car could only see the shape of his hat.

"You obeyed your orders. That is good. Come closer . . ."

The gun slipped silently out of the Scorpion's pocket, his forefinger curling quickly round the trigger as he drew it. He brought it up without a sound, so that the tip of the barrel rested on the ledge of the open window directly in line with the chest of the man twelve inches away. One lightning glance to left and right told him that the road was deserted.

"Now there is just one thing more—"

"There is," agreed Patricia Holm crisply. "Don't move!"

The Scorpion heard, and the glacial concentration of dispassionate unfriendliness in her voice froze him where he sat. He had not heard the noiseless turning of the handle of the door behind him, nor noticed the draught of cooler air that trickled through the car, but he felt the chilly hardness of the circle of steel that pressed into the base of his skull, and for a second he was paralysed. And in that second his target vanished.

"Drop that gun—outside the car. And let me hear it go!"

Again that crisp, commanding voice, as inclemently smooth as an arctic sea, whisked into his eardrums like a thin cold needle. He hesitated for a moment, and then, as the muzzle of the gun behind his neck increased its pressure by one warning ounce, he moved his hand obediently and relaxed his fingers. His automatic rattled on to the running board, and almost immediately the figure that he had taken for Long Harry rose into view again, and was framed in the square space of window.

But the voice that acknowledged the receipt of *item*, Colts, automatic, scorpions, for the use of, one, was not the voice of Long Harry. It was the most cavalier, the most mocking, the most cheerful voice that the Scorpion had ever heard—he noted those qualities about it subconsciously, for he was not in a position to revel in the discovery with any hilariously wholehearted abandon.

"O.K. . . . And how are you, my Scorpion?"

"Who are you?" asked the man in the car.

He still kept his head lowered, and under the brim of his hat his eyes were straining into the gloom for a glimpse of the man who had spoken, but the Saint's face was in shadow. Glancing away to one side, the Scorpion could focus the head of the girl whose gun continued to impress his cervical vertebræ with the sense of its rocklike steadiness, but a dark close-fitting hat covered the upper part of her head, and a scarf that was loosely knotted about her neck had been pulled up to veil her face from the eyes downwards.

The Saint's light laugh answered the question.

"I am the world's worst gunman, and the lady behind you is the next worst, but at this range we can say that we never miss. And that's all you need to worry about just now. The question that really arises is—who are you?"

"That is what you have still to discover," replied the man in the car impassively. "Where is Garrot?"

"Ah! That's what whole synods of experts are still trying to discover. Some would say that he was simply rotting, and others would say that that was simply rot. He might be floating around the glassy sea, clothed in white samite, mystic, wonderful, with his new regulation nightie flying in the breeze behind, or he might be attending to the central heating plant in the basement. I was never much of a theologian myself—"

"Is he dead?"

"Very," said the Saint cheerfully. "I organised the decease myself."

"You killed him?"

"Oh, no! Nothing like that about me. I merely arranged for him to die. If you survive to read your morning paper tomorrow, you may be informed that the body of an unknown man has been fished out of the Thames. That will be Long Harry. Now come out and take your curtain, sweetheart!"

The Saint stepped back and twitched open the door, pocketing the Scorpion's gun as he did so.

And at the same moment he had a queer feeling of futility. He knew that that was not the moment when he was destined to lay the Scorpion by the heels.

Once or twice before, in a life which had only lasted as long as it had by reason of a vigilance that never blinked for one split second, and a forethought that was accustomed to skid along half a dozen moves ahead of the opposition performers in every game with the agility of a startled streak of lightning zipping through space on ball bearings with the wind behind it, he had experienced the same sensation—of feeling as if an intangible shutter had guillotined down in front of one vitally receptive lens in his alertness. Something was going to happen—his trained intuition told him that beyond all possibility of argument, and an admixture of plain horse-sense told him what would be the general trend of that forthcoming event, equally beyond all possibility of argument—but exactly what shape that event would take was more than any faculty of his could divine.

A tingling stillness settled upon the scene, and in the stillness some fact that he should have been reckoning with seemed to hammer frantically upon that closed window in his mind. He knew that that was so, but his brain produced no other response. Just for that fractional instant of time a cog slipped one pinion, and the faultless machine was at fault. The blind spot that roams around somewhere in every human cerebral system suddenly broke its moorings, and drifted down over the one minute area of co-ordinating apparatus of which Simon Templar had most need, and no effort of his could dislodge it.

"Step out, Cuthbert," snapped the Saint, with a slight rasp in his voice.

In the darkness inside the car, a slight blur of white caught and interested Simon's eye. It lay on the seat beside the driver. With that premonition of failure dancing about in his subconscious and making faces at his helpless stupidity, the Saint grabbed at the straw. He got it away—a piece of paper—and the Scorpion, seeing it go, snatched wildly but not soon enough.

Simon stuffed the paper into his coat pocket, and with his other hand he took the Scorpion by the neck.

"Step!" repeated the Saint crisply.

And then his forebodings were fulfilled—simply and straightforwardly, as he had known they would be.

The Scorpion had never stopped the engine of his car—that was the infinitesimal yet sufficient fact that had been struggling ineffectively to register itself upon the Saint's brain. The sound was scarcely anything at all, even to the Saint's hypersensitive ears—scarcely more than a rhythmic pulsing disturbance of the stillness of the night.

Yet all at once—too late—it seemed to rise and racket in his mind like the thunder of a hundred dynamos, and it was then that he saw his mistake.

But that was after the Scorpion had let in the clutch.

In the blackness, his left hand must have been stealthily engaging the gears, and then, as a pair of swiftly growing lights pin-pointed in his driving-mirror, he unleashed the car with a bang.

The Saint, with one foot in the road and the other on the running-board, was flung off his balance. As he stumbled, the jamb of the door crashed agonisingly into the elbow of the arm that reached out to the driver's collar, and something like a thousand red-hot needles prickled right down his forearm to the tip of his little finger and numbed every muscle through which it passed.

As he dropped back into the road, he heard the crack of Patricia's gun.

The side of the car slid past him, gathering speed, and he whipped out the Scorpion's own automatic. Quite casually, he plugged the off-side back tyre, and then a glare of light came into the tail of his eye, and he stepped quickly across to Patricia.

"Walk on," he said quietly.

They fell into step and sauntered slowly on, and the headlights of the car behind threw their shadows thirty yards ahead.

"That jerk," said Patricia ruefully, "my shot missed him by a yard. I'm sorry."

Simon nodded.

"I know. It was my fault. I should have switched his engine off."

The other car flashed past them, and Simon cursed it fluently.

"The real joy of having the country full of automobiles," he said, "is that it makes gunning so easy. You can shoot anyone up anywhere, and everyone except the victim will think it was only a backfire. But it's when people can see the gun that the deception kind of disintegrates."

He gazed gloomily after the dwindling tail light of the unwelcome interruption. "If only that four-wheeled gas-crocodile had burst a blood-vessel two miles back, we mightn't have been on our way home yet."

"I heard you shoot once—"

"And he's still going—on the other three wheels. I'm not expecting he'll stop to mend that leak."

Patricia sighed.

"It was short and sweet, anyway," she said. "Couldn't you have stopped that other car and followed?"

He shook his head.

"Teal could have stopped it, but I'm not a policeman. I think this is a bit early for us to start gingering up our publicity campaign."

"I wish it had been a better show, boy," said Patricia wistfully, slipping her arm through his, and the Saint stopped to stare at her.

In the darkness, this was not very effective, but he did it.

"You bloodthirsty child!" he said.

And then he laughed.

"But that wasn't the final curtain," he said. "If you like to note it down, I'll make you a prophecy: the mortality among Scorpions is going to rise one unit, and for once it will not be my fault."

They were back in Hatfield before she had made up her mind to ask him if he was referring to Long Harry, and for once the Saint did not look innocently outraged at the suggestion.

"Long Harry is alive and well, to the best of my knowledge and belief," he said, "but I arranged the rough outline of his decease with Teal over the telephone. If we didn't kill Long Harry, the Scorpion would, and I figure our method will be less fatal. But as for the Scorpion himself—well, Pat, I'm dreadfully afraid I've promised to let them hang him according to the law. I'm getting so respectable these days that I feel I may be removed to Heaven in a fiery chariot at any moment."

THE SAINT VERSUS SCOTLAND YARD

He examined his souvenir of the evening in a corner of the deserted hotel smoking-room a little later, over a final and benedictory tankard of beer. It was an envelope, postmarked in the South-Western district at 11 a.m. that morning, and addressed to Wilfred Garniman, Esq., 28, Mallaby Road, Harrow. From it the Saint extracted a single sheet of paper, written in a feminine hand.

Dear Mr Garniman,

Can you come round for dinner and a game of bridge on Tuesday next? Colonel Barnes will be making a fourth.

Yours sincerely
(Mrs) R. Venables.

For a space he contemplated the missive with an exasperated scowl darkening the beauty of his features; then he passed it to Patricia, and reached out for the consolation of draught Bass with one hand and for a cigarette with the other. The scowl continued to darken.

Patricia read, and looked at him perplexedly.

"It looks perfectly ordinary," she said.

"It looks a damned sight too ordinary!" exploded the Saint. "How the devil can you blackmail a man for being invited to play bridge?"

The girl frowned.

"But I don't see. Why should this be anyone else's letter?"

"And why shouldn't Mr Wilfred Garniman be the man I want?"

"Of course. Didn't you get it from that man in the car?"

"I saw it on the seat beside him—it must have come out of his pocket when he pulled his gun."

"Well?" she prompted.

"Why shouldn't this be the beginning of the Scorpion's triumphal march towards the high jump?" asked the Saint.

"That's what I want to know."

Simon surveyed her in silence. And, as he did so, the scowl faded slowly from his face. Deep in his eyes a pair of little blue devils roused up, executed a tentative double-shuffle, and paused with their heads on one side.

"Why not?" insisted Patricia.

Slowly, gently, and with tremendous precision, the Saintly smile twitched at the corners of Simon's lips, expanded, grew, and irradiated his whole face.

"I'm blowed if I know why not," said the Saint seraphically. "It's just that I have a weakness for getting both feet on the bus before I tell the world I'm travelling. And the obvious deduction seemed too good to be true."

CHAPTER 7

Mallaby Road, Harrow, as the Saint discovered, was one of those jolly roads in which ladies and gentlemen live. Lords and ladies may be found in such places as Mayfair, Monte Carlo, and St Moritz; men and women may be found almost anywhere; but Ladies and Gentlemen blossom in their full beauty only in such places as Mallaby Road, Harrow. This was a road about two hundred yards long, containing thirty of the stately homes of England, each of them a miraculously preserved specimen of Elizabethan architecture, each of them exactly the same as the other twenty-nine, and each of them surrounded by identical lawns, flower-beds, and atmospheres of overpowering gentility.

Simon Templar, entering Mallaby Road at nine o'clock—an hour of the morning at which his vitality was always rather low—felt slightly stunned.

There being no other visible distinguishing marks or peculiarities about it, he discovered No. 28 by the simple process of looking at the figures on the garden gates, and found it after inspecting thirteen other numbers which were not 28. He started on the wrong side of the road.

To the maid who opened the door he gave a card bearing the name
of Mr Andrew Herrick and the official imprint of *The Daily Record*.
Simon Templar had no right whatever to either of these decorations,
which were the exclusive property of a reporter whom he had once
interviewed, but a little thing like that never bothered the Saint. He
kept every visiting card that was ever given him and a few that had not
been consciously donated, and drew appropriately upon his stock in
time of need.

"Mr Garniman is just finishing breakfast, sir," said the maid
doubtfully, "but I'll ask him if he'll see you."

"I'm sure he will," said the Saint, and he said it so winningly that
if the maid's name had been Mrs Garniman the prophecy would have
passed automatically into the realm of sublimely concrete certainties.

As it was, the prophecy merely proved to be correct.

Mr Garniman saw the Saint, and the Saint saw Mr Garniman.
These things happened simultaneously, but the Saint won on points.
There was a lot of Mr Garniman.

"I'm afraid I can't spare you very long, Mr Herrick," he said. "I
have to go out in a few minutes. What did you want to see me about?"

His restless grey eyes flittered shrewdly over the Saint as he spoke,
but Simon endured the scrutiny with the peaceful calm which only
the man who wears the suits of Anderson and Sheppard, the shirts
of Harman, the shoes of Lobb, and self-refrigerating conscience can
achieve.

"I came to ask you if you could tell us anything about the Scorpion,"
said the Saint calmly.

Well, that is one way of putting it. On the other hand, one could
say with equal truth that his manner would have made a sheet of plate
glass look like a futurist sculptor's impression of a bit of the Pacific
Ocean during a hurricane. And the innocence of the Saintly face would
have made a Botticelli angel look positively sinister in comparison.

His gaze rested on Mr Wilfred Garniman's fleshy prow with no more than a reasonable directness, but he saw the momentary flicker of expression that preceded Mr Garniman's blandly puzzled frown, and wistfully wondered whether, if he unsheathed his sword-stick and prodded it vigorously into Mr Garniman's immediate future, there would be a loud pop, or merely a faint sizzling sound. That he overcame this insidious temptation, and allowed no sign of the soul-shattering struggle to register itself on his face, was merely a tribute to the persistently sobering influence of Mr Lionel Delborn's official proclamation and the Saint's sternly practical devotion to business.

"Scorpion?" repeated Mr Garniman, frowning. "I'm afraid I don't quite—"

"Understand. Exactly. Well, I expected I should have to explain."

"I wish you would. I really don't know—"

"Why we should consider you an authority on scorpions. Precisely. The Editor told me you'd say that."

"If you'd—"

"Tell you the reason for this rather extraordinary procedure— "

"I should certainly see if I could help you in any way, but at the same time—"

"You don't see what use you could be. Absolutely. Now, shall we go on like this or shall we sing the rest in chorus?"

Mr Garniman blinked.

"Do you want to ask me some questions?"

"I should love to," said the Saint heartily. "You don't think Mrs Garniman will object?"

"Mrs Garniman?"

"Mrs Garniman."

Mr Garniman blinked again.

"Are you—"

"Certain—"

"Are you certain you haven't made a mistake? There is no Mrs Garniman."

"Don't mention it," said the Saint affably.

He turned the pages of an enormous notebook.

"*Interviewed Luis Cartaro. Diamond rings and Marcel wave. Query—Do Pimples Make Good Mothers? Said—*'Sorry, wrong page . . . Here we are: *'Memo. See Wilfred Garniman and ask the big—ask him about scorpions. 28 Mallaby Road, Harrow.'* That's right, isn't it?"

"That's my name and address," said Garniman shortly. "But I have still to learn the reason for this—er—"

"Visit," supplied the Saint. He was certainly feeling helpful this morning.

He closed his book and returned it to his pocket.

"As a matter of fact," he said, "we heard that the Saint was interested in you."

He was not even looking at Garniman as he spoke. But the mirror over the mantelpiece was in the tail of his eyes, and thus he saw the other's hands, which were clasped behind his back, close and unclose—once.

"The Saint?" said Garniman. "Really—"

"Are you sure I'm not detaining you?" asked the Saint, suddenly very brisk and solicitous. "If your staff will be anxious . . ."

"My staff can wait a few minutes."

"That's very good of you. But if we telephoned them—"

"I assure you—that is quite unnecessary."

"I shouldn't like to think of your office being disorganised—"

"You need not trouble," said Garniman. He moved across the room. "Will you smoke?"

"Thanks," said the Saint.

He had just taken the first puff from a cigarette when Garniman turned round with a carved ebony box in his hand.

"Oh," said Mr Garniman, a trifle blankly.

"Not at all," said the Saint, who was never embarrassed. "Have one of mine?"

He extended his case, but Garniman shook his head.

"I never smoke during the day. Would it be too early to offer you a drink?"

"I'm afraid so—much too late," agreed Simon blandly.

Garniman returned the ebony box to the side table from which he had taken it. Then he swung round abruptly.

"Well?" he demanded. "What's the idea?"

The Saint appeared perplexed.

"What's what idea?" he inquired innocently.

Garniman's eyebrows came down a little.

"What's all this about scorpions—and the Saint?"

"According to the Saint—"

"I don't understand you. I thought the Saint had disappeared long ago."

"Then you were grievously in error, dear heart," murmured Simon Templar coolly. "Because I am myself the Saint."

He lounged against a book-case, smiling and debonair, and his lazy blue eyes rested mockingly on the other's pale plump face.

"And I'm afraid you're the Scorpion, Wilfred," he said.

For a moment Mr Garniman stood quite still. And then he shrugged.

"I believe I read in the newspapers that you had been pardoned and had retired from business," he said, "so I suppose it would be useless for me to communicate your confession to the police. As for this scorpion that you have referred to several times—"

"Yourself," the Saint corrected him gently, and Garniman shrugged again.

"Whatever delusion you are suffering from—"

"Not a delusion, Wilfred."

"It is immaterial to me what you call it."

The Saint seemed to lounge even more languidly, his hands deep in his pockets, a thoughtful and reckless smile playing lightly about his lips.

"I call it a fact," he said softly. "And you will keep your hands away from that bell until I've finished talking . . . You are the Scorpion, Wilfred, and you're probably the most successful blackmailer of the age. I grant you that—your technique is novel and thorough. But blackmail is a nasty crime. Your ingenuity has already driven two men to suicide. That was stupid of them, but it was also very naughty of you. In fact, it would really give me great pleasure to peg you in your front garden and push this highly desirable residence over on top of you, but for one thing. I've promised to reserve you for the hangman and for another thing I've got my income tax to pay, so—Excuse me one moment."

Something like a flying chip of frozen quicksilver flashed across the room and plonked crisply into the wooden panel around the bell-push towards which Garniman's fingers were sidling. It actually passed between his second and third fingers, so that he felt the swift chill of its passage and snatched his hand away as if he had received an electric shock. But the Saint continued his languid propping up of the *Encyclopaedia Britannica*, and he did not appear to have moved.

"Just do what you're told, Wilfred, and everything will be quite all right—but I've got lots more of them there missiles packed in my pants," murmured the Saint soothingly, warningly, and untruthfully—though Mr Garniman had no means of perceiving this last adverb. "What was I saying? . . . Oh yes. I have my income tax to pay—"

Garniman took a sudden step forward, and his lips twisted in a snarl.

"Look here—"

"Where?" asked the Saint excitedly.

Mr Garniman swallowed. The Saint heard him distinctly.

"You thrust yourself in here under a false name—you behave like a raving lunatic—then you make the most wild and fantastic accusations—you—"

"Throw knives about the place—"

"What the devil," bellowed Mr Garniman, "do you mean by it?"

"Sir," suggested the Saint mildly.

"What the devil," bellowed Mr Garniman, "do you mean—'sir'?"

"Thank you," said the Saint.

Mr Garniman glared. "What the—"

"O.K.," said the Saint pleasantly. "I heard you the second time. So long as you go on calling me 'sir,' I shall know that everything is perfectly respectable and polite. And now we've lost the place again. Half a minute . . . Here we are: *'I have my income tax to pay—'*"

"Will you get out at once," asked Garniman, rather quietly, "or must I send for the police?"

Simon considered the question.

"I should send for the police," he suggested at length.

He hitched himself off the book-case and sauntered leisurely across the room. He detached his little knife from the bell panel, tested the point delicately on his thumb, and restored the weapon to the sheath under his left sleeve, and Wilfred Garniman watched him without speaking. And then the Saint turned.

"Certainly—I should send for the police," he drawled. "They will be interested. It's quite true that I had a pardon for some old offences, but whether I've gone out of business, or whether I'm simply just a little cleverer than Chief Inspector Teal, is a point that is often debated at Scotland Yard. I think that any light you could throw on the problem would be welcomed."

Garniman was still silent, and the Saint looked at him, and laughed caressingly.

"On the other hand—if you're bright enough to see a few objections to that idea—you might prefer to push quietly on to your beautiful office and think over some of the other things I've said. Particularly those pregnant words about my income tax."

"Is that all you have to say?" asked Garniman, in the same low voice, and the Saint nodded.

"It'll do for now," he said lightly. "And since you seem to have decided against the police, I think I'll beetle off and concentrate on the method by which you're going to be induced to contribute to the Inland Revenue."

The slightest glitter of expression came to Wilfred Garniman's eyes for a moment, and was gone again. He walked to the door and opened it.

"I'm obliged," he said.

"After you, dear old reed-warbler," said the Saint courteously.

He permitted Garniman to precede him out of the room, and stood in the hall adjusting the piratical slant of his hat.

"I presume we shall meet again?" Garniman remarked.

His tone was level and conversational. And the Saint smiled.

"You might even bet on it," he said.

"Then—*au revoir.*"

The Saint tilted back his hat and watched the other turn on his heels and go up the stairs.

Then he opened the door and stepped out, and the heavy ornamental stone flower-pot that began to gravitate earthwards at the same moment actually nicked the brim of his Stetson before it split thunderously on the flagged path an inch behind his right heel.

Simon revolved slowly, his hands still in his pockets, and cocked an eyebrow at the debris, and then he strolled back under the porch and applied his forefinger to the bell.

Presently the maid answered the door.

"I think Mr Garniman has dropped the aspidistra," he murmured chattily, and resumed his interrupted exit before the bulging eyes of an audience of one.

CHAPTER 8

"But what on earth," asked Patricia helplessly, "was the point of that?"

"It was an exercise in tact," said the Saint modestly.

The girl stared.

"If I could only see it," she began, and then the Saint laughed.

"You will, old darling," he said.

He leaned back and lighted another cigarette.

"Mr Wilfred Garniman," he remarked, "is a surprisingly intelligent sort of cove. There was very little nonsense—and most of what there was was my own free gift to the nation. I grant you he added to his present charge-sheet by offering me a cigarette and then a drink, but that's only because, as I've told you before, he's an amateur. I'm afraid he's been reading too many thrillers, and they've put ideas into his head. But on the really important point he was most professionally bright. The way the calm suddenly broke out in the middle of the storm was quite astonishing to watch."

"And by this time," said Patricia, "he's probably going on being calm a couple of hundred miles away."

Simon shook his head.

"Not Wilfred," he said confidently. "Except when he's loosing off six-shooters and throwing architecture about, Wilfred is a really first-class amateur. And he is so rapid on the uptake that if he fell off the fortieth floor of the Empire Building he would be sitting on the roof before he knew what had happened. Without any assistance from me, he divined that I had no intention of calling in the police. So he knew he wasn't very much worse off than he was before."

"Why?"

"He may be an amateur, as I keep telling you, but he's efficient. Long before his house started to fall to pieces on me, he'd begun to make friendly attempts to bump me off. That was because he'd surveyed all the risks before he started in business, and he figured that his graft was exactly the kind of graft that would make me sit up and take notice. In which he was darned right. I just breezed in and proved it to him. He told me himself that he was unmarried; I wasn't able to get him to tell me anything about his lawful affairs, but the butcher told me that he was supposed to be 'something in the City'—so I acquired two items of information. I also verified his home address, which was the most important thing, and I impressed him with my own brilliance and charm of personality, which was the next most important. I played the perfect clown, because that's the way these situations always get me, but in the intervals between laughs I did everything that I set out to do. And he knew it—as I meant him to."

"And what happens next?"

"The private war will go on," said the Saint comfortably.

His deductions, as usual, were precisely true, but there was one twist in the affairs of Wilfred Garniman of which he did not know, and if he had known of it he might not have taken life quite so easily as he did for the next few days. That is just possible.

On the morning of that first interview, he had hung around in the middle distances of Mallaby Road with intent to increase his store of information, but Mr Garniman had driven off to his righteous labours in a car which the Saint knew at a glance it would be useless to attempt to follow in a taxi. On the second morning, the Saint decorated the same middle distances at the wheel of his own car, but a traffic jam at Marble Arch baulked him of his quarry. On the third morning he tried again, and collected two punctures in the first half-mile, and when he got out to inspect the damage he found sharp steel spikes strewn all over the road. Then, fearing that four consecutive seven-o'clock breakfasts might affect his health, the Saint stayed in bed on the fourth morning and did some thinking.

One error in his own technique he perceived quite clearly.

"If I'd sleuthed him on the first morning, and postponed the backchat till the second, I should have been a bright lad," he said. "My genius seems to have gone off the boil."

That something of the sort had happened was also evidenced by the fact that during those four days the problem of evolving a really agile method of inducing Mr Garniman to part with a proportion of his ill-gotten gains continued to elude him.

Chief Inspector Teal heard the whole story when he called in on the evening of that fourth day to make inquiries, and was almost offensive.

The Saint sat at his desk after the detective had gone, and contemplated the net result of his ninety-six hours' cerebration moodily. This consisted of a twelve-line epilogue to the Epic History of Charles.

His will was read. His father learned
Charles wished his body to be burned.
With huge heroic flames of fire
Upon a Roman funeral pyre.
But Charles's pa, sole legatee,
Averse to such publicity,
Thought that, his bidding might be done

Without disturbing anyone,
And, in a highly touching scene,
Cremated him at Kensal Green.
And so Charles has his little shrine
With cavalier and concubine.

Simon Templar scowled sombrely at the sheet for some time, and then, with a sudden impatience, he heaved the inkpot out of the window and stood up.

"Pat," he said, "I feel that the time is ripe for us to push into a really wicked night club and drown our sorrows in iced ginger-beer."

The girl closed her book and smiled at him.

"Where shall we go?" she asked, and then the Saint suddenly shot across the room as if he had been touched with a hot iron.

"Holy Pete!" he yelled. "Pat—old sweetheart—old angel—"

Patricia blinked at him.

"My dear old lad—"

"Hell to all dear old lads!" cried the Saint recklessly.

He took her by the arms, swung her bodily out of her chair, put her down, rumpled her hair, and kissed her.

"Paddle on," he commanded breathlessly. "Go on—go and have a bath—dress—undress—glue your face on—anything. Sew a gun into the cami-whatnots, find a butterfly net—and let's go!"

"But what's the excitement about?"

"We're going entomo-botanising. We're going to prowl around the West End fishing for beetles. We're going to look at every night club in London—I'm a member of them all. If we don't catch anything, it won't be my fault. We're going to knock the L out of London and use it to tie the Home Secretary's ears together. The voice of the flatfooted periwinkle shall be heard in the land—"

He was still burbling foolishly when Patricia fled, but when she returned he was resplendent in Gents' Evening Wear and wielding a cocktail-shaker with a wild exuberance that made her almost giddy to watch.

"For Heaven's sake," she said, catching his arm, "pull yourself together and tell me something!"

"Sure," said the Saint daftly. "That nightie of yours is a dream. Or is it meant to be a dress? You can never tell, with these long skirts. And I don't want to be personal, but are you sure you haven't forgotten to put on the back or posterior part? I can see all your spine. Not that I mind, but . . . Talking of swine—spine—there was a very fine specimen at the Embassy the other night. Must have measured at least thirty-two inches from snout to—They say the man who landed it played it for three weeks. Ordinarily trout line and gaff, you know . . ."

Patricia Holm was almost hysterical by the time they reached the Carlton, where the Saint had decided to dine. And it was not until he had ordered an extravagant dinner, with appropriate wines, that she was able to make him listen to a sober question. And then he became the picture of innocent amazement.

"But didn't you get me?" he asked. "Hadn't you figured it out for yourself? I thought you were there long ago. Have you forgotten my little exploit at the Bird's Nest? Who d'you think paid for that bit of coloured mosquito-net you're wearing? Who bought these studs I'm wearing? Who, if it comes to that, is standing us this six-course indigestion? . . . Well, some people might say it was Montgomery Bird, but personally—"

The girl gasped. "You mean that other man at the Bird's Nest was the Scorpion?"

"Who else? . . . But I never rumbled to it till tonight! I told you he was busy putting the black on Montgomery when Teal and I butted in. I overheard the whole conversation, and I was certainly curious. I made a mental note at the time to investigate that bearded battleship, but it never came into my head that it must have been Wilfred himself—I'm damned if I know why!"

Patricia nodded.

"I'd forgotten to think of it myself," she said.

"And I must have been fast asleep the whole time! Of course it was the Scorpion—and his graft's a bigger one than I ever dreamed. He's got organisation, that guy. He probably has his finger in half the wicked pies that are being cooked in this big city. If he was on to Montgomery, there's no reason why he shouldn't have got on to a dozen others that you and I can think of, and he'll be drawing his percentage from the whole bunch. I grant you I put Montgomery out of business, but—"

"If you're right," said Patricia, "and the Scorpion hasn't done a bunk, we may find him anywhere."

"Tonight," said the Saint. "Or, if not tonight, some other night. And I'm prepared to keep on looking. But my income tax has got to be paid tomorrow, and so I want the reunion to be tonight."

"Have you got an idea?"

"I've got a dozen," said the Saint. "And one of them says that Wilfred is going to have an Evening!"

His brain had suddenly picked up its stride again. In a few minutes he had sketched out a plan of campaign as slick and agile as anything his fertile genius had ever devised. And once again he was proved a true prophet, though the proceedings took a slight twist which he had not foreseen.

For at a quarter past eleven they ran Wilfred Garniman to earth at the Golden Apple Club. And Wilfred Garniman certainly had an Evening.

He was standing at the door of the ballroom, sardonically surveying the clientèle, when a girl walked in and stopped beside him. He glanced round at her almost without thinking. Having done which, he stayed glancing—and thought a lot.

She was young, slim, fair-haired, and exquisite. Even Wilfred Garniman knew that. His rather tired eyes, taking in other details of her appearance, recognised the simple perfection of a fifty-guinea gown. And her face was utterly innocent of guile—Wilfred Garniman had a shrewd perception of these things also. She scanned the crowd anxiously, as though looking for someone, and in due course it became apparent that the someone was not present. Wilfred Garniman was the last man she looked at. Their glances met, and held for some seconds, and then the faintest ripple of a smile touched her lips.

And exactly one hour later, Simon Templar was ringing the bell at 28, Mallaby Road, Harrow.

He was not expecting a reply, but he always liked to be sure of his ground. He waited ten minutes, ringing the bell at intervals, and then he went in by a ground-floor window. It took him straight into Mr Garniman's study. And there, after carefully drawing the curtains, the Saint was busy for some time. For thirty-five minutes by his watch, to be exact.

And then he sat down in a chair and lighted a cigarette.

"Somewhere," he murmured thoughtfully, "there is a catch in this."

For the net result of a systematic and expert search had panned out at precisely nil.

And this the Saint was not expecting. Before he left the Carlton, he had propounded one theory with all the force of an incontestable fact.

"Wilfred may have decided to take my intrusion calmly, and trust that he'll be able to put me out of the way before I managed to strafe him good and proper, but he'd never leave himself without at least one line of retreat. And that implies being able to take his booty with him. He'd never have put it in a bank, because there'd always be the chance that someone might notice things and get curious. It will have been in a safe deposit, but it won't be there now."

Somewhere or other—somewhere within Wilfred Garniman's easy reach—there was a large quantity of good solid cash, ready and willing to be converted into all manner of music by anyone who picked it up and offered it a change of address. It might have been actually on Wilfred Garniman's person, but the Saint didn't think so. He had decided that it would most probably be somewhere in the house at Harrow, and as he drove out there he had prepared to save time by considering the potential hiding-places in advance. He had thought of many, and discarded them one by one, for various reasons, and his final judgment had led him unhesitatingly into the very room where he had spent thirty-five fruitless minutes . . . and where he was now getting set to spend some more.

"This is the Scorpion's sacred lair," he figured, "and Wilfred wouldn't let himself forget it. He'd play it up to himself for all it was worth. It's the inner sanctum of the great ruthless organisation that doesn't exist. He'd sit in that chair in the evenings—at that desk—there —thinking what a wonderful man he was. And he'd look at whatever innocent bit of interior decoration hides his secret cache, and gloat over the letters and dossiers that he's got hidden there, and the money they've brought in or are going to bring in—the fat, slimy, wallowing slug . . ."

Again his eyes travelled slowly round the room. The plainly papered walls could have hidden nothing, except behind the pictures, and he had tried every one of those. Dummy books he had ruled out at once, for a servant may always take down a book, but he had tested the back of every shelf—and found nothing. The whole floor was carpeted, and he gave that no more than a glance: his analysis of Wilfred Garniman's august meditations did not harmonise with the vision of the same gentleman crawling about on his hands and knees. And every drawer of the desk was already unlocked, and not one of them contained anything of compromising interest.

And that appeared to exhaust the possibilities. He stared speculatively at the fireplace—but he had done that before. It ignored the exterior architecture of the building and was a plain modern affair of blue tiles and tin, and it would have been difficult to work any grisly gadgets into its bluntly bourgeois lines. Or, it appeared, into the lines of anything else in that room.

"Which," said the Saint drowsily, "is absurd."

There remained of course, Wilfred Garniman's bedroom—the Saint had long since listed that as the only feasible alternative. But, somehow, he didn't like it. Plunder and pink poplin pyjamas didn't seem a psychologically satisfactory combination—particularly when the pyjamas must be presumed to surround something like Wilfred Garniman must have looked like without his Old Harrovian tie. The idea did not ring a bell. And yet, if the boodle and etceteral appurtenances thereof and howsoever were not in the bedroom, they must be in the study—some blistered whereabouts or what not . . .

"Which," burbled the Saint, "is *ab*sluly *pos*rous . . ."

The situation seemed less and less annoying . . . It really didn't matter very much . . . Wilfred Garniman, if one came to think of it, was even fatter than Teal . . . and one made allowances for detectives . . . Teal was fat, and Long Harry was long, and Patricia played around with Scorpions; which was all very odd and amusing, but nothing to get worked up about before breakfast, old dear . . .

CHAPTER 9

Somewhere in the infinite darkness appeared a tiny speck of white. It came hurtling towards him, and as it came it grew larger and whiter and more terrible, until it seemed as if it must smash and smother and pulp him into the squashed wreckage of the whole universe at his back. He let out a yell, and the upper half of the great white sky fell back like a shutter, sending a sudden blaze of dazzling light into his eyes. The lower bit of white touched his nose and mouth damply, and an acrid stinging smell stabbed right up into the top of his head and trickled down his throat like a thin stream of condensed fire. He gasped, coughed, choked—and saw Wilfred Garniman.

"Hullo, old toad," said the Saint weakly.

He breathed deeply, fanning out of his nasal passages the fiery tingle of the restorative that Garniman had made him inhale. His head cleared magically, so completely that for a few moments it felt as if a cold wind had blown clean through it, and the dazzle of the light dimmed out of his eyes. But he looked down, and saw that his wrists and ankles were securely bound.

"That's a pretty useful line of dope, Wilfred," he murmured huskily. "How did you do it?"

Garniman was folding up his handkerchief and returning it to his pocket, working with slow meticulous hands.

"The pressure of your head on the back of the chair released the gas," he replied calmly. "It's an idea of my own—I have always been prepared to have to entertain undesirable visitors. The lightest pressure is sufficient."

Simon nodded.

"It certainly is a great game," he remarked. "I never noticed a thing, though I remember now that I was blithering to myself rather inanely just before I went under. And so the little man works off his own bright ideas . . . Wilfred, you're coming on."

"I brought my dancing partner with me," said Garniman, quite casually.

He waved a fat indicative hand, and the Saint, squirming over to follow the gesture, saw Patricia in another chair. For a second or two he looked at her; then he turned slowly round again.

"There's no satisfying you jazz fiends, is there?" he drawled. "Now I suppose you'll wind up the gramophone and start again . . . But the girl seems to have lost the spirit of the thing . . ."

Garniman sat down at the desk and regarded the Saint with the heavy inscrutable face of a great gross image.

"I had seen her before, dancing with you at the Jericho, long before we first met—I never forget a face. After she had succeeded in planting herself on me, I spent a little time assuring myself that I was not mistaken, and then the solution was simple. A few drops from a bottle that I am never without—in her champagne—and the impression was that she became helplessly drunk. She will recover without our assistance, perhaps in five minutes, perhaps in half an hour—according to her strength." Wilfred Garniman's fleshy lips loosened in the travesty of a smile. "You underestimated me, Templar."

"That," said the Saint, "remains to be seen." Mr Garniman shrugged.

"Need I explain that you have come to the end of your interesting and adventurous life?"

Simon twitched an eyebrow, and slid his mouth mockingly sideways.

"What—not again?" he sighed, and Garniman's smooth forehead crinkled.

"I don't understand."

"But you haven't seen so many of these situations through as I have, old horse," said the Saint. "I've lost count of the number of times this sort of thing has happened to me. I know the tradition demands it, but I think they might give me a rest sometimes. What's the programme this time—do you sew me up in the bath and light the geyser, or am I run through the mangle and buried under the billiard-table? Or can you think of something really original?"

Garniman inclined his head ironically. "I trust you will find my method satisfactory," he said. He lighted a cigarette, and rose from the desk again, and as he picked up a length of rope from the floor and moved across to Patricia, the Saint warbled on in the same tone of gentle weariness.

"Mind how you fix those ankles, Wilfred. That gauzy silk stuff you see on the limbs costs about five pounds a leg, and it ladders if a fly settles on it. Oh, and while we're on the subject: don't let's have any nonsense about death or dishonour. The child mightn't want to die. And besides, that stuff is played out, anyway . . ."

Garniman made no reply.

He continued with his task in his ponderous methodical way, making every movement with immensely phlegmatic deliberation.

The Saint, who had known many criminals, and who was making no great exaggeration when he said that this particular situation had long since lost all its pristine charm for him, could recall no one in his experience who had ever been so dispassionate. Cold-blooded ruthlessness, a granite impassivity, he had met before, but through it all, deep as it might be, there had always run a perceptible taut thread of vindictive purpose. In Wilfred Garniman there showed nothing of this. He went about his work in the same way that he might have gone about the setting of a mouse-trap—with elephantine efficiency, and a complete blank in the teleological compartment of his brain. And Simon Templar knew with an eerie intuition that this was no pose, as it might have been in others. And then he knew that Wilfred Garniman was mad.

Garniman finished, and straightened up. And then, still without speaking, he picked Patricia up in his arms and carried her out of the room.

The Saint braced his muscles.

His whole body tightened to the effort like a tempered steel spring, and his arms swelled and corded up until the sleeves were stretched and strained around them. For an instant he was absolutely motionless, except for the tremors of titanic tension that shuddered down his frame like wind-ripples over a quiet pool . . . And then he relaxed and went limp, loosing his breath in a great gasp. And the Saintly smile crawled a trifle crookedly over his face.

"Which makes things difficult," he whispered—to the four unanswering walls.

For the cords about his wrists still held him firmly.

Free to move as he chose, he could have broken those ropes with his hands, but bound as he was, he could apply scarcely a quarter of his strength. And the ropes were good ones—new, half-inch, three-ply Manila. He had made the test, and he relaxed. To have struggled longer would have wasted valuable strength to no purpose. And he had come out without Belle, the little knife that ordinarily went with him everywhere, in a sheath strapped to his left forearm—the knife that had saved him on countless other occasions such as this.

Clumsily he pulled himself out of the chair, and rolled the few yards to the desk. There was a telephone there; he dragged himself to his knees and lifted the receiver. The exchange took an eternity to answer. He gave Teal's private number, and heard the preliminary buzz in the receiver as he was connected up, and then Wilfred Garniman spoke behind him, from the doorway.

"Ah! You are still active, Templar?"

He crossed the room with quick lumbering strides, and snatched the instrument away. For a second or two he listened with the receiver at his ear; then he hung it up and put the telephone down at the far end of the desk.

"You have not been at all successful this evening," he remarked stolidly.

"But you must admit we keep on trying," said the Saint cheerfully.

Wilfred Garniman took the cigarette from his mouth. His expressionless eyes contemplated the Saint abstractedly

"I am beginning to believe that your prowess was overrated. You came here hoping to find documents or money—perhaps both. You were unsuccessful."

"Er—temporarily."

"Yet a little ingenuity would have saved you from an unpleasant experience—and shown you quite another function of this piece of furniture."

Garniman pointed to the armchair. He tilted it over on its back, prised up a couple of tacks, and allowed the canvas finishing of the bottom to fall away. Underneath was a dark steel door, secured by three swivel catches.

"I made the whole chair myself—it was a clever piece of work," he said, and then he dismissed the subject almost as if it had never been raised. "I shall now require you to rejoin your friend, Templar. Will you be carried, or would you prefer to walk?"

"How far are we going?" asked the Saint cautiously.

"Only a few yards."

"I'll walk, thanks."

Garniman knelt down and tugged at the ankle ropes. A strand slipped under his manipulations, giving an eighteen-inch hobble.

"Stand up."

Simon obeyed. Garniman gripped his arm and led him out of the room. They went down the hall, and passed through a low door under the stairs. They stumbled down a flight of narrow stone steps. At the bottom, Garniman picked up a candlestick from a niche in the wall and steered the Saint along a short flagged passage.

"You know, Wilf," murmured the Saint conversationally, "this has happened to me twice before in the last six months. And each time it was gas. Is it going to be gas again this time, or are you breaking away from the rules?"

"It will not be gas," replied Garniman flatly.

He was as heavily passionless as a contented animal. And the Saint chattered on blithely.

"I hate to disappoint you—as the actress said to the bishop—but I really can't oblige you now. You must see it, Wilfred. I've got such a lot more to do before the end of the volume, and it'd wreck the whole show if I went and got bumped off in the first story. Have a heart, dear old Garbage-man!"

The other made no response, and the Saint sighed. In the matter of cross-talk comedy, Wilfred Garniman was a depressingly feeble performer. In the matter of murder, on the other hand, he was probably depressingly efficient, but the Saint couldn't help feeling that he made death a most gloomy business.

And then they came into a small low vault, and the Saint saw Patricia again.

Her eyes were open, and she looked at him steadily, with the faintest of smiles on her lips.

"Hullo, boy."

"Hullo, lass."

That was all.

Simon glanced round. In the centre of the floor there was a deep hole, and beside it was a great mound of earth. There was a dumpy white sack in one corner, and a neat conical heap of sand beside it.

Wilfred Garniman explained, in his monotonously apathetic way.

"We tried to sink a well here, but we gave it up. The hole is only about ten feet deep—it was not filled up again. I shall fill it up tonight."

He picked up the girl and took her to the hole in the floor. Dropping on one knee at the edge, he lowered her to the stretch of his arms and let go . . . He came back to the Saint, dusting his trousers.

"Will you continue to walk?" he inquired.

Simon stepped to the side of the pit, and turned. For a moment he gazed into the other man's eyes—the eyes of a man empty of the bowels of compassion. But the Saint's blue gaze was as cold and still as a polar sea.

"You're an over-fed, pot-bellied swamp-hog," he said, and then Garniman pushed him roughly backwards.

Quite unhurriedly, Wilfred Garniman took off his coat, unfastened his cuff-links, and rolled his sleeves up above his elbows. He opened the sack of cement and tipped out its contents into a hole that he trampled in the heap of sand. He picked up a spade, looked about him, and put it down again. Without the least variation of his heavily sedate stride he left the cellar, leaving the candle burning on the floor.

In three or four minutes he was back again, carrying a brimming pail of water in either hand, and with the help of these he continued his unaccustomed labour, splashing gouts of water on his materials and stirring them carefully with the spade.

It took him over half an hour to reduce the mixture to a consistency smooth enough to satisfy him, for he was an inexperienced worker and yet he could afford to make no mistake. At the end of that time he was streaming with sweat, and his immaculate white collar and shirt-front were grubbily wilting rags, but those facts did not trouble him. No one will ever know what was in his mind while he did that work: perhaps he did not know himself, for his face was blank and tranquil.

His flabby muscles must have been aching, but he did not stop to rest. He took the spade over to the hole in the floor. The candle sent no light down there, but in the darkness he could see an irregular blur of white—he was not interested to gloat over it. Bending his back again, he began to shovel the earth back into the hole. It took an astonishing time, and he was breathing stertorously long before he had filled the pit up loosely level with the floor. Then he dropped the spade and tramped over the surface, packing it down tight and hard.

And then he laid over it the cement that he had prepared, finishing it off smoothly level with the floor.

Even then he did not rest—he was busy for another hour, filling the pails with earth and carrying them up the stairs and out into the garden and emptying them over the flower-beds. He had a placidly accurate eye for detail and an enormous capacity for taking pains, had Mr Wilfred Garniman, but it is doubtful if he gave more than a passing thought to the eternal meaning of what he had done.

CHAPTER 10

To Mr Teal, who in those days knew the Saint's habits almost as well as he knew his own, it was merely axiomatic that breakfast and Simon Templar coincided somewhere between the hours of 11 a.m. and 1 p.m., and therefore it is not surprising that the visit which he paid to 7, Upper Berkeley Mews on one historic morning resulted in a severe shock to his system. For a few moments after the door had been opened to him he stood bovinely rooted to the mat, looking like some watcher of the skies who has just seen the Great Bear turn a back-somersault and march rapidly over the horizon in column of all fours. And when he had pulled himself together, he followed the Saint into the sitting-room with the air of a man who is not at all certain that there is no basin of water balanced over the door to await his entrance.

"Have some gum, old dear," invited the Saint hospitably, and Mr Teal stopped by the table and blinked at him.

"What's the idea?" he demanded suspiciously.

The Saint looked perplexed.

"What idea, brother?"

"Is your clock fast, or haven't you been to bed yet?"

Simon grinned.

"Neither. I'm going to travel, and Pat and I have got to push out and book passages and arrange for international overdrafts and all that sort of thing." He waved towards Patricia Holm, who was smoking a cigarette over *The Times*. "Pat, you have met Claud Eustace, haven't you? Made his pile in Consolidated Gas. Mr Teal, Miss Holm. Miss Holm, Mr Teal. Consider yourselves divorced."

Teal picked up the packet of spearmint that sat sedately in the centre of the table, and put it down again uneasily. He produced another packet from his own pocket.

"Did you say you were going away?" he asked.

"I did. I'm worn out, and I feel I need a complete rest—I did a couple of hours' work yesterday, and at my time of life . . ."

"Where were you going?"

The Saint shrugged.

"Doubtless Thomas Cook will provide. We thought of some nice warm islands. It may be the Canaries, the Balearic or Little by Little—"

"And what about the Scorpion?"

"Oh yes, the Scorpion . . . Well, you can have him all to yourself now, Claud."

Simon glanced towards the mantelpiece, and the detective followed his gaze. There was a raw puncture in the panelling where a stiletto had recently reposed, but the papers that had been pinned there were gone. The Saint took the sheaf from his pocket.

"I was just going to beetle along and pay my income tax," he said airily. "Are you walking Hanover Square way?"

Teal looked at him thoughtfully, and it may be recorded to the credit of the detective's somnolently cyclopean self-control that not a muscle of his face moved.

"Yes, I'll go with you—I expect you'll be wanting a drink," he said, and then his eyes fell on the Saint's wrist.

He motioned frantically at it.

"Did you sprain that trying to get the last drops out of the barrel?" he inquired.

Simon pulled down his sleeve.

"As a matter of fact, it was a burn," he said.

"The Scorpion?"

"Patricia."

Teal's eyes descended one millimetre. He looked at the girl, and she smiled at him in a seraphic way which made the detective's internal organs wriggle. Previously, he had been wont to console himself with the reflection that that peculiarly exasperating kind of sweetness in the smile was the original and unalienable copyright of one lone face out of all the faces in the wide world. He returned his gaze to the Saint.

"Domestic strife?" he queried, and Simon assumed an expression of pained reproach.

"We aren't married," he said.

Patricia flicked her cigarette into the fireplace and came over. She tucked one hand into the belt of her plain tweed suit, and laid the other on Simon Templar's shoulder. And she continued to smile seraphically upon the detective.

"You see, we were being buried alive," she explained simply.

"All down in the—er—what's-its of the earth," said the Saint.

"Simon hadn't got his knife, but he remembered his cigarette-lighter just in time. He couldn't reach it himself, so I had to do it. And he never made a sound—I never knew till afterwards—"

"It was a minor detail," said the Saint.

He twitched a small photograph from his pocket and passed it to Teal.

"From the Scorpion's passport," he said. "I found it in a drawer of his desk. That was before he caught me with as neat a trick as I've come across—the armchairs in his study will repay a sleuth-like investigation,

Claud. Then, if you pass on to the cellars, you'll find a piece of cement flooring that had only just begun to floor. Pat and I are supposed to be under there. Which reminds me—if you decide to dig down in the hope of finding us, you'll find my second-best boiled shirt somewhere in the depths. We had to leave it behind. I don't know if you've ever noticed it, but I can give you my word that even the most pliant rubber dickey rattles like a suit of armour when you're trying to move quietly."

For a space the detective stared at him.

Then he took out a notebook.

It was, in its way, one of the most heroic things he ever did.

"Where is this place?" he asked.

"Twenty-eight, Mallaby Road, Arrer. The name is Wilfred Garniman. And about that shirt—if you had it washed at the place where they do yours before you go toddling round the night clubs, and sent it on to me at Palma, I expect I could find a place to burn it. And I've got some old boots upstairs which I thought maybe you might like—"

Teal replaced his notebook and pencil.

"I don't want to ask too many questions," he said. "But if Garniman knows you got away—"

Simon shook his head.

"Wilfred does not know. He went out to fetch some water to dilute the concrete, and we moved while he was away. Later on I saw him carting out the surplus earth and dumping it on the gardening notes. When you were playing on the sands of Southend in a pair of pink shrimping drawers, Teal, did you ever notice that you can always dig more out of a hole than you can put back in it? Wilfred had quite enough mud left over to make him happy."

Teal nodded.

"That's all I wanted," he said, and the Saint smiled.

"Perhaps we can give you a lift," he suggested politely.

They drove to Hanover Square in the Saint's car. The Saint was in form. Teal knew that by the way he drove. Teal was not happy about it. Teal was even less happy when the Saint insisted on being escorted into the office.

"I insist on having police protection," he said. "Scorpions I can manage, but when it comes to tax collectors . . . Not that there's a great difference. The same threatening letters, the same merciless bleeding of the honest toiler, the same bleary eyes—"

"All right," said Teal wearily.

He climbed out of the car, and followed behind Patricia, and so they climbed to the general office. At the high counter which had been erected to protect the clerks from the savage assaults of their victims the Saint halted, and clamoured in a loud voice to be ushered into the presence of Mr Delborn.

Presently a scared little man came to the barrier.

"You wish to see Mr Delborn, sir?"

"I do."

"Yes, sir. What is your business, sir?"

"I'm a burglar," said the Saint innocently.

"Yes, sir. What did you wish to see Mr Delborn about, sir?"

"About the payment of my income tax, Algernon. I will see Mr Delborn himself and nobody else, and if I don't see him at once, I shall not only refuse to pay a penny of my tax, but I shall also take this hideous office to pieces and hide it in various drains belonging to the London County Council. By the way, do you know Chief Inspector Teal? Mr Teal, Mr Veal. Mr Veal—"

"Will you take a seat, sir?"

"Certainly," said the Saint.

He was half-way down the stairs when Teal caught him.

"Look here. Templar," said the detective, breathing heavily through the nose, "I don't care if you have got the Scorpion in your pocket, but if this is your idea of being funny—"

Simon put down the chair and scratched his head.

"I was only obeying instructions," he said plaintively. "I admit it seemed rather odd, but I thought maybe Lionel hadn't got a spare seat in his office."

Teal and Patricia between them got him as far as the top of the stairs where he put the chair down, sat on it, and refused to move.

"I'm going home," said Patricia finally.

"Bring some oranges back with you," said the Saint. "And don't forget your knitting. What time do the early doors open?"

The situation was only saved by the return of the harassed clerk.

"Mr Delborn will see you, sir."

He led the way through the general office and opened a door at the end.

"What name, sir?"

"Ghandi," said the Saint, and stalked into the room.

And there he stopped.

For the first time in his life, Simon Templar stood frozen into a kind of paralysis of sheer incredulous startlement.

In its own genre, that moment was the supremely flabbergasting instant of his life. Battle, murder, and sudden death of all kinds and varieties notwithstanding, the most hectic moments of the most earth-shaking cataclysms in which he had been involved paled their ineffectual fires beside the eye-shrivelling dazzle of that second. And the Saint stood utterly still, with every shadow of expression wiped from his face, momentarily robbed of even his facile power of speech, simply staring.

For the man at the desk was Wilfred Garniman.

Wilfred Garniman himself, exactly as the Saint had seen him on that very first expedition to Harrow—black-coated, black-tied, the perfect office gentleman with a fifty-two-inch waist. Wilfred Garniman sitting there in a breathless immobility that matched the Saint's, but with the prosperous colour draining from his face and his coarse lips going grey.

And then the Saint found his voice.

"Oh, it's you, Wilfred, is it?" The words trickled very softly into the deathly silence. "And this is Simon Templar speaking—not a ghost. I declined to turn into a ghost, even though I was buried. And Patricia Holm did the same. She's outside at this very moment, if you'd like to see her. And so is Chief Inspector Teal—with your photograph in his pocket . . . Do you know that this is very tough on me, sweetheart? I've promised you to Teal, and I ought to be killing you myself. Buried Pat alive, you did—or you meant to . . . And you're the greasy swine that's been pestering me to pay your knock-kneed taxes. No wonder you took to Scorping in your spare time. I wouldn't mind betting you began in this very office, and the capital you started with was the things you wormed out of people under the disguise of official inquiries . . . And I came in to give you one thousand, three hundred and thirty-seven pounds, nineteen and five-pence of your own money, all out of the strong-box under that very interesting chair, Wilfred—"

He saw the beginning of the movement that Garniman made, and hurled himself sideways. The bullet actually skinned one of his lower ribs, though he did not know it until later. He swerved into the heavy desk, and got his hands under the edge. For one weird instant he looked from a range of two yards into the eyes of Wilfred Garniman, who was in the act of rising out of his chair. Garniman's automatic was swinging round for a second shot, and the thunder of the first seemed to still be hanging in the air. And behind him Simon heard the rattle of the door.

And then—to say that he tipped the desk over would be absurd. To have done anything so feeble would have been a sentence of death pronounced simultaneously upon Patricia Holm and Claud Eustace Teal and himself—at least. The Saint knew that.

But as the others burst into the room, it seemed as if the Saint gathered up the whole desk in his two hands, from the precarious hold that he had on it, and flung it hugely and terrifically into the wall, and Wilfred Garniman was carried before it like a great bloated fly before a cannon-ball . . . And, really, that was that . . .

The story of the Old Bailey trial reached Palma about six weeks later, in an ancient newspaper which Patricia Holm produced one morning.

Simon Templar was not at all interested in the story, but he was vastly interested in an illustration thereto which he discovered at the top of the page. The Press photographer had done his worst, and Chief Inspector Teal, the hero of the case, caught unawares in the very act of inserting some fresh chewing gum in his mouth as he stepped out on to the pavement of Newgate Street, was featured looking almost libellously like an infuriated codfish afflicted with some strange uvular growth.

Simon clipped out the portrait and pasted it neatly at the head of a large plain postcard. Underneath it he wrote:

Claud Eustace Teal, when overjoyed,
Wiggled his dexter adenoid;
For well-bred policemen think it rude
To show their tonsils in the nude.

"That ought to come like a ray of sunshine into Claud's dreary life," said the Saint, surveying his handiwork.

He may have been right, for the postcard was delivered in error to an Assistant Commissioner who was gifted with a particularly acid tongue, and it is certain that Teal did not hear the last of it for many days.

THE MILLION POUND DAY

INTRODUCTION

Not very long ago I received a letter from a faithful follower of this series who had just discovered, it seemed with some distress, that the Saint was getting older.

"In *Meet the Tiger*," she wrote, "you say that the Saint is 26, and in one of the latest books he has aged to 35, and at that rate Patricia must be somewhere around 27 or 29, and that is not a nice age for a heroine. She should always be about 20, and the Saint should remain 26. They shouldn't age, because what are you going to do when the Saint gets about 40 and Patricia is nearly 30?"

This is not at all an easy question to answer, even apart from its slightly frantic arithmetic. It was, incidentally, a mild shock to an old gaffer like myself to learn that such comparatively adolescent years as the early thirties were regarded in some quarters as coming perilously close to the borders of senile decay.

Well, I thought, let us pretend that Patricia is thirty (she is ageing a little slower than the Saint, of course, skipping a birthday here and there with a feminine agility which my correspondent, being of the same sex, tactfully takes for granted). She will be, I tried to think, almost an Old Hag. But the only conclusion that this led to was that I myself must have quite a weakness for the company of Old Hags; which couldn't possibly be the right answer.

So the best I could do was to point out, as a matter of inexorable mathematics, that since all of the Saint's adventures have taken a definite period of time to happen, and since several of them had already called on him for a good deal of ground work before the points at which I began to chronicle them, and since I hoped that there were many other adventures yet to come, any such Peter Pan chronology as she suggested would ultimately lead to a transparent absurdity.

My own conception is diametrically opposite. I have never been able to see why a fictional character should not grow up, mature, and develop, the same as anyone else. The same, if you like, as his biographer. The only adequate reason is that so far as I know—no other fictional character in modern times has survived a sufficient number of years for these changes to be clearly observable. I must confess that a lot of my own selfish pleasure in the Saint has been in watching him grow up.

The book from which this story is taken, *The Holy Terror*, will always be one of my favourites. Perhaps I have done better since, at times, but not so much better that I am ashamed of the comparison. I am not so sure about the seven that went before it. For this was the first book in which I really felt that I had been able to bring him into three dimensions. It may have been in the nick of time, for I also feel that this was when the Saint himself took a long stride towards his own future.

—Leslie Charteris (1939)

CHAPTER 1

The scream pealed out at such point-blank range, and was strangled so swiftly and suddenly, that Simon Templar opened his eyes and wondered for a moment whether he had dreamed it.

The darkness inside the car was impenetrable, and outside, through the thin mist that a light frost had etched upon the windows, he could distinguish nothing but the dull shadows of a few trees silhouetted against the flat pallor of the sky. A glance at the luminous dial of his wrist-watch showed that it was a quarter to five; he had slept barely two hours.

A week-end visit to some friends who lived on the remote margin of Cornwall, about thirteen inches from Land's End, had terminated a little more than seven hours earlier, when the Saint, feeling slightly limp after three days in the company of two young souls who were convalescing from a recent honeymoon, had pulled out his car to make the best of a clear night road back to London. A few miles beyond Basingstoke he had backed into a side lane for a cigarette, a sandwich, and a nap. The cigarette and the sandwich he had had, but the nap should have lasted until the hands of his watch met at six-thirty and the sky was white and clear with the morning—he had fixed that time for himself, and had known that his eyes would not open one minute later.

And they hadn't. But they shouldn't have opened one minute earlier, either . . . And the Saint sat for a second or two without moving, straining his ears into the stillness for the faintest whisper of sound that might answer the question in his mind, and driving his memory backwards into those last blank moments of sleep to recall the sound that had woken him. And then, with a quick stealthy movement, he turned the handle of the door and slipped out into the road.

Before that, he had realised that that scream could never have been shaped in his imagination. The sheer shrieking horror of it still rang between his eardrums and his brain; the hideous high-pitched sob on which it had died seemed still to be quivering on the air. And the muffled patter of running feet which had reached him as he listened had served only to confirm what he already knew.

He stood in the shadow of the car with the cold damp smell of the dawn in his nostrils, and heard the footsteps coming closer. They were coming towards him down the main road—now that he was outside the car, they tapped into his brain with an unmistakable clearness. He heard them so distinctly, in the utter silence that lay all around, that he felt he could almost see the man who had made them. And he knew that that was the man who had screamed. The same stark terror that had gone shuddering through the very core of the scream was beating out the wild tattoo of those running feet—the same stomach-sinking dread translated into terms of muscular reaction. For the feet were not running as a man ordinarily runs. They were kicking, blinding, stumbling, hammering along in the mad muscle-binding heart-bursting flight of a man whose reason has tottered and cracked before a vision of all the tortures of the Pit . . .

Simon felt the hairs on the nape of his neck prickling. In another instant he could hear the gasping agony of the man's breathing, but he stayed waiting where he was. He had moved a little way from the car, and now he was crouched right by the corner of the lane, less than a yard from the road, completely hidden in the blackness under the hedge.

The most elementary process of deduction told him that no man would run like that unless the terror that drove him on was close upon his heels—and no man would have screamed like that unless he had felt cold upon his shoulder the clutching hand of an intolerable doom. Therefore the Saint waited.

And then the man readied the corner of the lane.

Simon got one glimpse of him—a man of middle height and build, coatless, with his head back and his fists working. Under the feebly lightening sky his face showed thin and hollow-cheeked, pointed at the chin by a small peaked beard, the eyes starting from their sockets.

He was done in—finished. He must have been finished two hundred yards back. But as he reached the corner the ultimate end came. His feet blundered again, and he plunged as if a trip-wire had caught him across the knees. And then it must have been the last instinct of the hunted animal that made him turn and reel round into the little lane, and the Saint's strong arms caught him as he fell.

The man stared up into the Saint's face. His lips tried to shape a word, but the breath whistled voicelessly in his throat. And then his eyes closed and his body went limp, and Simon lowered him gently to the ground.

The Saint straightened up again, and vanished once more into the gloom. The slow bleaching of the sky seemed only to intensify the blackness that sheltered him, while beyond the shadows a faint light was beginning to pick out the details of the road. And Simon heard the coming of the second man.

The footfalls were so soft that he was not surprised that he had not heard them before. At the moment when he picked them up they could only have been a few yards away, and to anyone less keen of hearing they would still have been inaudible. But the Saint heard them—heard the long-striding ghostly sureness of them padding over the macadam—and a second tingle of eerie understanding crawled over his scalp and glissaded down his spine like a needle-spray of ice-cold water. For the feet that made those sounds were human, but the feet were bare . . .

And the man turned the corner.

Simon saw him as clearly as he had seen the first—more clearly.

He stood huge and straight in the opening of the lane, gazing ahead into the darkness. The wan light in the sky fell evenly across the broad black primitive-featured face, and stippled glistening silver high-lights on the gigantic ebony limbs. Except for a loosely knotted loin-cloth he was naked, and the gleaming surfaces of his tremendous chest shifted rhythmically to the mighty movements of his breathing. And the third and last thrill of comprehension slithered clammily into the small of the Saint's back as he saw all these things—as he saw the savage ruthlessness of purpose behind the mere physical presence of that magnificent brute-man, sensed the primeval lust of cruelty in the parting of the thick lips and the glitter of the eyes. Almost he seemed to smell the sickly stench of rotting jungles seeping its fetid breath into the clean cold air of that English dawn, swelling in hot stifling waves about the figure of the pursuing beast that had taken the continents and the centuries in its bare-foot loping stride.

And while Simon watched, fascinated, the eyes of the negro fell on the sprawling figure that lay in the middle of the lane, and he stepped forward with a snarl of a beast rumbling in his throat.

And it was then that the Saint, with an effort which was as much physical as mental, tore from his mind the steely tentacles of the hypnotic spell that had held him paralysed for those few seconds—and also moved.

"Good morning," spoke the Saint politely, but that was the last polite speech he made that day. No one who had ever heard him talk had any illusions about the Saint's opinion of Simon Templar's physical prowess, and no one who had ever seen him fight had ever seriously questioned the accuracy of those opinions: but this was the kind of occasion on which the Saint knew that the paths of glory lead but to the grave. Which may help to explain why, after that single preliminary concession to the requirements of his manual of etiquette, he heaved the volume over the horizon and proceeded to lapse from grace in no uncertain manner.

After all, that encyclopedia of all the social virtues, though it had some cheering and helpful suggestions to offer on the subject of addressing letters to archdeacons, placing Grand Lamas in the correct relation of precedence to Herzegovinian Grossherzöge, and declining invitations to open bazaars in aid of Homes for Ichthyotic Vulcaniser's Mates, had never even envisaged such a situation as that which was then up for inspection, and the Saint figured that the rules allowed him a free hand.

The negro, crouching in the attitude in which the Saint's gentle voice had frozen him, was straining his eyes into the darkness. And out of that darkness, like a human cannon-ball, the Saint came at him.

He came in a weird kind of twisting leap that shot him out of the obscurity with no less startling a suddenness than if he had at that instant materialised out of the fourth dimension. And the negro simply had no time to do anything about it. For that suddenness was positively the only intangible quality about the movement. It had, for instance, a very tangible momentum, which must have been one of the most painfully concrete things that the victim of it had ever encountered. That momentum started from the five toes of the Saint's left foot; it rippled up his left calf, surged up his left thigh, and gathered to itself a final wave of power from the big muscles of his hips. And then, in that twisting action of his body, it was swung on into another channel: it travelled down the tautening fibres of his right leg, gathering new force in every inch of its progress, and came right out at the end of his shoe with all the smashing violence of a ten-ton stream of water cramped down into the finest nozzle of a garden hose. And at the very instant when every molecule of shattering velocity and weight was concentrated in the point of that right shoe, the point impacted precisely in the geometrical centre of the negro's stomach.

If there had been a football at that point of impact, a rag of shredded leather might reasonably have been expected to come to earth somewhere north of the Aberdeen Providential Society Buildings. And the effect upon the human target, colossus though it was, was just as devastating, even if a trifle less spectacular.

Simon heard the juicy *whuck!* of his shoe making contact, and saw the man travel three feet backwards as if he had been caught in the full fairway of a high-speed hydraulic battering-ram. The wheezy *phe-e-ew* of electrically emptied lungs merged into the synchronised sound effects, and ended in a little grunting cough. And then the negro seemed to dissolve on to the roadway like a statue of sculptured butter caught in the blast of a superheated furnace . . .

Simon jerked open one of the rear doors of the car, picked the bearded man lightly off the ground, heaved him upon the cushions, and slammed the door again.

Five seconds later he was behind the wheel, and the self-starter was whirring over the cold engine.

The headlights carved a blazing chunk of luminance out of the dimness as he touched a switch, and he saw the negro bucking up on to his hands and knees. He let in the clutch, and the car jerked away with a spluttering exhaust. One running-board rustled in the long grass of the banking as he lashed through the narrow gap, and then he was spinning round into the wide main road.

THE SAINT VERSUS SCOTLAND YARD

Ten yards ahead, in the full beam of the headlights a uniformed constable tumbled off his bicycle and ran to the middle of the road with outstretched hands, and Simon almost gasped.

Instantaneously he realised that the scream which had woken him must have been audible for some considerable distance—the policeman's attitude could not more clearly have indicated a curiosity which the Saint was at that moment instinctively disinclined to meet.

He eased up, and the constable guilelessly fell around to the side of the car.

And then the Saint revved up his engine, let in the clutch again with a bang, and went roaring on through the dawn with the policeman's shout tattered to futile fragments in the wind behind him.

CHAPTER 2

It was full daylight when he turned into Upper Berkeley Mews and stopped before his own front door, and the door opened even before he had switched off the engine.

"Hullo, boy!" said Patricia. "I wasn't expecting you for another hour."

"Neither was I," said the Saint.

He kissed her lightly on the lips, and stood there with his cap tilted rakishly to the back of his head and his leather coat swinging back from wide square shoulders, peeling off his gloves and smiling one of his most cryptic smiles.

"I've brought you a new pet," he said.

He twitched open the door behind him, and she peered puzzledly into the back of the car. The passenger was still unconscious, lolling back like a limb mummy in the travelling rug which the Saint had tucked round him, his white face turned blankly to the roof.

"But—who is he?"

"I haven't the faintest idea," said the Saint blandly. "But for the purposes of convenient reference I have christened him Beppo. His shirt has a Milan tab on it—Sherlock Holmes himself could deduce no more. And up to the present, he hasn't been sufficiently compos to offer any information."

Patricia Holm looked into his face, and saw the battle glint in his eye and a ghost of Saintliness flickering in the corners of his smile, and tilted her sweet fair head.

"Have you been in some more trouble?"

"It was rather a one-sided affair," said the Saint modestly. "Sambo never had a break—and I didn't mean him to have one, either. But the Queensberry Rules were strictly observed. There was no hitting below belts, which were worn loosely round the ankles—"

"Who's this you're talking about now?"

"Again, we are without information. But again for the purposes of convenient reference, you may call him His Beatitude the Negro Spiritual. And now listen."

Simon took her shoulders and swung her round.

"Somewhere between Basingstoke and Wintney," he said, "there's a gay game being played that's going to interest us a lot. And I came into it as a perfectly innocent party, for once in my life—but I haven't got time to tell you about it now. The big point at the moment is that a cop who arrived two minutes too late to be useful got my number. With Beppo in the back, I couldn't stop to hold converse with him, and you can bet he's jumped to the worst conclusions. In which he's damned right, but not in the way he thinks he is. There was a phone box twenty yards away, and unless the Negro Spiritual strangled him first he's referred my number to London most of an hour ago, and Teal will be snorting down a hot scent as soon as they can get him out of bed. Now, all you've got to know is this: I've just arrived, and I'm in my bath. Tell the glad news to anyone who rings up and anyone who calls, and if it's a call, hang a towel out of the window."

"But where are you going?"

"The Berkeley—to park the patient. I just dropped in to give you your cue." Simon Templar drew the end of a cigarette red, and snapped his lighter shut again. "And I'll be right back," he said, and wormed in behind the wheel.

A matter of seconds later the big car was in Berkeley Street, and he was pushing through the revolving doors of the hotel.

"Friend of mine had a bit of a car smash," he rapped at a sleepy reception clerk. "I wanna room for him now, and a doctor at eleven. Will you send a coupla men out to carry him in? Car at the door."

"One four eight," said the clerk, without batting an eyelid.

Simon saw the unconscious man carried upstairs, shot half-crowns into the hands of the men who performed the transportation, and closed the door on them.

Then he whipped from his pocket a thin nickelled case which he had brought from a pocket in the car. He snapped the neck of a small glass phial and drew up the colourless fluid it contained into the barrel of a hypodermic syringe. His latest protégé was still sleeping the sleep of sheer exhaustion, but Simon had no guarantee of how long that sleep would last. He proceeded to provide that guarantee himself, stabbing the needle into a limp arm and pressing home the plunger until the complete dose had been administered.

Then he closed and locked the door behind him and went quickly down the stairs.

Below, the reception clerk stopped him.

"What name shall I register, sir?"

"Teal," said the Saint, with a wry flick of humour. "Mr C. E. Teal. He'll sign your book later."

"Yes, sir . . . Er—has Mr Teal no luggage, sir?"

"Nope." A new ten-pound note drifted down to the desk. "On account," said the Saint. "And see that the doctor's waiting here for me at eleven, or I'll take the roof off your hotel and crown you with it."

He pulled his cap sideways and went back to his car. As he turned into Upper Berkeley Mews for the second time, he saw that his first homecoming had only just been soon enough. But that did not surprise him, for he had figured out his chances on that schedule almost to a second. A warning blink of white from an upper window caught his expectant eye at once, and he locked the wheel hard over and pulled up broadside on across the mews. In a flash he was out of his seat unlocking a pair of garage doors right at the street end of the mews, and in another second or two the car was hissing back into that garage with the cut-out firmly closed.

The Saint, without advertising the fact, had recently become the owner of one complete side of Upper Berkeley Mews, and he was in process of making some interesting structural alterations to that block of real estate of which the London County Council had not been informed and about which the District Surveyor had not even been consulted. The great work was not yet by any means completed, but even now it was capable of serving part of its purposes.

Simon went up a ladder into the bare empty room above. In one corner a hole had been roughly knocked through the wall; he went through it into another similar room, and on the far side of this was another hole in a wall; thus he passed in quick succession through numbers 1, 3, and 5, until the last plunge through the last hole and a curtain beyond it brought him into No. 7 and his own bedroom.

His tie was already off and his shirt unbuttoned by that time, and he tore off the rest of his clothes in little more than the time it took him to stroll through to the bathroom. And the bath was already full—filled long ago by Patricia.

"Thinks of everything!" sighed the Saint, with a wide grin of pure delight.

He slid into the bath like an otter, head and all, and came out of it almost in the same movement with a mighty splash, tweaking the plug out of the waste pipe as he did so. In another couple of seconds he was hauling himself into an enormously woolly blue bath-robe and grabbing a towel . . . and he went paddling down the stairs with his feet kicking about in a pair of gorgeously dilapidated moccasins, humming the hum of a man with a copper-plated liver and not one solitary little baby sin upon his conscience.

And thus he rolled into the sitting-room.

"Sorry to have kept you waiting, old dear," he murmured, and Chief Inspector Claud Eustace Teal rose from an armchair and surveyed him heavily.

"Good morning," said Mr Teal.

"Beautiful, isn't it?" agreed the Saint affably.

Patricia was smoking a cigarette in another chair. She should, according to the book of etiquette, have been beguiling the visitor's wait with some vivacious topical chatter, but the Saint, who was sensitive to atmosphere, had perceived nothing but a glutinously expanding silence as he entered the room. The perception failed to disturb him. He lifted the silver cover from a plate of bacon and eggs, and sniffed appreciatively. "You don't mind if I eat, do you, Claud?" he murmured.

The detective swallowed. If he had never been required to interview the Saint on business, he could have enjoyed a tolerably placid life. He was not by nature an excitable man, but these interviews never seemed to take the course which he intended them to take.

"Where were you last night?" he blurted.

"In Cornwall," said the Saint. "Charming county—full of area. Know it?"

"What time did you leave?"

"Nine-fifty-two pip."

"Did anybody see you go?"

"Everyone who had stayed the course observed my departure," said the Saint carefully. "A few of the male population had retired hurt a little earlier, and others were still enthusiastic but already blind. Apart from seven who had been ruled out earlier in the week by an epidemic of measles—"

"And where were you between ten and five minutes to five this morning?"

"I was on my way."

"Were you anywhere near Wintney?"

"That would be about it."

"Notice anything peculiar around there?"

Simon wrinkled his brow.

"I recall the scene distinctly. It was the hour before the dawn. The sleeping earth, still spell-bound by the magic of night, lay quiet beneath the paling skies. Over the peaceful scene brooded the expectant hush of all the mornings since the beginning of these days. The whole world, like a bride listening for the footfall of her lover, or a breakfast sausage hoping against hope—"

The movement with which Teal clamped a battered piece of spearmint between his molars was one of sheer ferocity.

"Now listen," he snarled. "Near Wintney, between ten and five minutes to five this morning, a Hirondel with your number plates on it was called on to stop by a police officer—and it drove straight past him!"

Simon nodded.

"Sure, that was me," he said innocently. "I was in a hurry. D'you mean I'm going to be summoned?"

"I mean more than that. Shortly before you came past, the constable heard a scream . . ."

Simon nodded again.

"Sure, I heard it too. Weird noises owls make sometimes. Did he want me to hold his hand?"

"That was no owl screaming—"

"Yeah? You were there as well, were you?"

"I've got the constable's telephoned report—"

"You can find a use for it." The Saint opened his mouth, inserted egg, bacon, and buttered toast in suitable proportions, and stood up. "And now you listen, Claud Eustace." He tapped the detective's stomach with his forefinger. "Have you got a warrant to come round and cross-examine me at this ungodly hour of the morning—or any other hour, for that matter?"

"It's part of my duty—"

"It's part of the blunt end of the pig of the aunt of the gardener. Let that pass for a minute. Is there one single crime that even your pop-eyed imagination can think of to charge me with? There is not. But we understand the functioning of your so-called brain. Some loutish cop thought he heard someone scream in Hampshire this morning, and because I happened to be passing through the same county you think I must have had something to do with it. If somebody tells you that a dud shilling has been found in a slot machine in Blackpool, the first thing you want to know is whether I was within a hundred miles of the spot within six months of the event. A drowned man is fished out of the ocean at Boston, and if you hear a rumour that I was staying beside the same ocean at Biarritz two years before—"

"I never—"

"You invariably. And now get another earful. You haven't a search-warrant, but we'll excuse that. Would you like to go upstairs and run through my wardrobe and see if you can find any bloodstains on my clothes? Because you're welcome. Would you like to push into the garage and take a look at my car and see if you can find a body under the back seat? Shove on. Make yourself absolutely at home. But digest this first." Again that dictatorial forefinger impressed its point on the preliminary concavity of the detective's waistcoat. "Make that search—accept my invitation—and if you can't find anything to justify it, you're going to wish your father had died a bachelor, which he may have done for all I know. You're becoming a nuisance, Claud, and I'm telling you that this is where you get off. Give me the small half of less than a quarter of a break, and I'm going to roast the hell out of you. I'm going to send you up to the sky on one big balloon, and when you come down you're not going to bounce—you're going to spread yourself out so flat that a short-sighted man will not be able to see you sideways. Got it?"

Teal gulped.

His cherubic countenance took on a slightly redder tinge, and he shuffled his feet like a truant schoolboy. But that, to do him justice, was the only childish thing about his attitude, and it was beyond Teal's power to control. For he gazed deep into the dancing, mocking, challenging blue eyes of the Saint standing there before him, lean and reckless and debonair even in that preposterous bath-robe outfit, and he understood the issue exactly.

And Chief Inspector Claud Eustace Teal nodded.

"Of course," he grunted, "if that's the way you take it, there's nothing more to be said."

"There isn't," agreed the Saint concisely. "And if there was, I'd say it."

He picked up the detective's bowler hat, dusted it with his towel, and handed it over. Teal accepted it, looked at it, and sighed. And he was still sighing when the Saint took him by the arm and ushered him politely but firmly to the door.

CHAPTER 3

"And if that," remarked the Saint, blithely returning to his interrupted breakfast, "doesn't shake up Claud Eustace from the Anzora downwards, nothing short of an earthquake will."

Patricia lighted another cigarette.

"So long as you didn't overdo it," she said. "*Quis s'excuse, s'accuse—*"

"And *honi soit qui mal y pense*," said the Saint cheerfully. "No, old sweetheart—that outburst had been on its way for a long while. We've been seeing a great deal too much of Claud Eustace lately, and I have a feeling that the Teal-baiting season is just getting into full swing."

"But what is the story about Beppo?"

Simon embarked upon his second egg.

"Oh, yes! Well, Beppo . . ."

He told her what he knew, and it is worth noting that she believed him. The recital, with necessary comment and decoration, ran out with the toast and marmalade, and at the end of it she knew as much as he did, which was not much.

"But in a little while we're going to know a whole lot more," he said.

He smoked a couple of cigarettes, glanced over the headlines of a newspaper, and went upstairs again. For several minutes he swung a pair of heavy Indian clubs with cheerful vigour; then a shave, a second and longer immersion in the bath with *savon* and *vox humana* accompaniment, and he felt ready to punch holes in three distinct and different heavy-weights. None of which being available, he selected a fresh outfit of clothes, dressed himself with leisurely care, and descended once more upon the sitting-room looking like one consolidated ray of sunshine.

"Cocktail at the Bruton at a quarter to one," he murmured, and drifted out again.

By that time, which was 10:44 precisely, if that matters a damn to anyone, the floating population of Upper Berkeley Mews had increased by one conspicuous unit, but that did not surprise the Saint. Such things had happened before, they were part of the inevitable paraphernalia of the attacks of virulent detectivosis which periodically afflicted the ponderous lucubrations of Chief Inspector Teal, and after the brief but comprehensive exchanges of pleasantries earlier that morning, Simon Templar would have been more disappointed than otherwise if he had seen no symptoms of a fresh outbreak of the disease.

Simon was not perturbed . . . He raised his hat politely to the sleuth, was cut dead, and remained unperturbed . . . And he sauntered imperturbably westwards through the smaller streets of Mayfair until, in one of the very smallest streets, he was able to collar the one and only visible taxi, in which he drove away, fluttering his handkerchief out of the window, and leaving a fuming plain-clothes man standing on the kerb glaring frantically around for another cab in which to continue the chase—and finding none.

At the Dover Street corner of Piccadilly, he paid off the driver and strolled back to the Piccadilly entrance of the Berkeley. It still wanted a few minutes to eleven, but the reception clerk, spurred on perhaps by the Saint's departing purposefulness, had a doctor already waiting for him.

Simon conducted the move to the patient's room himself, and had his first shock when he helped to remove the man's shirt.

He looked at what he saw in silence for some seconds, and then the doctor, who had also looked, turned to him with his ruddy face gone a shade paler.

"I was told that your friend had had an accident," he said bluntly, and the Saint nodded.

"Something unpleasant has certainly happened to him. Will you go on with your examination?"

He lighted a cigarette and went over to the window, where he stood gazing thoughtfully down into Berkeley Street until the doctor rejoined him.

"Your friend seems to have been given an injection of scopolamine and morphia—you have probably heard of 'twilight sleep.' His other injuries you've seen for yourself—I haven't found any more."

The Saint nodded.

"I gave him the injection myself. He should be waking up soon—he had rather less than one-hundredth of a grain of scopolamine. Will you want to move him to a nursing-home?"

"I don't think that will be necessary, unless he wishes it himself, Mr—"

"Travers."

"Mr Travers. He should have a nurse, of course—"

"I can get one."

The doctor inclined his head.

Then he removed his pince-nez and looked the Saint directly in the eyes.

"I presume you know how your friend received his injuries?" he said.

"I can guess." The Saint flicked a short cylinder of ash from his cigarette. "I should say that he had been beaten with a raw-hide whip, and that persuasion by hot irons had also been applied."

The doctor put his finger-tips together and blinked.

"You must admit, Mr Travers, that the circumstances are—er—somewhat unusual."

"You could say all that twice, and no one would accuse you of exaggerating," assented the Saint, with conviction. "But if that fact is bothering your professional conscience, I can only say that I'm as much in the dark as you are. The accident story was just to satisfy the birds below. As a matter of fact, I found our friend lying by the roadside in the small hours of this morning, and I sort of took charge. Doubtless the mystery will be cleared up in due course."

"Naturally, you have communicated with the police."

"I've already interviewed one detective, and I'm sure he's doing everything he can," said the Saint veraciously. He opened the door, and propelled the doctor decisively along the corridor. "Will you want to see the patient today?"

"I hardly think it will be necessary, Mr Travers. His dressing should be changed tonight—the nurse will see to that. I'll come in tomorrow morning—"

"Thanks very much. I shall expect you at the same time. Good-bye."

Simon shook the doctor warmly by the hand, swept him briskly into the waiting elevator, and watched him sink downwards out of view.

Then he went back to the room, poured out a glass of water, and sat down in a chair by the bedside. The patient was sleeping easily, and Simon, after a glance at his watch, prepared to await the natural working-off of the drug.

A quarter of an hour later he was extinguishing a cigarette when the patient stirred and groaned. A thin hand crawled up to the bare throat, and the man's head rolled sideways with his eyelids flickering. As Simon bent over him, a husky whisper of a word came through the relaxed lips.

"*Acqua . . .*"

"Sure thing, brother." Simon propped up the man's head and put the glass to his mouth.

"*Mille grazie.*"

"*Prego.*"

Presently the man sank back again. And then his eyes opened, and focused on the Saint.

For a number of seconds there was not the faintest glimmer of understanding in the eyes: they stared at and through their object like the eyes of a blind man. And then, slowly, they widened into round pools of shuddering horror, and the Italian shrank away with a thin cry rattling in his throat.

Simon gripped his arm and smiled.

"*Non tema. Sono un amico.*"

It was some time before he was able to calm the man into a dully incredulous quietness, but he won belief before he had finished, and at last the Italian sank back among the pillows and was silent.

Simon mopped his brow and fished out his cigarette-case.

And then the man spoke again, still weakly, but in a different voice.

"*Quanti ne abbiamo quest' oggi?*"

"*Eil due ottobre.*"

There was a pause.

"*Vuol favorire di dirmi il suo nome?*"

"Templar—Simon Templar."

There was another pause. And then the man rolled over and looked at the Saint again. And he spoke in almost perfect English.

"I have heard of you. You were called—"

"Many things. But that was a long time ago."

"How did you find me?"

"Well—I rather think that you found me."

The Italian passed a hand across his eyes.

"I remember now. I was running. I fell down. Someone caught me . . ." Suddenly he clutched the Saint's wrist. "Did you see—him?"

"Your gentleman friend?" murmured Simon lightly. "Sure I did. He also saw me, but not soon enough. Yes, we certainly met."

The grip of the trembling fingers loosened slowly, and the man lay still, breathing jerkily through his nose.

"*Voglia scusarmi,*" he said at length. "*Mi vergogno.*"

"Non ne val la pena."

"It is as if I had awoken from a terrible dream. Even now—" The Italian looked down at the bandages that swathed the whole of the upper part of his body, and shivered uncontrollably. "Did you put on these?" he asked.

"No—a doctor did that."

The man looked round the room.

"And this—?"

"This is the Berkeley Hotel, London."

The Italian nodded. He swallowed painfully, and Simon refilled his glass and passed it back. Another silence fell, which grew so long that the Saint wondered if his patient had fallen asleep again. He rose stealthily to his feet, and the Italian roused and caught his sleeve.

"Wait." The words came quite quietly and sanely. "I must talk to you."

"Sure." Simon smiled down at the man. "But do you want to do it now? Hadn't you better rest for a bit—maybe have something to eat—"

The Italian shook his head.

"Afterwards. Will you sit down again?"

And Simon Templar sat down.

And he listened, almost without movement, while the minute hand of his watch voyaged unobserved once round the dial. He listened in a perfect trance of concentration, while the short precise sentences of the Italian's story slid into the atmosphere and built themselves up into a shape that he had never even dreamed of.

It was past one o'clock when he walked slowly down the stairs with the inside story of one of the most stupendous crimes in history whirling round in his brain like the armature of a high-powered dynamo.

Wrapped up in the rumination of what he had heard, he passed out like a sleep-walker into Berkeley Street. And it so happened that in his abstraction he almost cannoned into a man who was at that moment walking down towards Piccadilly. He stepped aside with a muttered apology, absent-mindedly registering a kind of panoramic impression of a brilliantly purple suit, lemon-coloured gloves, a gold-mounted cane, a lavender shirt, spotted tie, and—

Just for an instant the Saint's gaze rested on the man's face. And then they were past each other, without a flicker of recognition, without the batting of an eyelid. But the Saint knew . . .

He knew that that savagely arrogant face, like a mask of black marble, was like no other black face that he had ever seen in his life before that morning. And he knew, with the same certainty, that the eyes in the black face had recognised him in the same moment as he had recognised them—and with no more betrayal of their knowledge. And as he wandered up into Berkeley Square, and the portals of the Bruton Club received him, he knew, though he had not looked back, that the black eyes were still behind him, and had seen where he went.

CHAPTER 4

But the smile with which the Saint greeted Patricia was as gay and carefree a smile as she had ever seen.

"I should like," said the Saint, sinking into an armchair, "three large double Martinis in a big glass. Just to line my stomach. After which, I shall be able to deal respectfully with a thirst which can only be satisfactorily slaked by two gallons of bitter beer."

"You will have one Martini, and then we'll have some lunch," said Patricia, and the Saint sighed.

"You have no soul," he complained.

Patricia put her magazine under the table.

"What's new, boy?" she asked.

"About Beppo? . . . Well, a whole heap of things are new about Beppo. I can tell you this, for instance: Beppo is no smaller a guy than the Duke of Fortezza, and he is the acting President of the Bank of Italy."

"He's—what?"

"He's the acting President of the Bank of Italy—and that's not the half of it. Pat, old girl, I told you at the start that there was some gay game being played, and, by the Lord, it's as gay a game as we may ever find!" Simon signed the chit on the waiter's tray with a flourish and settled back again, surveying his drink dreamily. "Remember reading in some paper recently that the Bank of Italy were preparing to put out an entirely new and original line of paper currency?" he asked.

"I saw something about it."

"It was so. The contract was placed with Crosby Dorman, one of our biggest printing firms—they do the thin cash and postal issues of half a dozen odd little countries. Beppo put the deal through. A while ago he brought over the plates and gave the order, and one week back he came on his second trip to take delivery of three million pounds' worth of coloured paper in a tin-lined box."

"And then?"

"I'll tell you what then. One whole extra million pounds' worth of mazuma is ordered, and that printing goes into a separate box. Ordered on official notepaper, too, with Beppo's own signature in the south-east corner. And meanwhile Beppo is indisposed. The first crate of spondulix departs in the golden galleon without him, completely surrounded by soldiers, secret service agents, and general detectives, all armed to the teeth and beyond. Another of those nice letters apologises for Beppo's absence, and instructs the guard to carry on; a third letter explains the circumstances, ditto and ditto, to the Bank—"

Patricia sat up.

"And the box is empty?"

"The box is packed tight under a hydraulic press, stiff to the sealing-wax with the genuine articles as per invoice."

"But—"

"But obviously. That box had got to go through. The new issue had to spread itself out. It's been on the market three days already. And the ground bait is now laid for the big haul—the second box, containing approximately one million hundred-lire bills convertible into equivalent sterling on sight. And the whole board of the Bank of Italy, the complete staff of cashiers, office-boys, and outside porters, the entire vigilance society of soldiers, secret service agents, and general detectives, all armed to the teeth and beyond, are as innocent of the existence of that million as the unborn daughter of the Caliph's washerwoman."

The girl looked at him with startled eyes.

"And do you mean Beppo was in this?"

"Does it seem that way?" Simon Templar swivelled round towards her with one eyebrow inquisitorially cocked and a long wisp of smoke trailing through his lips. "I wish you could have seen him . . . Sure he's in it. They turned him over to the Negro Spiritual, and let that big black swine pet him till he signed. If I told you what they'd done to him you wouldn't be in such a hurry for your lunch." For a moment the Saint's lips thinned fractionally. "He's just shot to pieces, and when you see him you'll know why. Sure, that bunch are like brothers to Beppo!"

Patricia sat in a thoughtful silence, and the Saint emptied his glass. Then she said, "Who are this bunch?"

Simon slithered his cigarette round to the corner of his mouth.

"Well, the actual bunch are mostly miscellaneous, as you might say," he answered. "But the big noise seems to be a bird named Kuzela, whom we haven't met before but whom I'm going to meet darn soon."

"And this money—"

"Is being delivered to Kuzela's men today." The Saint glanced at his watch. "Has been, by now. And within twenty-four hours parcels of it will be burning the sky over to his agents in Paris, Berlin, Vienna, and Madrid. Within the week it will be gravitating back to him through the same channels—big bouncing wads of it, translated into authentic wads of francs, marks, pesetas—while one million perfectly genuine hundred-lire bills whose numbers were never in the catalogue are drifting home to a Bank of Italy that will be wondering whether the whole world is falling to pieces round its ears . . . Do you get me, Pat?"

The clear blue eyes rested on her face with the twist of mocking hell-for-leather delight that she knew so well, and she asked her next question almost mechanically. "Is it your party?"

"It is, old Pat. And not a question asked. No living soul must ever know—there'd be a panic on the international exchanges if a word of it leaked out. But every single one of those extra million bills has got to be taken by hand and led gently back to Beppo's tender care—and the man who's going to do it is ready for his lunch."

And lunch it was without further comment, for the Saint was like that . . . But about his latest meeting with the Negro Spiritual he did not find it necessary to say anything at all—for, again, the Saint was that way . . . And after lunch, when Patricia was ordering coffee in the lounge, yet another incident which the Saint was inclined to regard as strictly private and personal clicked into its appointed socket in the energetic history of that day.

Simon had gone out to telephone a modest tenner on a horse for the 3:30, and was on his way back through the hall when a porter stopped him.

"Excuse me, sir, but did you come here from the Berkeley?"

The Saint fetched his right foot up alongside his left and lowered his brows one millimetre.

"Yeah—I have been in there this morning."

"A coloured gentleman brought these for you, sir. He said he saw you drop them as you came out of the hotel, but he lost you in the crowd while he was picking them up. And then, as he was walking through Lansdowne Passage, he happened to look up and see you at one of the windows, so he brought them in. From the description he gave me it seemed as if it must have been you, sir—"

"Oh, it was certainly me."

The Saint, who had never owned a pair of lemon-coloured gloves in his life, accepted the specimens gingerly, folded them, and slipped them into his pocket.

"Funny coincidence, sir, wasn't it?" said the porter chattily. "Him happening to pass by, and you happening to be in the window at that time."

"Quite remarkable," agreed the Saint gravely, recalling the care he had taken to avoid all windows, and, turning back, he retired rapidly to a remote sanctuary.

There he unfolded the gloves in an empty washbasin, contriving to work them cautiously inside out with his fountain pen in one hand and his propelling pencil in the other.

He had not the vaguest idea what kind of creeping West African frightfulness might be waiting for him in those citron-hued misdemeanours, but he was certainly a trifle surprised when he saw what fell out of the first glove that he tackled.

It was simply a thin splinter of wood, painted at both ends, and stained with some dark stain.

For a moment or two he looked at it expressionlessly.

Then he picked it up between two matches and stowed it carefully in his cigarette-case.

He turned his attention to the second glove, and extracted from it a soiled scrap of paper. He read:

If you will come to 85, Vandemeer Avenue, Hampstead, at midnight tonight, we may be able to reach some mutually satisfactory agreement. Otherwise, I fear that the consequences of your interference may be infinitely regrettable.

K.

Simon Templar held the message at arm's length, well up to the light, and gazed at it wall-eyed.

"And whales do so lay eggs," he articulated at last, when he could find a voice sufficiently impregnated with emotion.

And then he laughed and went back to Patricia.

"If Monday's Child comes home, you shall have a new hat," he said, and the girl smiled.

"What else happens before that?" she asked.

"We go on a little tour," said the Saint.

They left the club together, and boarded a taxi that had just been paid off at the door.

"Piccadilly Hotel," said the Saint.

He settled back, lighting a cigarette.

"I shook off Teal's man by Method One," he explained. "You are now going to see a demonstration of Method Two. If you can go on studying under my supervision, all the shadowers you will ever meet will mean nothing to you . . . The present performance may be a waste of energy"—he glanced back through the rear window—"or it may not. But the wise man is permanently suspicious."

They reached the Piccadilly entrance of the hotel in a few minutes, and the Saint opened the door. The exact fare, plus bonus, was ready in the Saint's hand, and he dropped it in the driver's palm and followed Patricia across the pavement—without any appearance of haste, but very briskly. As he reached the doors, he saw in one glass panel the reflection of another taxi pulling in to the kerb behind him.

"This way."

He steered the girl swiftly through the main hall, swung her through a short passage, across another hall, and up some steps, and brought her out through another door into Regent Street. A break in the traffic let them straight through to the taxi rank in the middle of the road.

"Berkeley Hotel," said the Saint.

He lounged deep in his corner and grinned at her.

"Method Two is not for use on a trained sleuth who knows you know he's after you," he murmured. "Other times, it's the whelk's knee-cap." He took her bag from her hands, slipped out the little mirror, and used it for a periscope to survey the south side pavement as they drove away. "This is one of those whens," he said complacently.

"Then why are we going to the Berkeley?"

"Because you are the nurse who is going to look after Beppo. His number is 148, and 149 is already booked for you. Incidentally, you might remember that he's registered in the name of Teal—C. E. Teal. I'll pack a bag and bring it along to you later, but once you're inside the Berkeley Arms you've got to stay put so long as it's daylight. The doctor's name is Branson and mine is Travers, and if anyone else applies for admission you will shoot him through the binder and ring for the bell-hop to remove the body."

"But what will you be doing?"

"I am the proud possessor of a Clue, and I'm going to be very busy tying a knot in its tail. Also I have an ambition to be humorous, and that will mean that I've got to push round to a shop I know of and purchase one of those mechanical jokes that are said to create roars of laughter. I've been remembering my younger days, and they've brought back to me the very thing I need . . . And here we are."

The cab had stopped at its destination, and they got out. Patricia hesitated in the doorway. "When will you be back?" she asked.

"I shall be along for dinner about eight," said the Saint. "Meanwhile, you'll be able to get acquainted with Beppo. Really, you'll find him quite human. Prattle gently to him, and he'll eat out of your hand. When he's stronger, you might even be allowed to sing to him—I'll ask the doctor about that tomorrow . . . So long, lass!"

And the Saint was gone.

And he did exactly what he had said he was going to do. He went to a shop in Regent Street and bought a little toy and took it back with him to Upper Berkeley Mews, and a certain alteration which he made to its inner functionings kept him busy for some time and afforded him considerable amusement.

For he had not the slightest doubt that there was going to be fun and games before the next dawn. The incident of those lemon-coloured gloves was a distinct encouragement. It showed a certain thoroughness on the part of the opposition, and that sort of thing always gave the Saint great pleasure.

"If one glove doesn't work, the other is expected to oblige," he figured it out, as he popped studs into a snowy white dress shirt. "And it would be a pity to disappoint anyone."

He elaborated this latter idea to Patricia Holm when he rejoined her at the Berkeley, having shaken off his official watcher again by Method Three. Before he left, he told her nearly everything.

"At midnight, all the dreams of the ungodly are coming true," he said. "Picture to yourself the scene. It will be the witching hour. The menace of dark deeds will veil the stars. And up the heights of Hampstead will come toiling the pitiful figure of the unsuspecting victim, with his bleary eyes bulging and his mouth hanging open and the green moss sprouting behind his ears, and that will be Little Boy . . ."

CHAPTER 5

Some men enjoy trouble; others just as definitely don't. And there are some who enjoy dreaming about the things they would do if they only dared—but they need not concern us.

Simon Templar came into Category A—straight and slick, with his name in a panel all to itself, and a full stop just where it hits hardest.

For there is a price ticket on everything that puts a whizz into life, and adventure follows the rule. It's distressing, but there you are. If there was no competition, everything would be quite all right. If you could be certain that you were the strongest man in the world, the most quick-witted, the most cunning, the most keen-sighted, the most vigilant, and simultaneously the possessor of the one and only lethal weapon in the whole wide universe, there wouldn't be much difficulty about it. You would just step out of your hutch and hammer the first thing that came along.

But it doesn't always pan out like that in practice. When you try the medicine on the dog, you are apt to discover some violent reactions which were not arranged for in the prescription. And then, when the guns give tongue and a spot of fur begins to fly, you are liable to arrive at the sudden and soul-shattering realisation that a couple of ounces of lead travelling with a given velocity will make precisely as deep an impression on your anatomical system as they will on that of the next man.

Which monumental fact the Saint had thoroughly digested a few days after mastering his alphabet. And the effect it had registered upon his unweaned peace of mind had been so near to absolute zero that a hair-line could not have been drawn between them—neither on the day of the discovery nor on any subsequent day in all his life.

In theory . . .

In theory, of course, he allowed the artillery to pop, and the fur to become volatile, without permitting a single lock of his own sleek dark hair to aberrate from the patent-leather discipline in which he disposed it, and thereby he became the Saint. But it is perfectly possible to appreciate and acknowledge the penetrating unpleasantness of high-velocity lead, and forthwith to adopt a debonairly philosophical attitude towards the same, without being in a tearing hurry to offer your own carcase for the purpose of practical demonstration; this also the Saint did, and by doing it with meticulous attention contrived to be spoken of in the present tense for many years longer than the most optimistic insurance broker would have backed him to achieve.

All of which has not a little to do with 85, Vandemeer Avenue, Hampstead.

Down this road strolled the Saint, his hands deep in the pockets of knife-edged trousers, the crook of his walking-stick hooked over his left wrist, and slanting sidelong over his right eye a filibustering black felt hat which alone was something very like a breach of the peace. A little song rollicked on his lips, and was inaudible two yards away. And as he walked, his lazy eyes absorbed every interesting item of the scenery.

Aspidistra, little herb.

Do you think it silly
When the botaniser's blurb
Links you with the lily?

Up in one window of the house, he caught the almost imperceptible sway of a shifting curtain, and knew that his approach had already been observed. "But it is nice," thought the Saint, "to be expected." And he sauntered on.

Up above your window-ledge
Streatham stars are gleaming:
Aspidistra, little veg.
Does your soul go dreaming?

A low iron gate opened from the road. He pushed it wide with his foot, and went up the steps to the porch. Beside the door was a bell-push set in a panel of polished brass tracery.

The Saint's fingers moved towards it . . . and travelled back again. He stooped and examined the filigree more closely, and a little smile lightened his face.

Then he cuddled himself into the extreme houseward corner of the porch, held his hat over the panel, and pressed the button with the ferrule of his stick. He heard a faint hiss, and turned his hat back to the light of a street lamp. A stained splinter of wood quivered in the white satin lining of the crown, and the Saint's smile became blindingly seraphic as he reached into a side pocket of his jacket for a pair of tweezers . . .

And then the door was opening slowly.

Deep in his angle of shadow, he watched the strip of yellow light widening across the porch and down the short flagged passage to the gate. The silhouette of a man loomed into it and stood motionless for a while behind the threshold.

Then it stepped out into full view—a big, heavy-shouldered close-cropped man, with thick bunched fists hanging loosely at his sides. He peered outwards down the shaft of light, and then to right and left, his battered face creasing to the strain of probing the darkness of either side. The Saint's white shirt-front caught his eye, and he licked his lips and spoke like an automaton.

"Comin' in?"

"Behind you, brother," said the Saint.

He stepped across the light, taking the bruiser by the elbows and spinning him adroitly round. They entered the house in the order of his own arrangement, and Simon kicked the door shut behind him.

There was no machine-gun at the far end of the hall, as he had half expected, but the Saint was unashamed.

"Windy?" sneered the bruiser, as the Saint released him, and Simon smiled.

"Never since taking soda-mint," he murmured. "Where do we go from here?"

The bruiser glanced sideways, jerking his head.

"Upstairs."

"Oh, yeah?"

Simon slanted a cigarette into his mouth and followed the glance. His eyes waved up the banisters and down the separate steps of the stairway.

"After you again," he drawled. "Just to be certain."

The bruiser led the way, and Simon followed discreetly. They arrived in procession at the upper landing, where a second bruiser, a trifle shorter than the first, but even heavier of shoulder, lounged beside an open door with an unlighted stump of cigar in his mouth.

The second man gestured with his lower jaw and the cigar.

"In there."

"Thanks," said the Saint.

He paused for a moment in the doorway and surveyed the room, one hand ostentatiously remaining in the pocket of his coat.

Facing him, in the centre of the rich brown carpet, was a broad flat-topped desk. It harmonised with the solid simplicity of the book-cases that broke the panelling of the bare walls, and with the long austere lines of the velvet hangings that covered the windows—even, perhaps, with the squat square materialism of the safe that stood in the corner behind it. And on the far side of the desk sat the man whom the Saint had come to see, leaning forward out of a straight-backed oak chair.

Simon moved forward, and the two bruisers closed the door and ranged themselves on either side of him.

"Good evening, Kuzela," said the Saint.

"Good evening, Mr Templar." The man behind the desk moved one white hand. "Sit down."

Simon looked at the chair that had been placed ready for him. Then he turned, and took one of the bruisers by the lapels of his coat. He shot the man into the chair, bounced him up and down a couple of times, swung him from side to side, and yanked him out again.

"Just to make *quite* certain," said the Saint sweetly. He beamed upon the glowering pugilist, felt his biceps, and patted him encouragingly on the shoulder. "You'll be a big man when you grow up, Cuthbert," he said affably.

Then he moved the chair a yard to one side and sat in it himself.

"I'm sure you'll excuse all these formalities," he remarked conversationally. "I have to be so careful these days. The most extraordinary things happen to me. Only the other day, a large spotted hypotenuse, overtaking on the wrong side—"

"I have already observed that you possess a well-developed instinct of self-preservation, Mr Templar," said Kuzela suavely.

He clasped his well-kept hands on the blotter before him, and studied the Saint interestedly.

Simon returned the compliment.

He saw a man in healthy middle age, broad-shouldered and strongly built. A high, firmly modelled forehead rose into a receding setting of clipped iron-grey hair. With his square jaw and slightly aquiline nose, he might have posed for a symbolical portrait of any successful business man. Only his eyes might have betrayed the imposture. Pale blue, deep-set, and unwinking, they levelled themselves upon the object of their scrutiny in a feline stare of utter ruthlessness . . . And the Saint looked into the blue eyes and laughed.

"You certainly win on the exchange," he said, and a slight frown came between the other's eyebrows.

"If you would explain—?"

"I'm good-looking," said the Saint easily, and centred his tie with elegance.

Kuzela leaned back.

"Your name is known to me, of course, but I think this is the first time we have had the pleasure of meeting."

"This is certainly the first time you've had the pleasure of meeting me," said the Saint carefully.

"Even now, the responsibility is yours. You have elected to interfere with my affairs—"

Simon shook his head sympathetically.

"It's most distressing, isn't it?" he murmured. "And your most strenuous efforts up to date have failed to dispose of the interference. Even when you sent me a pair of gloves that would have given a rhinoceros a headache to look at, I survived the shock. It must be Fate, old dear."

Kuzela pulled himself forward again.

"You are an enterprising young man," he said quietly. "An unusually enterprising young man. There are not many men living who could have overcome Ngano, even by the method which you adopted. The mere fact that you were able to enter this house is another testimony to your foresight—or your good luck."

"My foresight," said the Saint modestly.

"You moved your chair before you sat down—and that again showed remarkable intelligence. If you had sat where I intended you to sit, it would have been possible for me, by a slight movement of my foot, to send a bullet through the centre of your body."

"So I guessed."

"Since you arrived, your hand has been in your pocket several times. I presume you are armed—"

Simon Templar inspected the finger-nails of his two hands.

"If I had been born the day before yesterday," he observed mildly, "you'd find out everything you wanted to know in approximately two minutes."

"Again, a man of your reputation would not have communicated with the police—"

"But he would take great care of himself." The Saint's eyes met Kuzela's steadily. "I'll talk or fight, Kuzela, just as you like. Which is it to be?"

"You are prepared to deal?"

"Within limits—yes."

Kuzela drummed his knuckles together.

"On what terms?"

"They might be—one hundred thousand pounds."

Kuzela shrugged.

"If you came here in a week's time—"

"I should be very pleased to have a drink with you," said the Saint pointedly.

"Suppose," said Kuzela, "I gave you a cheque which you could cash tomorrow morning—"

"Or suppose," said the Saint calmly, "you gave me some cash with which I could buy jujubes on my way home."

Kuzela looked at him with a kind of admiration.

"Rumour has not lied about you, Mr Templar," he said. "I imagine you will have no objection to receiving this sum in—er—foreign currency?"

"None whatever," said the Saint blandly.

The other stood up, taking a little key from his waistcoat pocket. And the Saint, who for the moment had been looking at the delicately painted shade of the lamp that stood on one side of the desk, which was the sole dim illumination of the room, slewed round with a sudden start.

He knew that there was going to be a catch somewhere—that, with a man of Kuzela's type, a man who had sent those gloves and who had devised that extremely ingenious bell-push on the front door, a coup could never be quite so easy. How that last catch was going to be worked he had no idea, nor was he inclined to wait and learn it. In his own way, he had done as much as he had hoped to do, and, all things considered—

"Let me see that key!" he exclaimed.

Kuzela turned puzzledly.

"Really, Mr Templar—"

"Let me see it!" repeated the Saint excitedly.

He reached over the desk and took the key out of Kuzela's hands. For a second he gazed at it, and then he raised his eyes again with a dancing devil of mischief glinting out of their blueness.

"Sorry I must be going, souls," he said, and with one smashing sweep of his arm he sent the lamp flying off the desk and plunged the room into inky blackness.

CHAPTER 6

The phrase is neither original nor copyright, and may be performed in public without fee or licence. It remains, however, an excellent way of describing that particular phenomenon.

With the extinction of the single source of luminance, the darkness came down in all the drenching suddenness of an unleashed cataract of Stygian gloom. For an instant, it seemed to blot out not only the sense of sight, but also every other active faculty, and a frozen, throbbing stillness settled between the four walls. And in that stillness the Saint sank down without a sound upon his toes and the tips of his fingers . . .

He knew his bearings to the nth part of a degree, and he travelled to his destination with the noiseless precision of a cat. Around him he could hear the sounds of tensely restrained breathing, and the slithering caress of wary feet creeping over the carpet. Then, behind him, came the vibration of a violent movement, the thud of a heavy blow, a curse, a scuffle, a crashing fall, and a shrill yelp of startled anguish . . . and the Saint grinned gently.

"I got 'im," proclaimed a triumphant voice, out of the dark void. "Strike a light, Bill."

Through an undercurrent of muffled yammering sizzled the crisp kindling of a match. It was held in the hand of Kuzela himself, and by its light the two bruisers glared at each other, their reddened stares of hate aimed upwards and downwards respectively. And before the match went out the opinions of the foundation member found fervid utterance.

"You perishing bleeder," he said, in accents that literally wobbled with earnestness.

"Peep-bo," said the Saint, and heard the contortionist effects blasphemously disentangling themselves as he closed the door behind him.

A bullet splintered a panel two inches east of his neck as he shifted briskly westwards. The next door stood invitingly ajar: he went through it as the other door reopened, slammed it behind him, and turned the key.

In a few strides he was across the room and flinging up the window. He squirmed over the sill like an eel, curved his fingers over the edge, and hung at the full stretch of his arms. A foot below the level of his eyes there was a narrow stone ledge running along the side of the building: he transferred himself to it, and worked rapidly along to the nearest corner. As he rounded it, he looked down into the road, twenty feet below, and saw a car standing by the kerb.

Another window came over his head. He reached up, got a grip of the sill, and levered his elbows above the sill level with a skilful kick and an acrobatic twist of his body. From there he was able to make a grab for the top of the lower sash . . . And in another moment he was standing upright on the sill, pushing the upper sash cautiously downwards.

A murmur of dumbfounded voices drifted to his ears.

"Where the 'ell can 'e 'ave gorn to?"

"Think 'e jumped for it?"

"Jumped for it, yer silly fat-'ead? . . ."

And then the Saint lowered himself cat-footed to the carpet on the safe side of the curtains in the room he had recently left.

Through a narrow gap in the hangings he could see Kuzela replacing the shattered bulb of the table-lamp by the light of a match. The man's white efficient hands were perfectly steady; his face was without expression. He accomplished his task with the tremorless tranquility of a patient middle-aged gentleman whom no slight accident could seriously annoy—tested the switch . . .

And then, as the room lighted up again, he raised his eyes to the convex mirror panel on the opposite wall, and had one distorted glimpse of the figure behind him.

Then the Saint took him by the neck.

Fingers like bands of steel paralysed his larynx and choked back into his chest the cry he would have uttered. He fought like a maniac, but though his strength was above the average, he was as helpless as a puppet in that relentless grip. And almost affectionately Simon Templar's thumbs sidled round to their mark—the deadly pressure of the carotid arteries which is to crude ordinary throttling what foil play is to sabre work . . .

It was all over in a few seconds. And Kuzela was lying limply spread-eagled across the desk, and Simon Templar was fitting his key into the lock of the safe.

The plungers pistoned smoothly back, and the heavy door swung open. And the Saint sat back on his heels and gazed in rapture at what he saw.

Five small leather attaché cases stood in a neat row before his eyes. It was superb—splendiferous—it was just five times infinitely more than he had ever seriously dared to hope. That one hundred million lire were lying around somewhere in London he had been as sure as a man can be of anything—Kuzela would never have wasted time transporting his booty from the departure centre to the country house where the Duke of Fortezza had been kept—but that the most extempore bluff should have led him promptly and faultlessly to the hiding-place of all that merry mazuma was almost too good to be true. And for a few precious seconds the Saint stared entranced at the vision that his everlasting preposterous luck had ladled out for his delight . . .

And then he was swiftly hauling the valises out on to the floor.

He did not even have to attempt to open one of them. He knew . . .

Rapidly he ranged the bags in a happy little line across the carpet. He picked up his stick and he was adjusting his hat at its most effective angle when the two men who had pursued him returned through the door. But there was a wicked little automatic pivoting round in his free hand, and the two men noticed it in time.

"Restrain your enthusiasm, boys," said the Saint. "We're going on a journey. Pick up your luggage, and let's be moving."

He transferred one of the bags to his left hand, and his gun continued to conduct the orchestra. And under its gentle supervision the two men obeyed his orders. The delirious progress of events during the past couple of minutes had been a shade too much for their ivorine uptakes: their faces wore two uniformly blank expressions of pained bewilderment, vaguely reminiscent of the registers of a pair of precocious goldfish photographed immediately after signing their first talking-picture contract. Even the power of protest had temporarily drained out their vocal organs. They picked up two bags apiece and suffered themselves to be shepherded out of the room in the same bovine vacuity of acquiescence.

In the hall, Simon halted the fatigue party for a moment.

"Before we pass out into the night," he said, "I want you to be quite clear about one thing. Those bags you're carrying, as you may or may not know, are each supposed to contain the equivalent of two hundred thousand pounds in ready money, and I want you to know anything that you may be prepared to do to keep all those spondulix for yourselves is just so much tadpole-gizzard beside what I'm prepared to do to prise it off you. So you should think a long while before you do anything rash. I am the greatest gun artist in the world," said the Saint persuasively, but with a singular lack of honesty, "and I'm warning you here and now that at the first sign I see of any undue enterprise, I shall shoot each of you through the middle of the eleventh spinal vertebra, counting from the bottom. Move on, my children."

The procession moved on.

It went down the porch steps and through the iron wicket gate to the road, and the Saint brought up the rear with his right hand in his pocket. The comedy was played without witnesses: at that hour Vandemeer Avenue, a quiet backwater even at the height of the day, was absolutely deserted. A sum total of four lighted windows was visible along the whole length of the thoroughfare, and those were too far away to provide the slightest inconvenience in any conceivable circumstances. Hampstead was being good that night . . .

The car which Simon had observed on his prowl round the exterior of the house was parked right opposite the gate—which was where he had expected it to be. As the two men paused outside the gate, waiting for further instructions, a door of the car opened, and a slim supple figure decanted itself lightly on to the sidewalk. Patricia . . . She came forward with her swinging long-limbed stride.

"O.K., Simon?"

"O.K., lass."

"Gee, boy, I'm glad to see you."

"And I you. And the whole Wild West show was just a sitting rabbit, believe it or believe it not." The Saint's hand touched her arm. "Get back behind the wheel, Pat, start her up, and be ready to pull out as soon as the boodle's on board. It isn't every day we ferry a cool million across London, and I don't see why the honour of being the pilot shouldn't be your share of the act."

"Right-ho . . ."

The girl disappeared, and Simon opened another door.

He watched the cases being stowed one by one in the back of the car, and the forefinger of his right hand curled tensely over the trigger of his gun. He had meant every word of his threat to the two men who were doing the job, and they must have known it, for they carried out his orders with commendable alacrity.

And yet Simon felt a faint electric tingle of uneasiness fanning up his back and into the roots of his hair like the march of a thousand ghostly needle-points. He could not have described it in any other way, and he was as much at a loss to account for it as if the simile had been the actual fact. It was sheer blind instinct, a seventh sense born of a hundred breathless adventures, that touched him with single thrill of insufficient warning—and left it at that. And for once in his life he ignored the danger-sign. He heard the whine of the self-starter, followed by the low-pitched powerful pulsing of the eight cleanly balanced cylinders, and saw the door closed upon the last of the bags: and he turned smiling to the two bruisers. He pointed.

"If you keep straight on down that road," he said, "it ought to land you somewhere near Birmingham—if you travel far enough. You might make that your next stop."

One of the men took a pace towards him.

"You just listen a minute—"

"To what?" asked the Saint politely.

"I'm telling yer—"

"A bad habit," said the Saint disapprovingly. "You must try and break yourself of that. And now I'm sorry, but I can't stop. I hope you'll wash the back of your neck, see that your socks are aired, say your prayers every night, and get your face lifted at the first opportunity . . .

Now push your ears back, my cherubs, and let your feet chase each other."

His right hand moved significantly in his pocket, and there was an instant's perilous silence. And then the man who had spoken jerked his head at the other.

"Come on," he said.

The two men turned and lurched slowly away, looking back over their shoulders.

And the Saint put one foot on the running-board.

And somewhere, far away, he heard the sound of his own head being hit. It was as extraordinary an experience as any that had ever happened to him. Patricia was looking ahead down the road, while her hand eased the gears quietly into mesh; and the Saint himself had not heard the slightest movement that might have put him on his guard. And the premonitory crawling of his nerves which he had felt a few seconds earlier had performed what it considered to be its duty, and had subsided . . . He could have believed that the whole thing was an incredibly vivid hallucination—but for the sickening sharp stab of sudden agony that plunged through his brain like a spurt of molten metal and paralysed every milligram of strength in his body.

A great white light swelled up and exploded before his eyes, and after it came a wave of whirling blackness shot with rocketing flashes of dizzy, dazzling colour, and the blackness was filled with a thin high singing note that drilled into his eardrums. His knees seemed to melt away beneath him . . .

And then, from somewhere above the vast dark gulf into which he was sinking, he heard Patricia's voice cry out.

"Simon!"

The word seemed to spell itself into his dulled brain letter by letter, as if his mind read it off a slowly uncoiling scroll. But it touched a nerve centre that roused him for one fractional instant of time to fight back titanically against the numbing oblivion that was swallowing him up.

He knew that his eyes were open, but all he could see was one blurred segment of her face, as he might have seen her picture in a badly-focused fade-out that had gone askew. And to that isolated scrap of vision in the overwhelming blackness he found the blessed strength to croak two words:

"Drive on."

And then a second surge of blackness welled up around him and blotted out every sight and sound, and he fell away into the infinite black void.

CHAPTER 7

"So even your arrangements can break down, Templar—when your accomplice fails you," Kuzela remarked silkily. "My enterprising young friend, when you are older you will realise that it is always a mistake to rely upon a woman. I have never employed a woman myself for that reason."

"I'll bet that broke her heart," said the Saint.

Once again he sat in Kuzela's study, with his head still throbbing painfully from the crashing welt it had received, and a lump on the back of it feeling as if it were growing out of his skull like a great auk's egg. His hair was slightly disarranged, and straps on his wrists prevented him from rearranging it effectively, but the Saintly smile had not lost one iota of its charm.

"It remains, however, to decide whether you are going to be permitted to profit by this experience—whether you are going to live long enough to do so. Perhaps it has not occurred to you that you may have come to the end of your promising career," continued the man on the other side of the desk dispassionately, and the Saint sighed.

"What, not again?" he pleaded brokenly, and Kuzela frowned.

"I do not understand you."

"Only a few months ago I was listening to those very words," explained the Saint. "Alas, poor Wilfred! And he meant it, too. 'Wilf, old polecat,' I said, 'don't you realise that I can't be killed before page three hundred and twenty?' He didn't believe me. And he died. They put a rope round his neck and dropped him through a hole in the floor, and the consequences to his figure were very startling. Up to the base of the neck he was not so thin—but oh, boy, from then on . . . It was awfully sad."

And Simon Templar beamed around upon the congregation—upon Kuzela, and upon the two bruisers who loafed about the room, and upon the negro who stood behind his chair. And the negro he indicated with a nod.

"One of your little pets?" he inquired, and Kuzela's lips moved in the fraction of a smile.

"It was fortunate that Ngano heard some of the noise," he said. "He came out of the house just in time."

"To sock me over the head from behind?" drawled the Saint genially. "Doubtless, old dear. But apart from that—"

"Your accomplice escaped, with my property. True. But, my dear Templar, need that prove to be a tragedy? We have your own invaluable self still with us—and you, I am quite sure, know not only where the lady has gone, but also where you have hidden a gentleman whom I should very much like to have restored to me."

Simon raised languid eyebrows.

"When I was the Wallachian Vice-Consul at Pfaffenhausen," he said pleasantly, "our diplomacy was governed by a picturesque little Pomeranian poem, which begins:

> *Der Steiss des Elephanten*
> *Ist nicht, ist nicht so klein.*

If you get the idea—"

Kuzela nodded without animosity. His deliberate, ruthless white hands trimmed the end of a cigar.

"You must not think that I am unused to hearing remarks like that, Templar," he said equably. "In fact, I remember listening to a precisely similar speech from our friend the Duke of Fortezza. And yet—" He paused to blow a few minute flakes of tobacco leaf from the shining top of the desk, and then his pale bland eyes flicked up again to the Saint's face . . . "The Duke of Fortezza changed his mind," he said.

Simon blinked.

"Do you know," he said enthusiastically, "there's one of the great songs of the century there! I can just feel it. Something like this:

> *The Duke of Fortezza.*
> *Quite frequently gets a*
> *Nimpulse to go blithering off on to the blind,*
> *But the Duchess starts bimbling*
> *And wambling and wimbling*
> *And threatens to wallop his ducal behind;*
> *And her ladyship's threats are*
> *So fierce that he sweats*
> *And just sobs as he pets her*
> *With tearful regrets—Ah!*
> *The Duke of Fortezza*
> *Is changing his mind.*

We could polish up the idea a lot if we had time, but you must admit that for an impromptu effort—"

"You underrate my own sense of humour, Templar." Unemotionally Kuzela inspected the even reddening of the tip of his cigar, and waved his match slowly in the air till it went out. "But do you know another mistake which you also make?"

"I haven't the foggiest notion," said the Saint cheerfully.

"You underrate my sense of proportion."

The Saint smiled.

"In many ways," he murmured, "you remind me of the late Mr Garniman. I wonder how you'll get on together."

The other straightened up suddenly in his chair. For a moment the mask of amiable self-possession fell from him.

"I shall be interested to bandy words with you later—if you survive, my friend." He spoke without raising his voice, but two little specks of red burned in the cores of his eyes, and a shimmering marrow of vitriolic savagery edged up through his unalteringly level intonation. "For the present, our time is short, and you have already wasted more than your due allowance. But I think you understand me." Once again, a smooth evanescent trickle of honey over the bitingly measured syllables. "Come, now, my dear young friend, it would be a pity for us to quarrel. We have crossed swords, and you have lost. Let us reach an amicable armistice. You have only to give me a little information, and then, as soon as I have verified it, and have finished my work—say after seven days, during which time you would stay with me as an honoured guest—you would be as free as air. We would shake hands and go our ways." Kuzela smiled, and picked up a pencil. "Now firstly: where has your accomplice gone?"

"Naturally, she drove straight to Buckingham Palace," said the Saint.

Kuzela continued to smile.

"But you are suspicious. Possibly you think that some harm might befall her, and perhaps you would be unwilling to accept my assurance that she will be as safe as yourself. Well, it is a human suspicion after all, and I can understand it. But suppose we ask you another question . . .

Where is the Duke of Fortezza?" Kuzela drew a small memorandum block towards him, and poised his pencil with engaging expectancy. "Come, come! That is not a very difficult question to answer, is it? He is nothing to you—a man whom you met a few hours ago for the first time. If, say, you had never met him, and you had read in your newspaper that some fatal accident had overtaken him, you would not have been in the least disturbed. And if it is a decision between his temporary inconvenience and your own promising young life . . ." Kuzela shrugged. "I have no wish to use threats. But you, with your experience and imagination, must know that death does not always come easily. And very recently you did something which has mortally offended the invaluable Ngano. It would distress me to have to deliver you into his keeping . . . Now, now, let us make up our minds quickly. What have you done with the Duke?"

Simon dropped his chin and looked upwards across the desk.

"Nothing that I should be ashamed to tell my mother," he said winningly, and the other's eyes narrowed slowly.

"Do I, after all, understand you to refuse to tell me?"

The Saint crossed his left ankle over to his right knee.

"You know, laddie," he remarked, "you should be on the movies, really you should. As the strong silent man you'd be simply great, if you were a bit stronger and didn't talk so much."

For some seconds Kuzela looked at him.

Then he threw down his pencil and pushed away the pad.

"Very well, then," he said.

He snapped his fingers without turning his head, and one of the two bruisers came to his side. Kuzela spoke without giving the man a glance.

"Yelver, you will bring round the car. We shall require it very shortly."

The man nodded and went out, and Kuzela clasped his hands again on the desk before him.

"And you, Templar, will tell us where we are going," he said, and Simon raised his head.

His eyes gazed full and clear into Kuzela's face, bright with the reckless light of their indomitable mockery, and a sardonically Saintly smile curved the corners of his mouth.

"You're going to hell, old dear," he said coolly, and then the negro dragged him up out of his chair.

Simon went meekly down the stairs, with the negro gripping his arm and the second bruiser following behind, and his brain was weighing up the exterior circumstances with lightning accuracy.

Patricia had got away—that was the first and greatest thing. He praised the Lord who had inspired her with the sober far-sightedness and clearness of head not to attempt any futile heroism. There was nothing she could have done, and mercifully she'd had the sense to see it . . . But having got away, what would be her next move?

"Claud Eustace, presumably," thought the Saint, and a wry little twist roved across his lips, for he had always been the most incorrigible optimist in the world.

So he reached the hall, and there he was turned round, and hustled along towards the back of the house. As he went, he stole a glance at his wrist-watch . . . Patricia must have been gone for the best part of an hour, and that would have been more than long enough for Teal to get busy. Half of that time would have been sufficient to get Teal on the phone from the nearest call box and have the house surrounded by enough men to wipe up a brigade—if anything of that sort were going to be done. And not a sign of any such developments had interrupted the playing of the piece . . .

Down from the kitchen a flight of steps ran to the cellar, and as the Saint was led down them he had a vivid appreciation of another similarity between that adventure and a concluding episode in the history of the late Mr Garniman. The subterranean prospects in each case had been decidedly uninviting, and now the Saint held his fire and wondered what treat was going to be offered him this time.

The cigar-chewing escort stopped at the foot of the steps, and the Saint was led on alone into a small bare room. From the threshold, the negro flung him forward into a far corner, and turned to lock the door behind him. He put the key in his pocket, took off his coat, and rolled up his sleeves, and all the time his dark blazing eyes were riveted upon the Saint.

And then he picked up a great leather whip from the floor, and his thick lips curled back from his teeth in a ghastly grin.

"You will not talk, no?" he said.

He swung his arm, and the long lash whistled and crackled through the air, and snaked over the Saint's shoulders like the recoiling snap of an overstrained hawser.

CHAPTER 8

Simon reeled away in a slash of agony that ate into his chest as if a thin jet of boiling acid had been sprayed across his back.

And he went mad.

Never, otherwise, could he have accomplished what he did. For one blinding instant, which branded itself on his optic nerves with such an eye-aching clarity that it might have stood for an eternity of frozen stillness, he saw everything there was to see in that little room. He saw the stained grey walls and ceiling and the dusty paving underfoot; he saw the locked door; he saw the towering figure of the gigantic hate-vengeful negro before him, and the cyclopean muscles swelling and rippling under the thin texture of the lavender silk shirt; and he saw himself. Just for that instant he saw those things as he had never seen anything before, with every thought of everything else and every other living soul in the world wiped from his mind like chalk marks smeared from a smooth board . . .

And then a red fog bellied up before his eyes, and the stillness seemed to burst inwards like the smithereening of a great glass vacuum bulb.

He felt nothing more—in that white heat of berserk fury, the sense of pain was simply blotted out. He dodged round the room by instinct, ducking and swerving mechanically, and scarcely knew when he succeeded and when he failed.

And at his wrists he felt nothing at all.

The buckle of the strap there was out of reach of his teeth, but he twisted his hands inwards, one over the other, tightening up the leather with all his strength, till his muscles ached with the strain. He saw the edges of the strap biting into his skin, and the flesh, swelling whitely up on either side; the pain of that alone should have stopped him, but there was no such thing. And he stood still and twisted once again, with a concentrated passion of power that writhed over the whole of his upper body like the stirring of a volcano, and the leather broke before his eyes like a strip of tissue paper . . .

And the Saint laughed.

The whip sang around again, and he leapt in underneath it and caught it as it fell. And what he had intuitively expected happened. The negro jerked at it savagely—and Simon did not resist. But he kept his hold fast, and allowed all the vicious energy of that jerk to merge flowingly into his own unchecked rush, and it catapulted him to his mark like a stone from a sling. His right fist sogged full and square into the negro's throat with a force that jarred the Saint's own shoulder, and Simon found the whip hanging free in his hand.

He stepped back and watched the grin melting out of the contorted black face. The negro's chest heaved up to the encompassing of a great groaning breath, but the shattering mule-power of that pent-up super-auxiliated swipe in the gullet had stunned his thyro-arytenoids as effectively as if a bullet had gone through them. His mouth worked wildly, but he could produce nothing more than an inaudible whisper. And the Saint laughed again, gathering up the whip.

"The boys will be expecting some music," he said, very gently. "And you are going to provide it."

Then the negro sprang at him like a tiger.

That one single punch which had reversed the situation would have sent any living European swooning off into hours of tortured helplessness, but in this case the Saint had never expected any such result from it. It had done all that he had ever hoped that it would do—obliterated the negro's speaking voice, and given the Saint himself the advantage of the one unwieldy weapon in the room. And with the red mists of unholy rage still swilling across his vision, Simon Templar went grimly into the fight of his life.

He side-stepped the negro's first maniac charge as smoothly and easily as a practised pedestrian evading a two-horse dray, and as he swerved he brought the whip cracking round in a stroke that split the lavender silk shirt as crisply as if a razor had been scored across it.

The negro fetched up against the far wall with an animal scream, spun round, and sprang at him again. And again the Saint swayed lightly aside, and made the whip lick venomously home with a report like a gunshot . . .

He knew that that was the only earthly hope he had—to keep his opponent tearing blindly through a hazing madness of pain and fury that would scatter every idea of scientific fighting to the four winds. There were six feet eight inches of the negro, most of three hundred pounds of pitiless, clawing, blood-mad primitive malignity caged up with Simon Templar within those blank damp-blotched walls, and Simon knew, with a quiet cold certainty, that if once those six feet eight inches, those three hundred-odd pounds of bone and muscle resolved themselves into the same weight and size of logical, crafty, fighting precision, there was no man in the world who could have stood two minutes against them. And the Saint quietly and relentlessly crimped down his own strength and speed and fighting madness into the one narrow channel that would give it a fighting chance.

It was a duel between brute strength and animal ferocity on the one hand, and on the other hand the lithe swiftness and lightning eye of the trickiest fighting man alive—a duel with no referee, in which no foul was barred. Tirelessly the Saint went round the room, flitting airily beyond, around, even under the massive arms that grappled for him, bobbing and swooping and turning, up on his toes and supple as a dancer, as elusive as a drop of quicksilver on a plate, and always the tapered leather thong in his hand was whirling and hissing like an angry fer-de-lance, striking and coiling and striking again with a bitter deadliness of aim. Once the negro grabbed at the whip and found it, and the Saint broke his hold with a kick to the elbow that opened the man's fingers as if the tendons had been cut: once the Saint's foot slipped, and he battered his way out of a closing trap in a desperate flurry of rib-creaking body blows that made even the negro stagger for a sufficient moment, and the fight went on.

It went on till the negro's half-naked torso shone with a streaming lather of sweat and blood, and a sudden kicking lurch in his step shot into Simon's taut-strung brain the wild knowledge that the fight was won.

And for the first time the Saint stood his ground, with his back to one wall, holding the negro at bay by the flailing sweep of the lash alone.

Then Simon pressed forward, and the negro went back . . .

The Saint drove him into the opposite corner and beat him whimpering to his knees. And then, as the man spilled forward on to his face, Simon leapt in and got an ankle hold.

"Get your hands right up behind your back," he rasped incisively, "or I'll twist the leg off you!"

He applied his leverage vigorously, and the man obeyed him with a yelp. Simon locked the ankle with his knees and bent his weight over it. With quick deft fingers he knotted the tail of the whip round the negro's wrists, and passed the stock over one shoulder, round the neck, and back over the other shoulder into a slip-knot. A draught of air gulped noisily into the negro's straining lungs, and Simon gave the noose a yank.

"One word from you, and you graze in the Green Pastures," he stated pungently, and heard the lungful choke sibilantly out again. "And get this," said the Saint, with no increase of friendliness, "if you move the half of an inch in that hog-tie, you'll bowstring your own sweet self. That's all."

He fished the key of the door out of the negro's pocket and stood up, breathing deeply.

He himself was starting to look as if he had recently taken a warm shower-bath in his clothes, and now that the anaesthetic red mists were thinning out, a large part of his back was beginning to stiffen itself up into an identical acreage of ache, but he was not yet ready to sit down and be sorry about such minor discomforts. With the key snapping over in the lock, he brushed the hair back off his forehead and opened the door, and the cigar-chewer at the foot of the steps crawled upright like a slow-motion picture, with his jaw sagging nervelessly and his eyes popping from their orbits, gaping at the Saint as he might have gaped at his own ghost . . .

Smiling, and without any haste, Simon walked towards him.

And the man stood there staring at him, watching him come on, numbed with a bone-chilling superstitious terror. It was not until the Saint was within two yards of him that a sobbing little wail gurgled in his throat and he reached feebly round to his hip pocket.

Of the rest of the entertainment he knew little. He knew that a grip about which there was nothing ghostly seized upon his right wrist before he had time to draw, while another metallic clutch closed round his knees; he knew that the weight came suddenly off his feet, and then he seemed to go floating ethereally through space. Somewhere in the course of that flight an astonishingly hard quantity of concrete impinged upon his skull, but it did not seem an important incident. His soul went bimbering on, way out into the land of blissful dreams . . .

And the Saint went on up the steps.

He was half-way up when a bell jangled somewhere overhead, and he checked involuntarily. And then a tiny skew-eyed grin skimmed over his lips.

"Claud Eustace for the hell of it," he murmured, and went upwards very softly.

Right up by the door at the top of the stairs he stopped again and listened. He heard slow and watchful footsteps going down the hall, followed by the rattle of a latch and the cautious whine of slowly turning hinges. And then he heard the most perplexing thing of all, which was nothing more or less than an expansive and omnipotent silence.

The Saint put up one hand and gently scratched his ear, with a puzzled crease chiselling in between his eyebrows. He was prepared to hear almost anything else but that. And he didn't. The silence continued for some time, and then the front door closed again and the footsteps started back solo on the return journey.

And then, in the very opposite direction, the creak of a window-sash sliding up made him blink.

Someone was wriggling stealthily over the sill. With his ear glued to a panel of the door, he could visualise every movement as clearly as if he could have seen it. He heard the faint patter of the intruder's weight coming on to the floor, and then the equally faint sound of footsteps creeping over the linoleum. They connected up in his mind with the footsteps of the man who had gone to the door like the other part of a duet. Then the second set of footsteps died away, and there was only the sound of the man's returning from the hall. Another door opened . . . And then a voice uttered a corrosively quiet command.

"Keep still!"

Simon almost fell down the steps. And then he wind-milled dazedly back to his balance and hugged himself.

"Oh, Pat!" he breathed. "Mightn't I have known it? And you ring the bell to draw the fire, and sprint round and come in the back way . . . oh, you little treasure."

Grinning a great wide grin, he listened to the dialogue.

"Put your hands right up . . . That's fine . . . And now, where's Kuzela?"

Silence.

"Where is Kuzela?"

A shifting of feet, and then the grudging answer: "Upstairs."

"Lead on, sweetheart."

The sounds of reluctant movement . . .

And the whole of Simon Templar's inside squirmed with ecstasy at the pure poetic Saintliness of the technique. Not for a thousand million pounds would he have butted in just then—not one second before Kuzela himself had also had time to appreciate the full ripe beauty of the situation. He heard the footsteps travelling again: they came right past his door and went on into the hall, and the Saint pointed his toes in a few movements of an improvised cachucha.

And then, after a due pause, he opened the door and followed on.

He gave the others time to reach the upper landing, and then he went whisking up the first flight. Peeking round the banisters, he was just in time to get a sight of Patricia disappearing into Kuzela's study. Then the door slammed behind her, and the Saint raced on up and halted outside it.

While after the answering of the dud front-door call there had certainly been a silence, the stillness to which he listened now made all previous efforts in noiselessness sound like an artillery barrage. Against that background of devastating blankness, the clatter of a distant passing truck seemed to shake the earth, and the hoot of its klaxon sounded like the Last Trump.

And then Patricia spoke again, quite calmly, but with a lethal clearness that was hedged around on every side with the menace of every manner of murder.

"Where is the Saint?" she asked.

And upon those words Simon Templar figured that he had his cue.

He turned the handle soundlessly and pushed the door wide open.

Patricia's back was towards him. A little farther on to one side the second bruiser stood by with his hands high in the air. And behind the desk sat Kuzela, with his face still frozen in an expression of dumb, incredulous stupefaction . . . And as the door swung back, and the Saint advanced gracefully into the limelight, the eyes of the two men revolved and centred on him, and dilated slowly into petrified staring orbs of something near to panic.

"Good morning," said the Saint.

Patricia half turned. She could not help herself—the expressions on the faces of the two men in front of her were far too transparently heartfelt to leave her with any mistrust that they were part of a ruse to put her off her guard.

But the result of her movement was the same, for as she turned her eyes away, the smallest part in the cast had his moment. He awoke out of his groping comatosity, saw his chance, and grabbed it with both fists.

The automatic was wrested violently out of the girl's hands, and she was thrown stumbling back into the Saint's arms. And the Saint's gentle smile never altered.

He passed Patricia to one side, and cocked a derisive eye at the gun that was turned against him. And with no more heed for it than that, he continued on towards the desk.

"So nice to see you again," he said.

CHAPTER 9

Kuzela rose lingeringly to his feet.

There was a perceptible pause before he gained control of the faculty of speech. The two consecutive smacks that had been jolted into the very roots of his being within the space of the last forty seconds would have tottered the equilibrium of any man—of any man except, perhaps, the Saint himself . . . But the Saint was not at all disturbed. He waited in genteel silence, while the other schooled the flabby startlement out of his face and dragged up his mouth into an answering smile.

"My dear young friend!"

The voice, when Kuzela found it, had the same svelte timbre as before, and Simon bowed a mocking compliment to the other's nerve.

"My dear old comrade!" he murmured, open-armed.

"You have saved us the trouble of fetching you, Templar," Kuzela said blandly. "But where is Ngano?"

"The Negro Spiritual?" The Saint aligned his eyebrows banteringly. "I'm afraid he—er—met with a slight accident."

"Ah!"

"No—not exactly. I don't think he's quite dead yet, though he may easily have strangled himself by this time. But he hasn't enjoyed himself. I think if the circumstances had been reversed, he would have talked," said the Saint, with a glacial inclemency of quietness.

Kuzela stroked his chin.

"That is unfortunate," he said.

And then he smiled.

"But it is not fatal, my friend," he purred. "The lady has already solved one problem for us herself. And now that she is here, I am sure you would do anything rather than expose her to the slightest danger. So let us return to our previous conversation at once. Perhaps the lady will tell us herself where she went to when she drove away from here?"

Simon put his hands in his pockets.

"Why, yes," he said good-humouredly. "I should think she would."

The girl looked at him as if she could not quite believe her ears. And Simon met her puzzled gaze with blue eyes of such a blinding Saintly innocence that even she could read no enticement to deception in them.

"Do you mean that?" she asked.

"Of course," said the Saint. "There are one or two things I shouldn't mind knowing myself."

Patricia put a hand to her head.

"If you want to know—when I left here I drove straight to—"

"Buckingham Palace," drawled the Saint. "And then?"

"I had the bags taken up to Beppo's room, and I saw him myself. He was quite wide awake and sensible. I told him I was coming back here to get you out, and said that if I wasn't back by four o'clock, or one of us hadn't rung him up, he was to get in touch with Teal. I gave him Teal's private number. He didn't want me to go at all, but I insisted. That's all there is to tell. I picked up a puncture on the second trip out here, and that held me up a bit—"

"But who cares about that?" said the Saint.

He turned back to the desk.

The man with the gun stood less than a yard away on his right front, but the Saint, ignoring his very existence, leaned a little forward and looked from the distance of another yard into the face of Kuzela. The loose poise of his body somehow centred attention even while it disarmed suspicion. But the mockery had gone out of his eyes.

"You heard?" he asked.

Kuzela nodded. His mouth went up at one corner. "But I still see no reason for alarm my friend," he said, in that wheedling voice of stow malevolence. "After all, there is still time for much to happen. Before your friend Mr Teal arrives—"

"Before my friend Chief Inspector Teal arrives with a squad of policemen in a plain van, I shall be a long way from here," said the Saint.

Kuzela started.

"So you have invoked the police?" he snapped. And then again he recovered himself. "But that is your affair. By the time they arrive, as you say, you will have left here. But where do you think you will have gone?"

"Home, James," said the Saint.

He took one hand out of his pocket to straighten his coat, and smiled without mirth.

"Fortunately, the argument between us can be settled tonight," he said, "which will save me having to stage any reunions. Your black torturer has been dealt with. I have given him a dose of his own medicine which will, I think, put him in hospital for several weeks. But you remain. You are, after all, the man who gave Ngano his orders. I have seen what you did to the Duke of Fortezza, and I know what you wanted to have done to me . . . I hope you will get on well with Wilfred."

"And what do you think you are going to do to me?" asked Kuzela throatily, and Simon held him with his eyes.

"I'm going to kill you, Kuzela," he said simply.

"Ah! And how will you do that?"

Simon's fingers dipped into his pocket. They came out with an ordinary match-box, and he laid it on the desk.

"That is the answer to all questions," he said.

Kuzela stared down at the box. It sat there in the middle of his clean white blotter, yellow and oblong and angular, as commonplace a thing as any man could see on his desk—and the mystery of it seemed to leer up at him malignantly. He picked it up and shook it: it weighed light in his hand, and his mind balked at the idea that it should conceal any engine of destruction. And the Saint's manner of presenting it had been void of the most minute scintilla of excitement—and still was. He eyed Kuzela quizzically.

"Why not open it?" he suggested.

Kuzela looked at him blankly. And then, with a sudden impatience, he jabbed his thumb at the little sliding drawer . . .

In a dead silence, the box fell through the air and flopped half-open on the desk.

"What does this mean?" asked Kuzela, almost in a whisper.

"It means that you have four minutes to live," said the Saint.

Kuzela held up his hand and stared at it.

In the centre of the ball of his right thumb a little globule of blood was swelling up in the pinky-white of the surrounding skin. He gazed stupidly from it to the match-box and back again. In imagination, he felt a second time the asp-like prick that had bitten into his thumb as he moved the drawer of the box—and understood. "The answer to all questions . . ."

He stood there as powerless to move as a man in a nightmare, and watched the infinitely slow distention of the tiny crimson sphere under his eyes, his face going ashen with the knowledge of inescapable doom. The drop of blood hypnotised him, filled his vision till he could see nothing else but the microscopic reflections glistening over the surface of it—until all at once it seemed to grow magically into a coruscating red vesicle of enormous size, thrusting in upon him, bearing him down, filling the whole universe with the menace of its smothering scarlet magnitude. A roaring of mighty waters seethed up about his ears . . .

The others saw him brace himself on his feet as if to resist falling, and he remained quite still, with his eyes fixing and going dim. And then he took one step sideways, swayed, and crumpled down on to the floor with his limbs twitching convulsively and his chest labouring . . .

Quite calmly and casually the Saint put out a hand and clasped it on the gun wrist of the man who stood beside him.

The man seemed to come alive out of a dream. And without any noticeable interregnum of full consciousness, he seemed to pass right on into another kind of dream—the transition being effected by the contingence upon the point of his jaw of a tearing uppercut that started well below the Saint's waistline and consummated every erg of its weight and velocity at the most vital angle of the victim's face. With the results aforementioned. He went down in a heap and lay very still, even as his companion had done a little earlier, and Simon picked up the gun.

"Which finishes that," said the Saint, and found Patricia looking down again at Kuzela.

"What happened to him?" she asked, a trifle unsteadily.

"More or less what he tried to make happen to me. Ever come across those trick match-boxes that shoot a needle into you when you try to open them? I bought one last afternoon, and replaced the needle with something that was sent to me along with the message you know about. And I don't know that we shall want it again."

He took the little box of death over to the fireplace, dropped it in the grate, and raked the glowing embers over it. Then he took up his hat and stick, which he saw lying in a chair, and glanced around for the last time. Only Kuzela's fingers were twitching now, and a wet froth gleamed on his lips and dribbled down one cheek . . . Simon put an arm round the girl's shoulders.

"I guess we can be going," he said, and led her out of the room.

It was in the hall that the expression on the face of a clock caught his eye and pulled him up with a jerk.

"What time did you say Beppo was going to get in touch with Teal?" he inquired.

"Four o'clock." Patricia followed his gaze and then looked at her wrist. "That clock must be fast—"

"Or else you've stopped," said the Saint pithily. He turned back his sleeve and inspected his own watch. "And stopped you have, old darling. It's thirty-three minutes after four now—and to give Claud Eustace even a chance to think that he'd pulled me out of a mess would break my heart. Not to include another reason why he mustn't find us here. Where did you leave the car?"

"Just one block away."

"This is where we make greyhounds look lazy," said the Saint, and opened the front door.

They were at the gate when Simon saw the lights of a car slowing up and swinging in to the kerb on his left. Right in front of him, Kuzela's car was parked, and the Saint knew clairvoyantly that that was their only chance.

He caught Patricia's arm and flipped up the collar of her coat.

"Jump to it," he crisped.

He scudded round to the driving-seat, and the girl tumbled in beside him as he let in the clutch. He shot right past the police car with his head well down and his shoulders hunched. A tattered shout reached him as he went by, and then he was bucking off down a side street with the car heeling over on two wheels as he crammed it round the corner. The police car would have to be turned right round in a narrow road before it could get after him, and he knew he was well away. He dodged hectically south-east, and kept hard at it till he was sure he had left any pursuit far behind.

Somewhere in the northern hinterlands of the Tottenham Court Road he stopped the car and made some hurried repairs to his appearance with the aid of the driving-mirror, and ended up looking distinctly more presentable than he had been when they left Hampstead. He looked so presentable, in fact, that they abandoned the car on that spot, and walked boldly on until they met a taxi, which took them to Berkeley Square.

"For the night isn't nearly over yet," said the Saint, as they walked down Upper Berkeley Mews together after the taxi had chugged off out of sight.

It was one of those fool-proof prophecies which always delighted his sense of the slickness of things by the brisk promptness with which they fulfilled themselves. He had hardly closed the door of his house when the telephone bell began to ring, and he went to answer the call with a feeling of large and unalloyed contentment.

"Hullo-o? . . . Speaking . . . That's which? . . . Teal? . . . Well, blow me. Claud Eustace, this is very late for you to be out! Does your grandmother allow you —? What? . . . What have I been doing tonight? I've been drinking beer with Beppo . . . No, not a leper—BEPPO. B for bdellium, E for eiderdown, P for psychology, P for pneumonia, O for a muse of fire that would ascend the brightest heaven of . . . I beg your pardon? . . . You were called up and told I was in trouble? . . . Someone's been pulling your leg, Claud. I'm at peace with the world . . . Whassat? . . . Why, sure. I was just going to bed, but I guess I can stay up a few minutes longer. Will you be bringing your own gum? . . . Right-ho . . ."

He listened for a moment longer, and then he hung up the receiver and turned to Pat.

"Claud's coming right along," he said gleefully, and the laughter was lifting in his voice. "We're not to try to get away, because he'll have an armed guard at every sea and air port in the British Isles ten minutes after he gets here and finds we've done a bunk. Which will be tremendous fun for all concerned . . . And now, get through to Beppo as fast as you can spin the dial, old sweetheart, while I sprint upstairs and change my shirt—for there's going to be a great day!"

CHAPTER 10

Chief Inspector Claud Eustace Teal fixed his pudgy hands in the belt of his overcoat, and levelled his unfriendly gaze on the superbly elegant young man who lounged against the table in front of him.

"So that message I had was a fake, was it?" he snarled.

"It must have been, Claud."

Teal nodded fatly.

"Perhaps it was," he said. "But I went to the address it gave me— and what do you think I found?"

"The Shah of Persia playing Ludo," hazarded Simon Templar intelligently, and the detective glowered.

"In the cellar I found a nigger tied up with the whip that had beaten half the hide off his back. Outside, there was a white man with a fractured skull—he's gone to hospital as well. In a room upstairs there was another man laid out with a broken jaw, and a fourth man in the same room—dead."

The Saint raised his eyebrows.

"But, my dear old sturgeon!" he protested reasonably. "What on earth do you think I am? A sort of human earthquake?"

"Both the nigger and the man with the broken jaw," Teal continued stonily, "gave me a description of the man responsible, and it fits you like a glove. The man with the broken jaw also added the description of the woman who couldn't be distinguished apart from Miss Holm."

"Then we obviously have doubles, Claud."

"He also heard the woman say, 'Where is the Saint?'"

Simon frowned.

"That's certainly odd," he admitted. "Where did you say this was?"

"You know darned well where it was! And I'll tell you some more. Just as I got there in the police car, a man and a woman dashed out of the house and got away. And who do you suppose they looked like?"

"The same doubles, obviously," said the Saint with great brilliance.

"And just one block away from that house we found a blue saloon Hirondel, which the two people I saw would have got away in if they'd had time to reach it. The number of it was ZX1257. Is that the number of your car?"

The Saint sat up.

"Claud, you're a blessing in disguise! That certainly is my car—and I was thinking I'd lost her! Pinched outside May Fair only yesterday afternoon, she was, in broad daylight. I was meaning to ring up Vine Street before, but what with one thing and another—"

Teal drew a deep breath—and then he exploded.

"Now would you like to know what I think of your defence?" he blurted out, in a boiling gust of righteous wrath. And he went on without waiting for encouragement. "I think it's the most weak-kneed tangle of moonshine I've ever had to listen to in my life. I think it's so drivelling that if any jury will listen to it for ten minutes, I'll walk right out of the court and have myself certified. I've got two men who'll swear to you on their dying oaths, and another one to put beside them if he recovers, and I know what I saw myself and what the men who were with me saw, and I think everything you've got to say is so maudlin that I'm going to take you straight back to Scotland Yard with me and have it put in writing before we lock you up. I think I've landed you at last, Mr Saint, and after what you said to me this morning I'm damned glad I've done it."

The Saint took out his cigarette-case and flopped off the table into an armchair, sprawling one long leg comfortably over the arm.

"Well, that does express your point of view quite clearly," he conceded. He lighted a cigarette, and looked up brightly. "Claud, you're getting almost fluent in your old age. But you've got to mind you don't let your new-found eloquence run away with you."

"Oh, have I?" The detective took the bait right down into his oesophagus, and clinched his teeth on the line. "Very well. Then while all these extraordinary things were being done by your double—while half a dozen sober men were seeing you and listening to you and being beaten up by you and getting messages from you—maybe you'll tell me what you were doing and who else knows it besides yourself?"

Simon inhaled luxuriously, and smiled.

"Why, sure. As I told you over the phone, I was drinking beer with Beppo."

"And who's he?"

"The Duke of Fortezza."

"Oh yes?" Teal grew sarcastic. "And where was the King of Spain and the Prime Minister of Jugoslavia?"

"Blowed if I know," said the Saint ingenuously. "But there were some other distinguished people present. The Count of Montalano, and Prince Marco d'Ombria, and the Italian Ambassador—"

"The Italian what?"

"Ambassador. You know. Gent with top hat and spats."

"And where was this?"

"At the Italian Embassy. It was just a little private party, but it went on for a long time. We started about midnight, and didn't break up till half-past four—I hadn't been home two minutes when you phoned."

Teal almost choked.

"What sort of bluff are you trying to pull on me now?" he demanded. "Have you got hold of the idea that I've gone dotty? Are you sitting there believing that I'll soak up that story, along with everything else you've told me, and just go home and ask no questions?" Teal snorted savagely. "You must have gone daft!" he blared.

The Saint came slowly out of his chair. He posed himself before the detective, feet astraddle, his left hand on his hip, loose-limbed and smiling and dangerous, and the long dictatorial forefinger which Teal had seen and hated before drove a straight and peremptory line into the third button of the detective's waistcoat.

"And now you listen to me again, Claud," said the Saint waspily. "Do you know what you're letting yourself in for?"

"Do I know what I'm—"

"Do you know what you're letting yourself in for? You burst into my house and make wild accusations against me. You shout at me, you bully me, you tell me I'm either lying or dippy, and you threaten to arrest me. I'm very sensitive, Claud," said the Saint, "and you hurt me. You hurt me so much that I've a damned good mind to let you run me in—and then, when you'd put the rope right round your own neck and drawn it up as tight as it'd go, I'd pull down such a schemozzle around your bat ears that you'd want nothing more in life than to hand in your resignation and get away to some forgotten corner of earth where they've never seen a newspaper. That's what's coming your way so fast that you're going to have to jump like a kangaroo to get from under it. It's only because I'm of a godly and forgiving disposition," said the Saint virtuously, "that I'm giving you a chance to save your skin. I'm going to let you verify my alibi before you arrest me, instead of having it fed into you with a stomach-pump afterwards, and then you are going to apologise to me and go home," said the Saint.

He picked up a telephone directory, found a place, and thrust the book under Teal's oscillating eyes.

"There's the number," he said. "Mayfair three two three O. Check it up for yourself now, and save yourself the trouble of telling me I'm just ringing up an accomplice."

He left the detective blinking at the volume, and went to the telephone.

Teal read off the number, put down the book, and pulled at his collar.

Once again the situation had passed out of his control. He gazed at the Saint purply, and the beginnings of a despondent weariness pouched up under his eyes. It was starting to be borne in upon him, with a preposterous certitude, that he had just been listening to something more than bluff. And the irony of it made him want to burst into tears. It was unfair. It was brutal. It outraged every cannon of logic and justice. He knew his case was watertight, knew that against the evidence he could put into a witness-box there could simply be no human way of escape—he could have sworn it on the rack, and would have gone to his death still swearing it. And he knew that it wasn't going to work.

Through a haze of almost homicidal futility, he heard the Saint speaking.

"Oh, is that you, Signor Ravelli? . . . Simon Templar speaking. Listen: there's some weird eruption going on in the brains of Scotland Yard. Some crime or other was committed somewhere tonight, and for some blithering reason they seem to think I was mixed up in it. I'm sorry to have to stop you on your way to bed, but a fat policeman has just barged in here—"

"Give me that telephone!" snarled Teal.

He snatched the instrument away and rammed the receiver against his ear.

"Hullo!" he barked. "This is Chief Inspector Teal, Criminal Investigation Department, speaking. I have every reason to believe that this man Templar was concerned in a murder which took place in Hampstead shortly after four o'clock this morning. He's tried to tell me some cock-and-bull story about . . . What? . . . But damn it . . . I beg your pardon, sir, but I definitely know . . . From twelve o'clock till half-past four? . . . But . . . But . . . But oh, hell, I . . . No, sir, I said . . . But he . . . Who? . . ."

The diaphragm of the receiver clacked and chattered and Teal's round red face sagged sickly.

And then:

"All right, sir. Thank you very much, sir," he said in a strangled voice, and slammed the microphone back on its bracket.

The Saint smoothed his hair.

"We might get on to Beppo next," he suggested hopefully. "He's staying at the Berkeley. Then you can have a word with Prince d'Ombria—"

"Can I?" Teal had eaten wormwood, and his voice was thick and raw with the bitterness of it. "Well, I haven't got time. I know when I'm licked. I know where I am when half a dozen princes and ambassadors will go into the witness-box and swear that you're chasing them round the equator at the very moment when I know that I'm talking to you here in this room. I don't even ask how you worked it. I expect you rang up the President of the United States and got him to fix it for you. But I'll be seeing you another time—don't worry."

He hitched his coat round, and grabbed up his hat.

"Bye-bye," sang the Saint.

"And you remember this," Teal gulped out. "I'm not through with you yet. You're not going to sit back on your laurels. You wouldn't. And that's what's going to be the finish of you. You'll be up to something else soon enough—and maybe you won't have the entire Italian Diplomatic Service primed to lie you out of it next time. From this minute, you're not even going to blow your nose without I know it. I'll have you watched closer than the Crown Jewels, and the next mistake you make is going to be the last."

"Cheerio, dear heart," said the Saint, and heard the vicious bang of the front door before he sank back into his chair in hysterics of helpless laughter.

But the epilogue of that story was not written until some weeks later, when a registered packet bearing an Italian postmark was delivered at No. 7, Upper Berkeley Mews.

Simon opened it after breakfast.

First came a smaller envelope, which contained a draft on the Bank of Italy for a sum whose proportions made even Simon Templar blink.

And then he took out a small shagreen case, and turned it over curiously. He pressed his thumbnail into the little spring catch, and the lid flew up and left him staring.

Patricia put a hand on his shoulder.

"What is it?" she asked, and the Saint looked at her.

"It's the medallion of the Order of the Annunziata—and I think we shall both have to have new hats on this," he said.

THE MELANCHOLY JOURNEY OF MR TEAL

CHAPTER 1

Now there was a day when the Saint went quite mad.

Of course, one might with considerable justification say that he always had been mad, anyway, so that the metamorphosis suggested by that first sentence would be difficult for the ordinary observer to discover. Patricia Holm said so, quite definitely, and the Saint only smiled.

"Neverwithstanding," he said, "I am convinced that the season is ripe for Isadore to make his contribution to our bank balance."

"You must be potty," said his lady, for the second time, and the Saint nodded blandly.

"I am. That was the everlasting fact with which we started the day's philosophy and meditation. If you remember—"

Patricia looked at the calendar on the wall, and her sweet lips came together in the obstinate little line that her man knew so well.

"Exactly six months ago," she said, "Teal was in here giving such a slick imitation of the sorest man on earth that anyone might have thought it was no impersonation at all. Two of his best men have been hanging around outside for twenty-four hours a day ever since. They're out there now. If you think six months is as far as his memory will go—"

"I don't."

"Then what are you thinking?"

The Saint lighted his second cigarette, and blew a streamer of smoke towards the ceiling. His blue eyes laughed.

"I think," he answered carefully, "that Claud Eustace is just getting set for his come-back. I think he's just finished nursing the flea I shot into his ear last time so tenderly that it's now big and bloodthirsty enough to annihilate anything smaller than an elephant—and maybe that plus. And I'm darned sure that if we lie low much longer, Claud Eustace will be getting ideas into his head, which would be very bad for him indeed."

"But—"

"There are," said the Saint, "no buts. I had a look at my pass-book yesterday, and it seems to be one of the eternal verities of this uncertain life that I could this day write a cheque for ninety-six thousand, two hundred and forty-seven pounds, eleven shillings, and four-pence— and have it honoured. Which is very nice, but just not quite nice enough. When I started this racket, I promised myself I wasn't coming out with one penny less than a hundred thousand pounds. I didn't say I'd come out even then, but I did think that when I reached that figure I might sit down for a bit and consider the possible advantages of respectability. And I feel that the time is getting ripe for me to have that think."

This was after a certain breakfast. Half a dozen volumes might be written around nothing else but those after-breakfast séances in Upper Berkeley Mews. They occupied most of the early afternoon in days of leisure, for the Saint had his own opinions about the correct hours for meals, and they were the times when ninety per cent of his coups were schemed. Towards noon the Saint would arise like a giant refreshed, robe himself in furiously patterned foulard, and enter with an immense earnestness of concentration upon the task of shattering his fast. And after that had been accomplished in a properly solemn silence, Simon Templar lighted a cigarette, slanted his eyebrows, shifted back his ears, and metaphorically rolled up his sleeves and looked around for something to knock sideways. A new day—or what was left of it— loomed up on his horizon like a fresh world waiting to be conquered, and the Saint stanced himself to sail into it with an irrepressible impetuosity of hair-brained devilment that was never too tired or short-winded to lavish itself on the minutest detail as cheerfully and generously as it would have spread itself over the most momentous affair in the whole solar system.

And in those moods of reckless unrepentance he smiled with shameless Saintliness right into that stubborn alignment of his lady's mouth, challenged it, teased it, dared it, laughed it into confusion, kissed it in a way that would have melted the mouth of a marble statue, and won her again and again, as he always would, into his own inimitable madness. As he said then . . .

"There's money and trouble to be had for the asking," said the Saint, when it was all over. "And what more could anyone want, old dear? . . . More trouble even than that, maybe. Well, I heard last night that Claud Eustace was also interested in Isadore, though I haven't the foggiest idea how much he knows. Tell me, Pat, old sweetheart, isn't it our cue?"

And Patricia sighed.

When Frankie Hormer landed at Southampton, he figured that his arrival was as secret as human ingenuity could make it. Even Detective Inspector Peters, who had been waiting for him for years, on and off, knew nothing about it—and he was at Southampton at the time. Frankie walked straight past him, securely hidden behind a beard which had sprouted to very respectable dimensions since he last set foot in England, and showed a passport made out in a name that his godfathers and godmother had never thought of. Admittedly, there had been a little difficulty with the tall dark man who had entered his life in Johannesburg and followed him all the way to Durban— inconspicuously, but not quite inconspicuously enough. But Frankie had dealt with that intrusion the night before he sailed. He carried two guns, and knew how to use them both.

And after that had been settled, the only man who should have known anything at all was Elberman, the genial little fellow who had financed the expedition at a staggering rate of interest, and who had personally procured the passport aforementioned, which was absolutely indistinguishable from the genuine article although it had never been inside the Foreign Office in its life.

Frankie had made that trip a number of times before—often enough to acquire a fairly extensive knowledge of the possible pitfalls. And this time he was reckoning to clean up, and he was taking no chances. The man from Johannesburg had bothered him more than a little, but the voyage back to England had given him time to forget that. And in the train that was speeding him towards Waterloo, Frankie thought ahead into a pleasant and peaceful future—with a chalet in Switzerland, probably, and a villa on the Riviera thrown in, and an endless immunity from the anxieties that are inseparable from what those who have never tried to earn it call "easy money."

And so, perhaps, his vigilance relaxed a trifle on the last lap of the journey—which was a pity, because he was quite a likeable man in spite of his sins. Perrigo got him somewhere between Southampton and Waterloo—Perrigo of the big coarse hands that were so quick and skilful with the knife. Thus Frankie Hormer enters the story and departs, and two men have been killed in the first four pages, which is good going.

Of this, Simon Templar knew nothing at the moment. His absorbing interest in Mr Perrigo, and particularly in Mr Perrigo's trousers, developed a little later. But he knew a whole lot of other things closely connected with the dramatis personnæ already introduced, for it was part of the Saint's business to know something about everything that was happening in certain circles, and on the strength of that he went after Isadore Elberman in quest of further information.

The structural alterations along the south side of Upper Berkeley Mews, which had recently been providing the Saint with as much exercise as he wanted, were now completed, and by means of a slight elaboration of his original scheme, he was able to enter and leave his home without in any way disturbing the stolid vigil of the two plain-clothes men who prowled before his front door, day and night, in a variety of disguises which afforded him continuous entertainment.

At nine o'clock that night he went upstairs to his bedroom, slid back the tall pier-glass which adorned one wall, and stepped into a narrow dimly-lighted passage, closing the panel again behind him. Thus with his feet making no sound on the thick felt matting that was laid over the floor, he passed down the corridor between the back of the mews and the dummy wall which he had built with his own hands, through numbers 5 and 3—which highly desirable residences had already been re-let to two impeccably respectable tenants who never knew that their landlord had a secret right-of-way through their homes. So the Saint came (through the false back of a wardrobe) into the bedroom of No. 1, which was occupied by the chauffeur of a Mr Joshua Pond, who was the owner of No. 104, Berkeley Square, which adjoined the corner of the mews. Mr Pond was not otherwise known to the police as Simon Templar, but he would have been if the police had been clever enough to discover the fact. And the Saint left No. 1, Upper Berkeley Mews through another cupboard in the room at which he had entered it, and reappeared out of a similar cupboard in one of the bathrooms of No. 104, Berkeley Square, and so became a free man again, while Chief Inspector Teal's watchers went on patrolling Upper Berkeley Mews in an ineffable magnificence of futility which can't really have done them any harm.

This was one of the things that Perrigo didn't know, and the possibility that the Saint might have any business with Isadore Elberman that night was another.

Perrigo had got what he wanted. It had been easier than he had expected, for Frankie Hormer had made the mistake of occupying a reserved compartment all by himself on the boat train. Perrigo walked in on him with some gold braid pinned to his overcoat and a guard's cap on his head, and took him by surprise. The trouble had started at Waterloo—a detective had recognised him in the station, and he had only just managed to make his getaway.

He reached Elberman's house at Regent's Park by a roundabout route, and morsed out the prearranged signal on the bell with feverish haste. The entrance of the house was at the back, in a little courtyard which contained the doorways of four other houses that also overlooked the Park. While he waited for the summons to be answered, Perrigo's eyes searched the shadows with the unsleeping instinct of his calling. But he did not see the Saint, for the simple reason that the Saint was at that moment slipping through a first-floor window on the Park side.

Elberman himself opened the door, and recognised his visitor.

"You're late," he said.

His pale bird-like face, behind the owlish spectacles, expressed no more agitation than his voice. He merely stated the fact—a perkily unemotional little man.

"I had to run for it at Waterloo," said Perrigo shortly.

He pushed into the hall, and shed his overcoat while Elberman barred the door behind him. Divested of that voluminous garment, he seemed even huskier than when he was wearing it. His jaw was square and pugnacious, and his nose had been broken years ago.

Elberman came back and looked up at him inquiringly.

"You weren't followed?"

"Not far."

"Everything else all right?"

Perrigo grunted a curt affirmative. He clapped his hat on a peg and thrust out his jaw.

"What you're talking about's O.K.," he said. "It's the follow-up that's not Jake. When Henderson hears about Frankie, he'll remember the way I ran—and there's a warrant for me over that Hammersmith job already."

"You killed Frankie?"

All Elberman's questions were phrased in the same way: they were flat statements, with the slightest of perfunctory interrogation marks tacked on to the last syllable.

"Had to," Perrigo said briefly. "Let's get on—I want a drink."

He was as barren of emotion as Elberman, but for a different reason. Habit had a hand in Perrigo's callousness. In the course of his chequered career he had been one of Chicago's star torpedoes, until a spot of trouble that could not be squared had forced him to jump the Canadian border and thence remove himself from the American continent. There were fourteen notches on his gun—but he was not by nature a boastful man.

Elberman led the way up the stairs, and Perrigo followed at his shoulder.

"Did you get that ticket?"

"Yes, I got you a berth. It's on the *Berengaria*. She sails tomorrow afternoon. You're in a hurry to leave?"

"I'll say I am. I guess it's safe for me to go back now, and I know a dealer in Detroit who'll give me a good price for my share. I'll get enough to give me a big start, and I'll make it grow. There's no money in this durned country."

Elberman shrugged, and opened a door.

He took two paces into the room, and Perrigo took one. And then and there the pair of them halted in their tracks like a Punch and Judy show whose operator has heard the lunch-hour siren, the muscles of their jaws going limp with sheer incredulous astonishment.

CHAPTER 2

"Come right in, boys," said the Saint breezily.

He reclined gracefully in Isadore Elberman's own sacrosanct armchair. Between the fingers of one hand was a freshly lighted cigarette; the fingers of the other hand curved round the butt of a .38 lead-pump that looked as if it could do everything the makers claimed for it and then some. It was as unsociable-looking a piece of armament as Perrigo had ever seen—and he knew what he was talking about. The sight of it kept his hands straight down and flaccid at his sides, as innocuous as the fists of something out of a waxwork exhibition.

If further pictorial detail is required, it may be provided by mentioning that the Saint was wearing a light grey suit and a silk shirt, both of which showed no traces of ever having been worn before, and an unwary angel might have been pardoned for turning round and hurriedly overhauling its own conscience after getting one glimpse of the radiant innocence of his face.

But most of these interesting points were wasted on the single-track minds of the two men in the doorway. Their retinas, certainly, registered a photographic impression of the general homoscape, but the spotlight of their attention merely oscillated momentarily over the broader features of the picture, and settled back in focus on the salient factor of the whole scenery—the starkly-fashioned chunk of blued steel that stared unwinkingly into the exact centre of the six-inch space between them, only too plainly ready and eager to concentrate its entire affection upon whichever of them first put in a bid for the monopoly.

"Make yourselves at home, boys," murmured the Saint. "Perrigo, you may close the door—how did you leave Frankie, by the way?"

Perrigo, with one hand dumbly obedient on the knob, started as if he had received an electric shock. The casual question needled with such an uncanny precision slick into the very core of things that he stared back at the Saint in the dim beginnings of a kind of vengeful terror.

"What do you know about Frankie?" he croaked.

"This and that," said the Saint, nonchalantly unhelpful. "Carry on shutting the door, brother, and afterwards you may keep on talking." He listened to the click of the latch, and spilled a quantity of cigarette-ash on to Mr Elberman's priceless carpet. "It was tough on your pal being bumped off in Durban," he continued conversationally, as if he had no other object but to put his victims at their ease. "Also, in my opinion, unnecessary. I know Frankie was inclined to be cagey, but I think a clever man could have found out what ship he was sailing home on without sending a man out to South Africa to spy on him . . . Come in, boys, come in. Sit down. Have a drink. I want you to feel happy."

"Who are you?" snarled Perrigo.

Simon shifted his mocking gaze to Elberman.

"Do you know, Isadore?" he asked.

Elberman shook his head, moistening his lips mechanically.

Simon smiled, and stood up. "Sit down," he said.

He ushered the two men forcefully into chairs, relieving Perrigo of a shooting-iron during the process. And then he put his back to the fire and leaned against the mantelpiece, spinning his gun gently round one finger hooked in the trigger-guard.

"I might deceive you," he said with disarming candour, "but I won't. I am the Saint." He absorbed the reflex ripples of expression that jerked over the seated men, and smiled again. "Yes—I'm the guy you've been wanting to meet all these years. I am the man with the load of mischief. I," said the Saint, who was partial to the personal pronoun, and apt to become loquacious when he found that it could start a good sentence, "am the Holy Terror, and the only thing for you boys to do is to try and look pleased about it. I'm on the point of taking a longish holiday, and my bank balance is just a few pounds shy of the amount I'd fixed for my pension. You may not have heard anything about it before, but you are going to make a donation to the fund."

The two men digested his speech in silence. It took them a little time, which the Saint did not begrudge them. He always enjoyed these moments. He allowed the gist of the idea to percolate deeply into their brains, timing the seconds by the regular spinning of his gun. There were six of them. Then—

"What d'you want?" snarled Perrigo.

"Diamonds," said the Saint succinctly.

"What diamonds?"

Perrigo's voice cracked on the question. The boil of belligerent animosity within him split through the thin overlay of puzzlement in which he tried to clothe his words, and tore the flimsy bluff to shreds. And the Saint's eyes danced.

"The illicit diamonds," he said, "which Frankie Hormer was bringing over by arrangement with Isadore. The diamonds for which Isadore double-crossed Frankie and took you into partnership, my pet. The boodle that you've got on your person right now, pretty Perrigo!"

"I don't know what you're talking about."

"No? Then perhaps Isadore will explain."

Again the Saint's bantering attention transferred itself to the owner of the house, but Elberman said nothing.

And Simon shook his head sadly.

"You may be the hell of a bright conspirator, Isadore," he remarked, "but you seem to be the odd man out of this conversazione. Pardon me while I do my Wild West stuff."

He unbuttoned his coat and took a length of light cord from an inside pocket. There was a running bowline ready at one end of it; he crossed to Elberman's chair and dropped the noose over his head, letting it settle down to his waist. With a brisk yank and a couple of twists he had the man's arms pinioned to his sides and the complete exhibit attached to the chair, finishing off with a pair of non-skid knots. He performed the entire operation with his left hand, and the gun in his right hand never ceased to keep the situation under effective control.

Then he returned to Perrigo.

"Where are they, sweetheart?" he inquired laconically, and the man tightened up a vicious lower lip.

"They're where you won't find them," he said.

Simon shrugged.

"The place does not exist," he said.

His glance quartered Perrigo with leisurely approbation—north to south, east to west. Somewhere in the area it covered was a hundred thousand pounds' worth of crystallised carbon, which wouldn't take up much room. A search through the man's pockets would only have taken a few seconds, but the Saint rather liked being clever. And sometimes he had inspirations of uncanny brilliance.

"Your trousers and coat don't match," he said abruptly.

The inspiration grew larger, whizzing out of the back of beyond with the acceleration of something off Daytona Beach, and the jump that Perrigo gave kicked it slap into the immediate urgent present.

"And I'll bet Frankie Hormer's don't, either," said the Saint.

The words came out in a snap.

And then he laughed. He couldn't help it. His long shot had gone welting through the bull's-eye with point-blank accuracy, and the scoring of the hit was registered on Perrigo's face as plainly as if a battery of coloured lamps had lighted up and a steam organ had begun to play *Down among the Dead Men* to celebrate the event.

"What's the joke?" demanded Perrigo harshly, and Simon pulled himself together.

"Let me reconstruct it. Diamonds are precious things—especially when they're the kind about which possession is the whole ten points of the law. If you're packing a load of that variety around with you, you don't take chances with 'em. You keep 'em as close to you as they'll go. You don't even carry them in your pockets, because pockets have their dangers. You sew them into your clothes. Frankie did, anyway. Wait a minute!" The Saint was working back like lightning over the ground he knew. He grabbed another thread and hauled it out of the skein— and it matched. "Why didn't you cut the diamonds out of Frankie's clothes? If you had time to trade clothes, you had time to do that. Then it must have been because it was dangerous. Why so? Because Frankie was dead! Because you didn't want to leave a clue to your motive. You killed Frankie, and—Hold the line, Perrigo!" The gangster was coming out of his chair, but Simon's gun checked him half-way. "You killed Frankie," said the Saint, "and you changed your coat for his."

Perrigo relaxed slowly.

"I don't know what you're talking about," he said.

"You do. You're three minutes late with your bluff. The train has pulled out and left you in the gentleman's cloakroom. Where you have no right to be. Take off that coat!"

Perrigo hesitated for a moment, and then, sullenly, he obeyed.

He threw the garment down at the Saint's feet, and Simon dropped on one knee. With the flat of his hand he went padding over every inch of the coat, feeling for the patch of tell-tale hardness that would indicate the whereabouts of Frankie Hormer's half-million-dollar cargo.

That was the sort of happy harvest that it was an unadulterated pleasure for the Saint to reap—the kind in which you just winked at the ears, and they hopped down off their stalks and marched in an orderly fashion into the barn. It made him feel at peace with the world . . . Down the sleeves he went, with tingling fingers, and over the lapels . . . Almost like lifting shoe-laces out of a blind beggar's tray, it was . . . He went along the bottom of the coat and up the back. He turned the pockets inside out, and investigated a wallet which he found in one of them.

And then, with a power-driven vacuum pump starting work on his interior, he turned the coat over and began again. He couldn't have been mistaken. He'd been as sure of his deductions as any man can be. The aptness of them had been placarded all over the place. And never in his life before had one of those moments of inspiration led him astray. He had grown to accept the conclusions they drew and the procedures they dictated as things no less inevitable and infallible than the laws of Nature that make water run downhill and mountains sit about the world with their fat ends undermost. And now, with a direct controversion of his faith right under his groping hands, he felt as if he was seeing Niagara Falls squirting upwards into Lake Ontario, while the Peak of Teneriffe perambulated about on its head with its splayed roots waving among the clouds.

For the first search had yielded nothing at all.

And the second search produced no more.

"Is—that—really—so!" drawled the Saint.

He stared at Perrigo without goodwill, and read the sneer in the other's eyes. It touched the rawest part of the Saint's most personal vanity—but he didn't tell the world.

"Thinking again?" Perrigo gibed.

"Why, yes," said the Saint mildly. "I often do it."

He stood up unconcernedly, fishing for his cigarette-case, and lighted another cigarette, still allowing nothing to distract the relentless aim of his automatic.

Somewhere there was a leak in the pipe, and his brain was humming out to locate it.

From Elberman there was nothing to be learned—he sat placidly where the Saint had roped him, outwardly unperturbed by what was happening, apparently satisfied to leave what small chance there was of effective opposition in the hands of Perrigo. And Elberman probably knew no more than the Saint, anyhow.

No—the secret was locked up behind the narrowed glinting eyes of Perrigo. Somewhere in the mind of that tough baby was stored the sole living human knowledge of the fate of the biggest packet of illicit diamonds ever brought into England in one batch, and Simon Templar was going to extract that knowledge if he had to carve it out with dynamite and rock-drills.

CHAPTER 3

"I heard you were clever." Perrigo spoke again, rasping into the breach in a voice that was jagged with spiteful triumph. "Got a reputation, haven't you? I'll say you must have earned it."

"Sure I did," assented the Saint, with a gaze like twin pinpoints of blue fire.

And then a thunder of knocking on the front door drummed up through the house and froze the three of them into an instant's bewildered immobility. It was, if the Saint had but known it at that moment, the herald of an interruption that was destined to turn that exceedingly simple adventure into the most riotous procession that the chronicler has yet been called upon to record. It was the starting-gun for the wildest of all wild-goose chases. It was, in its essence, the beginning of the Melancholy Journey of Mr Teal. If the Saint had known it, he would have chalked up the exact time on the wall and drawn a halo round it. But he did not know.

He stiffened up like a pointer, with his head cocked on one side and two short vertical lines etching in between his eyebrows. The clamorous insistence of that knocking boded no welcome visitor.

There was nothing furtive or sympathetic about it—nothing that one could associate with any possible client of a receiver of stolen goods. It hammered up the stairway in an atmosphere of case-hardened determination. And then it stopped, and grimly awaited results.

Simon looked from Elberman to Perrigo, and back again. He intercepted the glances that passed between them, and gathered from them a joint nescience equal to his own. In Perrigo's eyes there was suspicion and interrogation, in Elberman's nothing but an answering blank.

"Throwing a party?" murmured the Saint.

In silence he inhaled from his cigarette, and flicked it backwards into the fire. Listening intently, he heard through the window on his left the single sharp pip of a motor-horn sounding on a peculiar note. And the knocking below started again.

There was no doubt about its intentions this time. It signified its uncompromising determination to be noticed, and added a rider to the effect that if it wasn't noticed damned quickly it was perfectly prepared to bust down the door and march in regardless.

"So you've brought the cops, have you?" grated Perrigo.

He came recklessly out of his chair.

The obvious solution had dawned upon him a second after it dawned upon the Saint, and he acted accordingly. His interpretation was all wrong, but his reasoning process was simple.

To the Saint, however, the situation remained the same, whatever Perrigo thought. With the police outside, his gun was temporarily as useless as a piece of scrap-iron. And besides, he wanted further converse with Perrigo. Those three hundred carats of compact mazuma were still somewhere in Perrigo's charge, and Simon Templar was not going home without them. Therefore the bluff was called. Perrigo had got to stay alive, æsthetically distressing as his continued existence might be.

Simon pocketed his gun and stood foursquare to the fact. He slipped his head under Perrigo's smashing fist, and lammed into the gangster's solar plexus a half-arm jolt that sogged home like a battering-ram punching into a lump of putty. Perrigo gasped and went down writhing, and the Saint grinned.

"Sing to him, Isadore," he instructed hopefully, and went briskly out on to the landing.

That toot on the horn outside the window had been Patricia's signal to say that something troublesome was looming up and that she was wide awake, but the first item of information was becoming increasingly self-evident. As Simon went down the stairs, the clattering on the front door broke out again, reinforced by impatient peals on the bell, and the door itself was shaking before an onslaught of ponderous shoulders as the Saint turned out the light and drew the bolts.

A small avalanche of men launched themselves at him out of the gloom. Simon hacked one of them on the shins and secured a crippling grip on the nose of another, and then someone found the switch and put the light on again, and the Saint looked along his arm and found that his fingers were firmly clamped on the proboscis of Chief Inspector Teal himself.

"Why, it's Claud Eustace!" cried the Saint, without moving.

Teal shook the hand savagely off his nose, and wiped his streaming eyes.

"What the hell are you doing here?" he brayed.

"Playing dingbat through the daisies," said the Saint.

All the debonair gay impudence that he possessed was glimmering around his presence like a sort of invisible aurora borealis, and the perception of it made something seethe up through the detective like a gush of boiling lava. His brows knitted down over a glare of actual malevolence.

"Yes? And where's Perrigo?"

"He's upstairs."

"Since when?"

"About half an hour."

"And when did you arrive?"

"Roughly simultaneous, I should say."

"What for?"

"Well, if you must know," said the Saint, "I heard a rumour that Perrigo had discovered the second rhyme to 'Putney,' which I wanted for a limerick I was trying to compose. I thought of an old retired colonel of Putney, who lived on dill pickles and chutney, till one day he tried chilis boiled with carbide, tiddy dum tiddy dum didy utney. It's all very difficult."

Teal unfastened his coat and signed to one of the men who were with him.

"Take him," he ordered curtly.

Simon put his hands in his pockets and leaned against the wall with an air of injury.

"In your own words—what for?" he inquired, and a little of Chief Inspector Teal's old pose of heavy sleepiness returned. It was an affectation on which the detective had lately been losing a lot of his grip.

"A man named Hormer, a diamond smuggler, was murdered on the train between Southampton and Waterloo this evening. Perrigo was seen at Waterloo. I want him on suspicion of having committed the murder, and I'm going to take you on suspicion of being an accessory."

"Sorry," said the Saint, and something about the way he said it made Teal's baby blue eyes go dark and beady.

"Going to tell me you've got another alibi?"

"I am."

"I'll hear about that later."

"You'll hear about it now." The arrogant forefinger which Teal had learned to hate as personally as if it had a separate individual existence prodded into the gibbosity of his waistline with unequivocal emphasis. "From seven o'clock till eight-fifteen I was having dinner at Dorchester House—which includes the time that train got in. I had two friends with me. I talked to the head waiter, I discussed vintages with the wine waiter, and I gave the *maître d'hôtel* a personal lesson in the art of making perfect *crêpes suzette*. Go and ask 'em. And ask your own flat-footed oaf outside my house what time he saw me come in."

Teal champed grimly on his gum.

"I didn't accuse you of committing the murder," he said. "I'm having you for an accessory, and you can prove you were in Nova Scotia at the time for all that'll help you. Tell me you're going to prove you're in Nova Scotia right now, and perhaps I'll listen."

The Saint's brain functioned at racing speed.

A neat handful of spiky little facts prickled into its machinery, graded themselves, and were dealt with. One—that Perrigo had still got the diamonds. Two—that the diamonds must be detached from Perrigo. Three—that the detaching must not be done by Claud Eustace Teal. Four—that the Saint must therefore remain a free agent. Five— that the Saint would not remain a free agent if Claud Eustace Teal could help it.

Item five was fairly crackling about in the subtler undertones of the detective's drowsy voice, and it was that item which finally administered the upward heave to the balloon. The Teal-Templar feud was blowing up to bursting-point, and nobody knew it better than the Saint. But he also knew something else, which was that the burst was going to spray out into the maddest and merriest rodeo that ever was. Simon Templar proposed personally to supervise the spray.

He slipped his hands out of his pockets, and a very Saintly smile touched his lips.

"I might even prove something like that," he said.

And then he pushed Teal backwards and went away in one wild leap.

He had reached the foot of the stairs before the detectives had fully grasped what was happening, and he took the steps in flights of four at a pace that no detective in England could have approached. He made the upper landing before they were properly started. There was a big oak chest on that landing—Simon had noticed it on his way down—and he hulked it off the wall and ran it to the top of the stairs.

"Watch your toes, boys," he sang out, and shoved.

The three men below looked up and saw the chest hurtling down upon them. Having no time to get from under, they braced themselves and took the shock. And there they stuck, half-way up and half-way down. The huge iron-bound coffer tobogganed massively into them, two hundredweight of it if there was an ounce, and jammed them in their tracks. They couldn't go round, they couldn't go over, and it was several seconds before some incandescent intellect conceived the idea of going back.

Which was some time after the Saint had renewed his hectic acquaintance with Gunner Perrigo.

He found the gangster on his feet by a side table, cramming some papers into a shabby wallet. Perrigo's face was still contorted with agony, but he turned and crouched for a fight as the Saint burst in. As a matter of fact, the Saint was the last person he had ever expected to see again that night, and his puzzled amazement combined with the gesture of the Saint's upraised hand to check him where he was.

"Hold everything, Beautiful," said the Saint. "The police are in, and you and I are pulling our freight together."

He locked the door and strode coolly past the dumbfounded hoodlum. Flinging the window wide, he looked down into the private gardens that adjoined Gloucester Terrace and the park beyond. He saw shadows that moved, and knew that the house was surrounded. Simon waved a cheery hand to the cordon and closed the window again.

He turned back to Perrigo.

"Is there a way over the roof, or a back staircase?" he asked.

The man looked at him, his underlip jutting.

"What's the idea, Templar?"

"The idea is to get to hell out of here," said the Saint crisply. "Tell me what you know—and tell it quick!"

Perrigo glowered at him uncertainly, and in the silence they heard Teal's invading contingent arriving profanely on the landing.

And Perrigo made up his mind.

"There's no way out," he said.

He spoke the truth as far as he knew it, but the Saint laughed.

"Then we'll go out that way."

The door-handle rattled, and the woodwork creaked under an impacting weight, and Elberman suddenly roused out of his long retirement.

"And vot happens to me?" he squeaked, with his labouriously cultivated accent scattering to the four winds. "Vot do I say ven dey com' in?"

Simon walked to the mantelpiece and picked up a large globular vase, from which he removed the artificial flowers.

"You stay here and sing," he said, and forced the pot down firmly over the receiver's ears.

Outside, Chief Inspector Teal settled his hat and stepped back a pace. The casket that had delayed him was at the bottom of the stairs then, but if Teal could have had his way with it, it would have been at the bottom of the nethermost basement in Gehenna.

"All together," he snapped.

Three brawny shoulders moved as one, and the door splintered inwards.

Except for Isadore Elberman, struggling like a maniac to shake the porcelain cowl off his head, the room was empty of humanity.

Teal's glance scorched round it. There was plenty of furniture, but not a thing that would have given cover to a full-grown man. Then he saw a communicating door in another wall, and swore.

He dashed through, leaving his men to deal with the easy prisoner. Curtains flapping before an open window caught his eye, and instinctively he went over and stuck his head out. A man standing by a bush below looked up.

"Seen anyone?" Teal shouted.

"No, sir."

Teal withdrew his head and noticed a second door standing ajar. He went through it and found himself back on the landing he had just left, and his language became lurid.

Simon Templar and Perrigo stopped for a moment in the hall. Perrigo was a tough guy from the Uskides upwards, but Simon felt personally responsible for his safety and he took the responsibility seriously. There were irrefutable financial reasons for his solicitude— one hundred thousand of them. And for the duration of the fast-travelling episode he had got Perrigo's confidence. He tapped the gangster's bosom impressively.

"In case we should get separated, 7, Upper Berkeley Mews is the address," he stated. "See you remember it."

Perrigo gloomed sidelong at him, still fuddled with suspicious perplexity.

"I don't want to see you again," he growled.

"You will," said the Saint, and pushed him onwards.

Chief Inspector Teal floundered to the top of the stairs, and two of his men pressed close behind him. They looked down and saw Simon Templar alone in the hall, hands on hips, with his back to the door and an angelic smile on his upturned face.

"About that rhyme," said the Saint. "I've just thought of something. Suppose the old colonel 'went up in smoke for his gluttony'? Would the Poet Laureate pass it? Would Wilhelmina Stitch approve?"

"Get him!" snapped Teal.

The detectives swept down in a bunch.

They saw the Saint open the door, and heard outside the sharp pipping of a motor-horn. Patricia Holm was cruising round. But this they did not know. The door slammed shut again, and as a kind of multiple echo to the slam came the splattering cackle of an automatic. It fired four times, and then Teal got the door open.

He faced a considerable volume of pitchy darkness, out of which spoke the voice of one of the men he had posted to guard the courtyard.

"I'm sorry, sir—they got away."

"What happened?"

"Shot out the lights and slipped us in the dark, sir." Way down the road, a horn tooted seven times, derisively.

CHAPTER 4

A tinge of old beetroot suffused Mr Teal's rubicund complexion.

To say that his goat was completely and omnipotently got conveys nothing at all. In the last ten minutes his goat had been utterly annihilated, and the remains spirited away to the exact point in space where (so Einstein says) eternity changes its socks and starts back on the return journey. He was as comprehensively de-goated as a man can be.

With a foaming cauldron of fury bubbling just below his collar, he stood and watched his two outposts come up the steps towards him.

"Did you see Perrigo?" he rasped.

"Yes, sir. He came out first, and waited. I didn't recognise him at once—thought it was one of our own men. Then another bloke came out—"

Teal turned on the men behind him.

"And what are you loafing about here for?" he stormed. "D'you want your nannies to hold your hands when you go out at night? Get after them!"

He left the pursuit in their hands, and fumed back up the stairs. There he found a bedraggled Isadore Elberman, released at last from his eccentric headgear, in charge of a plain-clothes constable. The receiver was as loquacious as Teal allowed him to be.

"You can't hold me for nothing, Mr Teal. Those men attacked me and tied me up. You saw how I was fixed when you came in."

"I know all about you," said Teal unpleasantly.

Elberman blinked rapidly.

"Now you listen and I tell you somethings, Mr Teal. I don't like Perrigo. He's stole some tickets and never pay me for them, nor nothing else vot he owes me. You catch him and I'll tell you all about him. I'm an innocent man vot's been robbed. Now I'll tell you."

"You can tell the magistrate in the morning," said Teal.

He was in no mood to listen patiently to anyone. His temper had been jagged over with a cross-cut saw. Simon Templar had tweaked his nose for the umpteenth time, literally and figuratively, and the realisation of it was making Teal's palms sweat. It mattered nothing that a warrant to arrest the Saint could be obtained for the trouble of asking for it, and that the Saint could probably be located in fifteen minutes by the elementary process of going to No. 7, Upper Berkeley Mews and ringing the bell. Time after time Teal had thought his task was just as easy, and time after time he had found a flourishing colony of bluebottles using his ointment for a breeding-ground. It had gone on until Teal was past feeling the faintest tremor of optimism over anything less than a capture of the Saint red-handed, with stereoscopic cameras trained on the scene and a board of bishops standing by for witnesses. And something dimly approaching that ideal had offered itself that night—only to slither through his fingers and flip him in the eye with its departing tail.

He had no real enthusiasm for the arrest of Elberman, and even his interest in Perrigo had waned. The Saint filled his horizon to the exclusion of everything else. With a morose detachment he watched Elberman removed in a taxi, and stayed on in the same spirit to receive the reports of the men who had been down the road. These were not helpful.

"We went as far as Euston Road in the squad car, sir, but it wasn't any use. They had too long a start."

Teal had expected no better. He gave his subordinates one crowded minute of the caustic edge of his tongue for not having got on the job more promptly, and was mad with himself for doing it. Then he dismissed them.

"And give my love to your Divisional Inspector," he said. "Tell him I like his officers. And when I want some dumbbell exercise, I'll send for you again."

He made his exit on that line, and was sourly aware that their surprised and reproachful glances followed him out of the house.

He realised that the Saint had got under his skin more deeply than he knew. Never in any ordinary circumstances could the stoical and even-tempered Mr Teal have been moved to pass the buck to his helpless underlings in such a fashion.

And Teal didn't care. As he climbed into his car, the broiling crucibles of fury within him were simmering down to a steady white hot calidity of purpose. By the time he got to grips with his man again, the Saint would probably have another peck of dust ready to throw in his eyes, some new smooth piece of hokum laid out for him to skate over. Teal was prepared for it. It made no difference to him. His whole universe at that moment comprised but one ambition—to hound Simon Templar into a corner from which there could be no escape, corral him there, and proceed to baste into him every form of discourtesy and dolour permitted by the laws of England. And he was going to do it if it took him forty years and travelled him four thousand miles.

Some of which it did—but this prophecy was hidden from him.

The most inexorably wrathful detective in the British Isles, Chief Inspector Claud Eustace Teal, stepped on the gas and walloped into the second lap of his odyssey, heading for Upper Berkeley Mews.

CHAPTER 5

Simon Templar garaged his gat in a side pocket and leapt into the darkness. The men outside were on their toes for concerted action, but the dousing of the lights beat them. Simon swerved nimbly round the noises of their blundering, and sprinted for the square patch of twilight that indicated the way out of the courtyard.

His fingers hooked on the brickwork at the side of the opening as he reached it, and he fetched round into the road on a tight hair-pin turn that brought him up with his back to the wall outside. A yard or two to his left he saw the parking lights of a car gliding along the kerb.

Then Perrigo came plunging out. He skidded round the same turn and picked up his stride again without a pause. Simon shot off the wall and closed alongside him. He grabbed Perrigo's arm.

"The car—you won't make it on foot!"

He sprang for the running-board as he spoke—Patricia was keeping level, with the Hirondel dawdling easily along in second. Perrigo looked round hesitantly, making the pace flat-footed. Then he also hauled himself aboard.

"Right away, lass," said the Saint.

The great car surged forward, sprawling Perrigo head over heels on to the cushions of the back seat. Patricia changed up without a click, and Simon swung himself lightly over into place beside her.

"Well?" she asked calmly, and the Saint laughed.

"Oh, we had quite a jolly little party."

"What happened?"

Simon lighted a cigarette, and inhaled with deep satisfaction.

"Claud Eustace Teal's stomach walked in, closely followed by Claud Eustace. It was most extraordinary. Subsequently, I walked out. Claud Eustace is now thinking that that was even more extraordinary."

Patricia nodded.

"I saw the men getting into the gardens, and then I drove round to the back and saw the squad car. Did you have much trouble?"

"Nothing to speak of." The Saint was slewed round in his seat, his keen eyes searching back up the road. "I pulled Teal's nose, told him a perfectly drawing-room limerick, and left him to think it over . . . I should turn off again here, old darling—they're certain to be after us."

The girl obeyed.

And then she flashed the Saint a smile, and she said:

"Boy, I was all set to crash that squad car if they'd tried to take you away in it."

The Saint stared.

"You were which?"

"Sure, I'd have wrecked that car all right."

"And then?"

"I'd have got you out somehow."

"Pat, have you gone loco?"

She laughed, and shook her head, hustling the car recklessly down the long clear street.

Simon gazed at her thoughtfully.

It was typical of him that even then he was able to do that—and do it with his whole attention on the job. But the longer you knew him, the more amazing did that characteristic of light-hearted insouciance become. The most tempestuous incidents of his turbulent life occupied just as much of his mind as he allotted to them, and no more. And their claims were repudiated altogether by such a mood of scapegrace devilment as descended upon him at that instant.

He took in the features that he knew even better than his own with a new sense of delight. They stood out fair and clean-cut against the speeding background of sombre buildings—the small nose, the finely modelled forehead, the firm chin, the red lips slightly parted, the eyes gay and shining. The wind whipped a faint flush into her cheeks and swept back her hair like a golden mane. Under her short leather jacket the small high breasts seemed to be pressing forward with the eagerness of youth.

She turned to him, knowing his eyes were on her.

"What are you thinking, lad?"

"I'm thinking that I shall always want to remember you as I'm seeing you now," said the Saint.

One of the small strong hands came off the wheel and rested on his knee. He covered it with his own.

"I'm glad I was never a gentleman," he said.

They raced on, carving a wide circle out of the map of London. Traffic crossings delayed them here and there, but they kept as much as possible to unfrequented side streets, and moved fast. Perrigo sat in the back and brooded, with his coat collar turned up over his ears. His cosmos was still in a dizzy whirl, which he was trying to reduce to some sort of coherence. The vicissitudes that had somersaulted upon him from all angles during the past forty-five minutes had hopelessly dislocated his bearings. One minute the Saint was thumping him in the stomach, the next minute he was helping him on with his hat. One minute the Saint was preparing to hoist him, the next minute he was yanking him out of a splice. One minute the Saint seemed to have a direct hook-up with the police, the next minute he was leading the duck-out with all the zeal of an honest citizen avoiding contact with a Member of Parliament. It was a bit too much for Gunner Perrigo, a simple soul for whom the solution of all reasonable problems lay in the breech of a Smith-Wesson.

But out of the chaos one imperishable thought emerged to the forefront of his consciousness, and it was that which motivated his eventual decision. One bifurcated fact stood indefeasible amid the maelstrom. The Saint knew too much, and the Saint had at one time announced his intention of hijacking a certain parcel of diamonds. And the two prongs of that fact linked up and pointed to a single certainty: that the safest course for Gunner Perrigo was to get the hell out of any place where the Saint might be—and to make the voyage alone.

The car was held up at an Oxford Street crossing, and the Saint's back was towards him. Perrigo thought he had it all his own way.

But he had reckoned without the driving-mirror. For several minutes past the Saint had been doing a lot of Perrigo's thinking for him, and the imminence of some such manœuvre as that had been keeping him on the tip-toe of alertness. Throughout that time the driving-mirror had never been out of the tail of his eye, and he spotted Perrigo's stealthy movement almost before it had begun.

He turned his head and smiled sweetly.

"No," he said.

Perrigo squinted at him, sinking back a trifle.

"I can look after myself now," he grunted.

"You can't," said the Saint.

He was turning round again when Perrigo set his teeth, jumped up, and wrenched at the handle of the door.

It flew open, and then the Saint put one foot on the front seat and went over into the tonneau in a flying tackle.

He took Perrigo with him. They pelted over into the back seat in a lashing welter of legs and arms, fighting like savages. Perrigo had the weight, and brute strength, but Simon had the speed and cunning. The car lurched forward again while they rolled over and over in a flailing thudding tangle. After a few seconds of it, the Saint got an arm loose and whipped in a couple of pile-driving rib-binders; the effects of them put him on top of the mess, and he wedged Perrigo vigorously into a corner and held him there with a knee in his chest.

Then he looked up at the familiar helmet of a police constable, and found that the car had stopped.

They were in one of the narrow streets in the triangle of which Regent and Oxford form two sides. A heavy truck and a brace of taxis had combined to put a temporary plug in the meagre passage, and the constable happened to be standing by. Patricia was looking round helplessly.

"Wot's this?" demanded the Law, and Simon smiled winningly.

"We are secret emissaries of the Sheik Ali ben Dova, and we have sworn to place the sacred domestic utensil of the Caliph on top of the Albert Memorial."

"Wot?"

"Well, what I mean is that my friend is rather drunk, and that's his idea."

The Law produced a notebook.

"Any'ow," he said, "you got no right to be treating 'im like that."

Perrigo's mouth opened, and Simon shifted some more weight on to his knee. Perrigo choked and went red in the face.

"Ah, but you've no idea how violent he gets when he's had a few," said the Saint. "Goes quite bats. I'm trying to get him home now before he does any damage."

"Help!" yapped Perrigo feebly.

"Gets delusions, and all that sort of thing," said the Saint. "Thinks people are trying to kidnap him and murder him and so forth. Fancies everyone he meets is a notorious criminal. Doesn't even recognise his own wife—this is his wife, officer. Leads her an awful life. I don't know why she married the fool. And yet if you met him when he was sober, you'd take him for the most respectable gentleman you ever saluted. And he is, too. Man with a big diamond business. Right now, he's worth more money than you could save out of your salary if you were in the Force another three hundred years and lived on air."

Patricia leaned over pleadingly.

"Oh, officer, it's dreadful," she cried. "Please try to understand— please help me to save a scandal! Last time, the magistrate said he'd send my husband to prison if it happened again."

"I'm not your husband!" howled Perrigo. "I'm being robbed! Officer—"

"You see," said the Saint. "Just what I told you. Three weeks ago he fired a shot-gun at the postman because he said he was trying to put a bomb in the letter-box."

The policeman looked doubtfully from him to the lovely anxious face of Patricia, and was visibly moved. And then Perrigo heaved up again.

"Don't you know who this guy is?" he blurted. "He's the Sgloogphwf—"

This was not what Perrigo meant to say, but Simon clapped a hand over his mouth.

"Uses the most frightful language, too, when he's like this," said the Saint confidentially. "I couldn't even repeat what he called the cook when he thought she was sprinkling arsenic on the potatoes. If I had my way he'd be locked up. He's a dangerous lunatic, that's what he is—"

Suddenly the policeman's eyes glazed.

"Wot's that?" he barked.

Simon glanced round. His automatic lay in a corner of the seat, clear to view—it must have fallen out of his pocket during the scramble. It gleamed up accusingly from the glossy green-leather upholstery, and every milligram of the accusation was reflected in the constable's fixed and goggling eyes . . .

Simon drew a deep breath.

"Oh, that's just one of the props. We've been to a rehearsal of one of these amateur dramatic shows—"

The constable's head ducked with unexpected quickness. It pressed down close to the face of Perrigo, and when it raised itself again there was a blunt certitude written all over it.

"That man ain't bin drinking," it pronounced.

"Deodorised gin," explained the Saint easily. "A new invention for the benefit of a AWOL matrimoniates. Wonderful stuff. No longer can it be said that the wages of gin is breath."

The policeman straightened up.

"Ho, yus? Well, I think you'd better come round to the station, and let's 'ear some more about this."

The Saint shook his head.

He looked over the front of the car, and saw that the jam ahead had sorted itself out, and the road was clear. One hand touched Patricia's shoulder. And he smiled very seraphically.

"Sorry," he said. "We've got that date with the Albert Memorial."

He struck flat-handed at the policeman's shoulder, sending him staggering back, and as he did so Patricia engaged the gears and the Hirondel rocketed off the mark again like a shell from a howitzer.

Simon and Perrigo spilled over in another wild flurry. This time the objective was the gun on the seat. Simon got it. He also got Perrigo effectively screwed down to the mat, and knelt heavily on his biceps. The cold muzzle of the automatic rammed up under Perrigo's chin.

"That will be the end of your bonehead act, brother," said the Saint tersely. "You'd better understand that the only chance you've got is with me. You're a stranger over here. If I left you on your own, Teal would have you behind bars in record time. You wouldn't last twenty-four hours. And if you'd been able to make that cop take notice of you the way you wanted, you wouldn't have lasted twenty-four minutes—he'd have lugged you off to the station with the rest of us, and that would have been your finale. Get that up under your skull. And then put this beside it: you can't make your getaway now without consulting me. I've got your passport and your ticket to New York right next to my heart—dipped them out of your pocket before we left Isadore's. Which is why you're going to stick as close to me as you know how. When I'm through with you, I'll give you the bum's rush, quick enough—but not before!"

CHAPTER 6

The Hirondel skimmed round a corner and flashed out into Regent Street. The bows of an omnibus loomed up, bearing down upon them. Patricia spun the wheel coolly; they swerved round the wrong side of an island, dodged a taxi and a private car, and dived off the main road again.

Perrigo, on the floor of the tonneau, digested the fresh set of facts that the Saint had streamed into him. However apocryphal the first sheaf that he had meditated had been, these new ones were definitely concise and concrete—as was the circle of steel that bored steadily into his dewlap. He assimilated them in a momentous silence, while the stars gyrated giddily above him.

"All right," he said at length. "Let me up."

Simon hitched himself on to the seat; his gun went into his pocket, but retained command of the situation. As they entered Berkeley Square he watched Perrigo looking out to left and right, and was prompted to utter an additional warning.

"Stepping off moving vehicles," he said, "is the cause of umpteen street accidents per annum. If you left us now, it would be the cause of umpteen plus one. Ponder the equation, brother . . . And besides," said the Saint, who was starting to feel expansive again, "we've only just begun to know each other. The warbling and the woofling dies, so to speak, and we settle down to get acquainted. We approach the peaceful interlude.

> *When the cakes and ale are over*
> *And the buns and beer runs dry*
> *And the pigs are all in clover*
> *Up above the bright blue sky—*

as the poet hath it. Do you ever write poetry?" Perrigo said nothing.

"He does not write poetry," said the Saint.

The car stopped a few yards from the entrance of Upper Berkeley Mews, and Simon leaned forward and put his elbows on the back of the front seat. He rested his chin on his hands.

"When we were interrupted, darling," he said, "I was on the point of making some remarks about your mouth. It is, bar none, the most bewitching, alluring, tempting, maddening, seductive mouth I've ever kiss—set eyes on. The idea that it should ever be used for eating kippers is sacrilegious. You will oblige me by eating no more kippers. The way your lips curl at the corners when you're not sure whether you'll smile or not—"

Patricia turned with demure eyes.

"What do we do now?" she asked, and the Saint sighed.

"Teal's bloodhound saw you go out?"

"Yes."

"Then he'd better see you go in again. It'll set his mind at rest. Bertie and I will go our ways."

He opened the door and stepped out, Perrigo followed, constrained to do so by a grip which the Saint had fastened on the scruff of his neck. Maintaining possession of Perrigo, Simon leaned on the side of the car.

"When we get a minute or two to ourselves, Pat," he said, "remind me that my discourse on your eyes, which occupies about two hundred and fifty well-chosen words—"

"Is to be continued in our next," said Patricia happily, and let in the clutch.

Simon stood for a moment where she had left him, watching the car swing round into the mews.

And he was realising that the warbling and the woofling were very near their end. His flippant parody had struck home into the truth.

It was a queer moment for that blithe young cavalier of fortune. Out of the clear sky of the completely commonplace, it had flashed down upon him with a blinding brightness. The lights pointed to the end. No tremendous battle had done it, no breathless race for life, no cataclysmic instant of vision when all the intangible battlements of Paradise were shown up under the shadow of the sword. Fate, in the cussedness of its own inscrutable designs, had ordained that the revelation should be otherwise. Something simple and startling, a thing seen so often and grown so tranquilly familiar that the sudden unmasking of its inner portent would sweep away all the foundations of his disbelief like a tidal wave; something that would sheer ruthlessly through all sophistries and lies. A girl's profile against the streaking backcloth of smoke-stained stone. Yellow lamp-light rippling on a flying mane of golden hair. *Commedia.*

On the night of the third of April, at 10:30 p.m., Simon Templar stood on the pavement of Berkeley Square and looked life squarely in the eyes.

Just for that moment. And then the Hirondel was gone, and the moment was past. But all that there was to be done was done. The

207

High Gods had spoken. Simon turned. There was a new light in his eyes. "Let's go," he said.

They went. His step was light and swift, and the blood laughed in his veins. He had drunk the magic wine of the High Gods at one draught, down to the last dregs. It is a brave man who can do that, and he has his reward.

Perrigo walked tamely by his side. Simon had less than no idea what was passing in the gangster's mind just then. And he cared less than nothing. He would have taken on a hundred Perrigos that night, one after another or in two squads of fifty, just as they pleased—blipped them, bounced them, boned them, rolled them, trussed them up, wrapped them in greaseproof paper, and laid them out in a row to be called for by the corporation scavengers. And if Perrigo didn't believe it, Perrigo had only got to start something and see what happened. Simon thought less of Perrigo than a resolute rhinoceros would think of a small worm.

He ran up the steps of 104, Berkeley Square, turned his key in the lock, and switched on the lights. He made way for Perrigo with a courtly gesture. "In," he said.

Perrigo walked in very slowly. Some fresh plan of campaign was formulating behind the gangster's sullen compliance. Simon knew it. He knew that the ice was very thin—that only the two trump cards of passport and tickets, and the superb assurance with which they had been played, had driven Perrigo so far without a third bid for freedom. And he was not interested. As Perrigo's rear-ward foot lifted over the threshold, Simon shoved him on, followed him in a flash, and put his back to the closed door.

"You're thinking," he murmured, "that this is where you slug me over the head with the umbrella-stand, recover your property, and fade out. You're wrong."

He pushed Perrigo backwards. It seemed quite an effortless push, but there was an unsuspected kick of strength behind it. It flung Perrigo three paces towards the stairs, and then the hoodlum stopped on his heels and returned in a savage recoil.

Simon slipped the gun out of his pocket, and Perrigo reined in.

"You daren't shoot," he blustered.

"Again you're wrong," said the Saint metallically. "It would give me great pleasure to shoot. I haven't shot anyone for months. Perhaps you're thinking I'll be scared of the noise. Once more you're wrong. This gun isn't silenced, but the first three cartridges are only half-charged. No one in the street would hear a sound." For a tense second the Saint's gaze snapped daggers across the space between them. "You still think I'm bluffing. You've half a mind to test it out. Right. This is your chance. You've only to take one step towards me. One little step . . . I'm waiting for you!"

And Perrigo took the step.

The automatic slanted up, and hiccoughed. It made less noise than opening up a bottle of champagne, but Perrigo's hat whisked off his head and floated down to the carpet behind him. The gunman looked round stupidly at it, his face going a shade paler.

"Of course," said the Saint, relapsing into the conversational style, "I'm not a very good shot. I've been practising a bit lately, but I've a long way to go yet before I get into your class. Another time I might sort of kill you accidental like, and that would be very distressing. And then the question arises, Perrigo; would you go to Heaven? I doubt it. They're so particular about the people they let in. I don't think they'd like that check suit you're wearing. And can you play a harp? Do you know your psalms? Have you got a white nightie?"

Perrigo's fists clenched.

"What game are you playing?" he snarled.

"You know me," said the Saint rhetorically. "I am the man who knocked the 'L' out of London, and at any moment I may become the man who knocked the 'P' out of Perrigo. My game hasn't changed since we first met. It's a private party, and the police seemed to want to interfere, so we commuted to another site. That's the only reason why we're here, and why I took the trouble to get you away from Regent's Park. In short, if you haven't guessed it already, I'm still after those diamonds, my pet. They mean the beginning of a new chapter in my career, and a brief interlude of peace for Chief Inspector Teal. They are my old-age pension. I want that packet of boodle more than I've ever wanted any loot before, and if you imagine I'm not going to have them, your name is Mug. And now you can pass on—this hall's getting draughty."

"I'll see you in hell first," grated Perrigo.

"You won't see me in hell at all," said the Saint. "I like warm climates, but I'm very musical, and I think the harps have it. Forward march!"

He propelled Perrigo down the hall to a door which opened on to a flight of stone steps. At the bottom of these steps there was a small square cellar furnished with a chair and a camp bed. The door, Perrigo noticed, was of three-inch oak, and a broad iron bar slid in grooves across it. Simon pointed, and Perrigo went in and sat on the bed.

"When you know me better," said the Saint, "you'll discover that I have a cellar complex. So many people have taken me into cellars in order to do me grievous bodily harm that the infection has got into my system. There's something very sinister and thrilling about a cellar, don't you think?"

Perrigo hazarded no opinion.

"How long do I stay here?" he asked.

"Until tomorrow," Simon told him. "You'll find the place rather damp and stuffy, but there's enough ventilation to save you from suffocating. If you decide to strangle yourself with your braces, you might do it under that loose flagstone in the corner, which conceals a deep grave all ready dug for any corpses I might have on my hands. And in the morning I'll be along with some breakfast and a pair of thumbscrews, and we'll have a little chat. Night-night, old dear."

He left Perrigo with those cheering thoughts to chew over, and went out, bolting the iron bar into place and securing it with a steel staple.

A silver-noted buzzer was purring somewhere above him as he ran up the stairs, and he knew that the next development was already on its way. He was not surprised—he had been expecting it—but the promptitude with which his expectations had been realised argued a tenacious implacability on the part of Chief Inspector Teal that would have unsettled the serenity of anyone but a Simon Templar. But the Saint was lining up to the starting-gate of an odyssey quite different from that of Mr Teal. He let himself through the linen cupboard of the first-floor bathroom into No. 1, Upper Berkeley Mews, and went quickly down the runway to No. 7, and he was smiling as he stepped out of it into his own bedroom and slid the mirror panel shut behind him.

Patricia was waiting for him there.

"Teal's on his way," she said.

"Alone?"

"He was talking to his sleuth-hound when I gave you the signal. There wasn't anyone else with him."

"Splendid."

His coat off, the Saint was over at the dressing-table, putting a lightning polish on his hair with brush and comb. Under Patricia's eyes, the traces of his recent rough-and-tumble in the car disappeared miraculously. In a matter of seconds he was his old spruce self, lean and immaculate and alert, a laughing storm-centre of hell-for-leather mischief, flipping into a blue velvet smoking-gown . . .

"Darling—"

She stopped him, with a hand on his arm. She was quite serious.

"Listen, boy. I've never questioned you before, but this time there's no Duke of Fortezza to frame you out."

"Maybe not."

"Are you sure there isn't going to be real trouble?"

"I'm sure there is. For one thing, our beautiful little bolt-hole has done its stuff. Never again will it make that sleuth-hound outside my perfect alibi. After tonight, Claud Eustace will know that I've got a spare exit, and he'll come back with a search warrant and a gang of navvies to find it. But we'll have had our money's worth out of it. Sure, there's going to be trouble. I asked for it—by special delivery!"

"And what then?"

Simon clapped his hands on her shoulders, smiling the old Saintly smile.

"Have you ever known any trouble that I couldn't get out of?" he demanded. "Have you ever seen me beaten?"

She thrilled to his madcap buoyancy—she did not know why.

"Never!" she cried.

Downstairs, the front door bell rang. The Saint took no notice. He held her with his eyes, near to laughing, vibrant with impetuous audacity, magnificently mad.

"Is there anything that can put me down?"

"I can't imagine it."

He swept her to him and kissed her red lips.

The bell rang again. Simon pointed, with one of his wide gestures.

"Down there," he said, "there's an out-size detective whose one aim in life is to spike the holiday that's coming to us. Our own Claud Eustace Teal, with his mouth full of gum and his wattles crimsoning, paying us his last professional call. Let's go and swipe him on the jaw."

CHAPTER 7

In the sitting-room, Patricia closed her book and looked up as Chief Inspector Teal waddled in. Simon followed the visitor. It was inevitable that he should dramatise himself—that he should extract the last molecule of diversion from the scene by playing his part as strenuously as if life and death depended on it. He was an artist. And that night the zest of his self-appointed task tingled electrically in all his fibres. Teal, chewing stolidly through a few seconds' portentous pause, thought that he had never seen the Saint so debonair and dangerous.

"I hope I don't intrude," he said at last, heavily.

"Not at all," murmured the Saint. "You see before you a scene of domestic repose. Have some beer?"

Teal took a tight hold on himself. He knew that there was a toe-to-toe scrap in front of him, and he wasn't going to put himself at a disadvantage sooner than he could help. The searing vials of righteous indignation within him had simmered down still further during the drive from Regent's Park, and out of the travail caution had been born. His purpose hadn't weakened in the least, but he wasn't going to trip over his own feet in the attempt to achieve it. The lights of battle glittering about in the Saint's blue eyes augured a heap of snags along the route that was to be paddled, and for once Chief Inspector Teal was trying to take the hint.

"Coming quietly?" he asked.

The feeler went out, gruffly non-committal, and Simon smiled.

"You're expecting me to ask why," he drawled, "but I refuse to do anything that's expected of me. Besides, I know."

"How do you know?"

"My spies are everywhere. Sit down, Claud. That's a collapsible chair we bought specially for you, and the cigars in that box explode when you light them. Oh, and would you mind taking off your hat?— it doesn't go with the wallpaper."

Teal removed his bowler with savage tenderness. He realised that he was going to have an uphill fight to keep the promise he had made to himself. There was the faintest thickening in his lethargic voice as he repeated his question.

"How do you know what I want you for?"

"My dear soul, how else could I have known except by being with you when you first conceived the idea of wanting me?" answered the Saint blandly.

"So you're going to admit it really was you I was talking to at Regent's Park?"

"Between ourselves—it was."

"Got some underground way out of here, haven't you?"

"The place is a rabbit-warren."

"And where's Perrigo?"

"He's playing bunny."

Teal twiddled a button, and his eyelids lowered. The leading tentacles of a nasty cold sensation were starting to weave clammily up his spine. It was something akin to the sensation experienced by a man who, in the prelude to a nightmare, has been cavorting happily about in the middle of a bridge over a fathomless abyss, and who suddenly discovers that the bridge has turned into a thin slab of toffee and the temperature is rising.

Something was springing a leak. He hadn't the ghost of a presentiment of what the leak was going to be, but the symptoms of its approach were bristling all over the situation like the quills on a porcupine.

"You helped Perrigo to escape at Regent's Park, didn't you?" He tried to make his voice sleepier and more bored than it had ever been before, but the strain clipped minute snippets off the ends of the syllables. "You're admitting that you caused a wilful breach of the peace by discharging firearms in a public thoroughfare, and you obstructed and assaulted the police in the execution of their duty, and that you became an accessory to wilful murder?"

"Between these four walls," said the Saint, "and in these trousers, I cannot tell a lie."

"Very well." Teal's knuckles whitened over the brim of his hat. "Templar, I arrest you—"

"Oh, no," said the Saint. "Oh, no, Claud, you don't."

The detective tautened up as if he had received a blow. But Simon Templar wasn't even looking at him. He was selecting a cigarette from a box on the centre table. He flicked it into the air and caught it between his lips, with his hands complacently outspread. "My only parlour trick," he remarked, changing the subject.

Teal spoke through his teeth.

"And why?" he flared.

"Only one I ever learnt," explained the Saint naively.

"Why don't I arrest you?"

Simon ranged himself side-saddle on the table. He stroked the cog of an automatic lighter and put his cigarette in the flame.

"Because, Claud, what I say to you now, between these four walls and in these trousers, and what I'd say in the witness-box, are two things so totally different you'd hardly believe they came from the same rosebud mouth."

Teal snorted.

"Perjury, eh? I thought something cleverer than that was coming from you, Saint."

"You needn't be disappointed."

"Got a speech that you think'll let you out?"

"I have, Claud. I've got a peach of a speech. Put me in the dock, and I'll lie like a newspaper proprietor. Any idea what that means?"

The detective shrugged.

"That's your affair," he grunted. "If you want to be run for perjury as well as other things, I'm afraid I can't stop you."

Simon leaned forward, his left hand on his hip and his right hand on his knee. The deep-blue danger lights were glinting more brightly than ever in his eyes, and there was fight in every line of him. A back-to-the-wall, buccaneering fight, rollicking out to damn the odds.

"Claud, did you think you'd got me at last?"

"I did. And I still think so."

"Thought that the great day had dawned when my name was coming out of the Unfinished Business ledger, and you were going to sleep nights?"

"I did."

"That's too bad, Claud," said the Saint.

Teal pursed his lips tolerantly, but there were pinpoints of red luminance darting about in his gaze.

"I'm still waiting to hear why," he said flatly.

Simon stood up.

"O.K.," he said, and a new indefinable timbre of menace was pulsing into his easy drawl. "I'll tell you why. You asked for a showdown.

I'll tell you what you've been thinking. There was a feather you wanted for that hat of yours: you tried all manner of ways to get it, but it wasn't having you. You were too dumb. And then you thought you'd got it. Tonight was your big night. You were going to collect the Saint on the most footling break he ever made. I've got away with everything from murder downwards under your bloodshot eyes, but you were going to run me for stealing four-pence out of the Bank of England."

"That's not what I said."

"It goes for what you meant. You get what you asked for, Claud. Thought I was the World's Wet Smack, did you? Figured that I was so busy crashing the mountains that I'd never have time to put a tab on all the molehills? Well, you asked for something. Now would you like to know what I've really been doing tonight?"

"I'll hear it."

"I've been entertaining a dozen friends, and I'll give you from now till Kingdom Come to prove it's a lie!"

The detective glared.

"D'you think I was born yesterday?" he yelped.

"I don't know," said the Saint lazily. "Maybe you weren't born at all. Maybe you were just dug up. What's that got to do with it?"

Teal choked. His restraint split into small pieces, and the winds of his wrath began to twitch the bits out of his grasp, one by one.

"What's the idea?" he demanded heatedly, and the Saint smiled.

"Only the usual alibi, old corpuscle. Like it?"

"Alibi?" Teal rent the words with sadistic violence. "Oh, yes, you've got an alibi! Six men saw you at Regent's Park alone, but you've got twelve men to give you an alibi. And where was this alibi?"

"In the house that communicates with this one by the secret passage you wot of."

"You aren't going to change your mind about that passage?"

217

"Why should I? It may be eccentric, but there's nothing in the Statute Book to say it's illegal."

"And that's the alibi you're going to try and put over on me?"

"It's more," said the Saint comfortably. "It's the alibi that's going to dish you."

"Is it?"

Simon dropped his cigarette into an ashtray and put his hands in his pockets. He stood in front of the detective, six feet two inches of hair-trigger disorder—with a smile.

"Claud," he said, "you're missing the opportunity of a lifetime. I'm letting you in on the ground floor. Out of the kindness of my heart I'm presenting you with a low-down on the organisation of a master criminal that hundreds would give their ears to get. I'm not doing it without expense to myself, either. I'm giving away my labyrinth of secret passages, which means that if I want to be troublesome again I shall have to look for a new headquarters. I'm showing you the works of my emergency alibi, guaranteed to rescue anyone from any predicament: there are four lords, a knight, and three officers of field rank in it—they've taken me years to collect, and now I shall have to fossick around for a new bunch. But what are trifles like that between friends? Now be sensible, Claud. It becomes increasingly evident that someone is impersonating me."

"Yes, and I know who it is!"

"But it was bound to happen, wasn't it?" said the Saint, continuing in that philosophically persuasive strain under which the razor-keen knife-edges were gliding about like hungry sharks in a smooth tropical sea. "In my misguided efforts to do good, I once made myself so notorious that someone or other was bound to think of hanging his sins on me. The wonder is that it wasn't thought of years ago. Now look at that recent affair in Hampstead—"

"I don't want to know any more about that affair in Hampstead," said Teal torridly. "I want to know how you're going to swing it on me this time. Come on. Let me have the names and addresses of these twelve liars. I'll run them for perjury at the same time as I'm running you."

"You won't. But I'll tell you what *I'll* do—"

The Saint's forefinger shot out. Teal struck it aside.

"Don't do that!" he yapped.

"I have to," said the Saint. "I love the way your tummy dents in and pops out again. Talking of tummies—"

"You tell me what you think you're going to do."

"I'll run you for bribery, corruption, and blackmail!" said the Saint.

His languid voice lightened up on the sentence with a sudden crispness that had the effect of a gunshot. It rocked the atmosphere like an exploding bomb. And it was followed by a silence that was ear-splitting.

The detective gaped at him with goggling eyes, while a substratum of dull scarlet sapped up under the skin of his face. It was the most flabbergasting utterance that Chief Inspector Teal had listened to. He blinked as if he had been smitten with doubts of his own sanity.

"Have you gone off your head?" he hooted.

"Not that I know of."

"And who's supposed to have been bribing me?"

"I have."

"*You?*"

"Yeah." The Saint took another cigarette from the box, and lighted it composedly. "Haven't seen your pass-book lately, have you? You'd better ask for it tomorrow morning. You'll discover that in the last six weeks alone you've taken eight hundred and fifty pounds off me. Two hundred pounds on February the sixteenth, two-fifty on March the sixth, four hundred on March the twenty-second—apart from smaller regular payments extending over the previous six months. All the cheques have got your endorsement on 'em, and they've all been passed through your account: they're back in my bank now, available for inspection by any authorised person. It's quite a tidy little sum, Claud—eighteen hundred quid altogether. You'll have a grand time explaining it away."

Some of the colour ebbed slowly out of Teal's plump cheeks, and he seemed to sag inside his overcoat. Only the expression in his eyes remained the same—a stare of blank, frozen, incredulous stupefaction.

"You framed me for that?" he got out.

"I'm afraid I did." Simon inhaled, and blew a smoke-ring. "It was just another of my brilliant ideas. Are you thinking you can deny the endorsements? It won't be easy. Eight hundred and fifty pounds in six weeks is real money. I wrote it off as insurance, but I still hated parting with it. And how many juries would believe that I paid a detective eighteen hundred pounds inside six months just with the idea of being funny? It'd be a steep gamble for you if we had to go through the courts, old dear. I admit it was very naughty of me to bribe you, but there it is . . . Unfortunately, you couldn't be content with what I gave you. You wanted more, and you tried all sorts of persecutions to get it. First that Hampstead affair, and then this show tonight . . . Oh, well, Claud, it looks as if we shall have to swing together."

CHAPTER 8

The detective seemed to have shrunk. His complexion had gone lined and blotchy, and there was a dazed look in his eyes that stabbed the Saint with a twinge of pity.

Teal was a man facing the end. The bombshell that the Saint had flung at him had knocked the underpinning from the very foundations of his universe. The fight and bluster had gone out of him. He knew, better than anyone, the full and devastating significance of the trap that had been laid for him. There was no way out of it—no human bluff or subterfuge that would let him out. He could stick to his guns and give battle to the last ditch—arrest the Saint as he had intended, take his chance with the threatened alibi, fight out the counter-charge of bribery and corruption when it came along, perhaps even win an acquittal—but it would still be the end of his career. Even if he won, he would be a ruined man. A police officer must be above suspicion. And those endorsed and cancelled cheques of which the Saint had spoken, produced in court, would be damning evidence. Acquitted, Teal would still be under a cloud. Ever afterwards, there would be gossips to point to him and whisper that he was a man who had broken the eleventh commandment and escaped the consequences by the skin of his teeth. And he was not so young as he had been—not so young that he could snap his fingers at the gossips and buckle grimly back into the task of making good again. He would have to resign. He would be through.

He stood there, going paler, but not flinching, and the Saint blew two more smoke-rings.

Teal was trying to think, but he couldn't. The suddenness with which the blow had fallen had pulverised his wits. He felt himself going mentally and physically numb. Under the surveillance of those devilishly bleak blue eyes, and in the vivid presence of what they stood for, he couldn't do any consecutive and sober thinking.

Abruptly, he settled his belt and shook down his coat.

"I'll see you in the morning," he said, in a sort of gulp, and walked jerkily out of the room.

Simon heard the front door close, and listened to the detective's footsteps clumping past the window and dying away towards Berkeley Square. Something seemed to have paralysed their ordinary ponderous self-reliance. There was the least little tell-tale drag in them . . . And the Saint turned, and found Patricia watching him.

"A notable triumph," he said quietly.

The girl stood up.

"Were you bluffing?" she asked.

"Of course not. I knew that Teal and I were certain to have that showdown sooner or later, and I was prepared for it. I'd got half a dozen more shocks waiting for him, if he'd stayed to hear them. I just wanted to put the wind up him. But I'd no idea it'd be such a smash."

Patricia looked away.

"It was pathetic," she said. "Oh, I could see him go ten years older while you were talking."

Simon nodded. The fruits of victory were strangely bitter.

"Pat, did you know that an hour or so ago I was planning for this to be the sorriest show Teal ever stuck his nose into? The noble game of Teal-baiting was going to be played as it had never been played before. That's all I've got to say . . . What a damn-fool racket it is!"

He turned on his heel, and left her without another word.

His mind was too full to talk. Upstairs, he threw off his clothes and tumbled into bed, and almost instantly he fell asleep. That gift of sleep is one that all great adventurers have shared—a sleep that heals the mind and solves all problems. Patricia, coming up later, found his face as peaceful as a child's.

He must have slept very soundly, for the sound of a stealthy rustle only half roused him. Then he heard a click, and he was wide awake.

He opened his eyes and glanced round the room. There was enough light for him to see that there was no unusual shadow anywhere. He looked at his watch, and saw that it was nearly seven o'clock in the morning. For some moments he lay still, gazing at the indicator panel on the opposite wall. An ingenious system of invisible alarms connected up with that panel from every part of the house, and it was impossible for anyone to move about inside No. 7, Upper Berkeley Mews at night without every yard of his progress being charted by winking little coloured bulbs on the panel. But not one bulb was flickering, and the auxiliary buzzer under the Saint's pillow was silent.

Simon frowned puzzledly, wondering if his imagination had deceived him. And then a breath-taking duet of inspirations whirled into his brain, and he wriggled noiselessly from between the sheets.

He pushed the pier-glass aside, and touched a switch that illuminated the secret passage. Right at his feet, he saw a charred match-end lying on the felt matting, and his lips tightened. He sped down the corridor, and entered the end house. In front of him, the door of a cupboard, and its false back communicating with the bathroom in 104, Berkeley Square, were both wide open, and he remembered that he had left them ajar behind him on the previous night, in his haste to get home and resume the feud with Chief Inspector Teal. The bathroom door was also ajar; he slipped through it, and emerged on the landing. A tiny glow of light farther down the stairs caught his eye, and vanished immediately.

Then he established a second link between the two parts of the duet that had brought him to where he was and wished he had delayed the chase while he picked up his gun. He crept downwards, and saw a shadow that moved.

"Stay where you are," he rapped. "I've got you covered!"

The shadow leapt away, and Simon hurled himself after it. He was still four steps behind when he sprang through the air and landed on the man's shoulders. They crashed down together, rolled down the remaining treads, and reached the bottom with a bump. The Saint groped for a strangle-hold. He had found it with one hand when he saw a dull gleam of steel in the light of a street lamp that flung a faint nimbus of rays through the transom above the front door. He squirmed aside, and the point ripped his pyjamas and thudded into the floor. Then a bony knee picked up into his stomach, and he gasped and went limp with agony. The front door banged while he lay there twisting helplessly.

It was ten minutes before he was able to stagger to his feet and go on a tour of investigation. Down in the basement, he found the cellar door wide open. A hole big enough for a man's arm to pass through had been carved out of it a foot above the massive bolt, and the flagstones were littered with chips of wood. Simon realised that he had been incredibly careless.

He returned to his bedroom and looked at the coat he had been wearing. It had been moved from where he had thrown it down— that had been the cause of the soft rustling that had first disturbed his slumbers. A further investigation showed that Perrigo's passport and tickets were missing from the pocket where Simon had left them. This was no worse than the Saint had expected.

Aching, he went back to bed and slept again. And this time he dreamed a dream.

He was running up the wrong side of a narrow moving stairway. Patricia was in front of him, and he couldn't go fast enough; he had to keep pushing her. He wanted to get past her and catch Perrigo, who was dancing about just out of his grasp. Perrigo was dressed something like an organ-grinder's monkey, in a ridiculous straw hat, a tail coat, and a pair of white flannel trousers. There was an enormous diamond necklace over his collar, and he jeered and grimaced, and bawled, "Not in these trousers." Then the scene changed, and Teal came riding by on a giraffe, wearing a pair of plus fours, and he also said, "Not in these trousers."

Then the Saint woke up, and saw that it was half-past eight. He jumped out of bed, lighted a cigarette, and made for the bathroom. He soaped his face and shaved, haunted by his dream for some reason that he could not nail down, and he was wallowing in bath salts when the interpretation of it flashed upon him with an aptness that made him erupt out of the water with an almighty splash.

Ten minutes later, gorgeously apparelled in his new spring suit, he tore down the stairs and found bacon and eggs on the table and Patricia reading a newspaper.

"Perrigo has left us," he said.

The girl looked up with startled eyes, but Simon was laughing.

"He's left us, but I know where he's gone," said the Saint. "He collected his papers before he went. I forgot that he carried a knife, and locked him up without fanning him—he spent the night digging his way through the door, and came through here for his passport in the early morning. I was just too slow to catch him. We'll meet him again on the boat train—it leaves at ten o'clock."

"How do you know he'll be on it?"

"If he didn't mean to do that, why did he come back for his ticket? No—I know exactly what's in his head. He knows that he's only got one way out, now that he's bereaved of Isadore, and he's going to try to make the grade. He's made up his mind that I'm not helping the police, and he's going to take his chance on a straight duck with me—and I'll bet he'll park himself in the most crowded compartment he can find, just to give himself the turn of the odds. And I'll say some more; I know where those diamonds are now!"

"Have you got them?"

"Not yet. But up at Isadore's I spotted that Perrigo's costume was assorted. I thought he'd changed coats with Frankie Hormer, and I went over his jacket twice before Teal buzzed in. Naturally, I didn't find anything. I must have been half-witted. It wasn't coats he'd swapped— it was trousers. Those diamonds are sewn up somewhere in Bertie's leg draperies!"

Patricia came over to the table.

"Have you thought any more about Teal?" she asked.

Simon strode across to a book-case and took down a small leather-bound volume. There were months of painstaking work in its unassuming compass—names, addresses, personal data, means of approach, sources of evidence, all the laboriously perfected groundwork that enabled the Saint's raids upon the underworld to be carried through so smoothly and made their meteoric audacity possible.

"Pat," said the Saint, "I'm going to make Teal a great man. It may be extravagant, but what the hell? Can you have the whole earth for ten cents? This party has already cost us our home, our prize alibi, and one of our shrewdest counter-attacks—but who cares? Let's finish the thing in style. I'm the cleverest man in the world. Can't I find six more homes, work out fourteen bigger and better alibis, and invent seventy-nine more stratagems and spoils? Can't I fill two more books like this if I want to?"

Patricia put her arms round his neck.

"Are you going to give Teal that book?"

The Saint nodded. He was radiant.

"I'm going to steal Perrigo's pants, Claud Eustace is going to smile again, and you and I are going away together."

CHAPTER 9

The Saint was in a thaumaturgical mood. He performed a minor sorcery on a Pullman attendant that materialised seats where none had been before, and ensconced himself with the air of a wizard taking his ease. After a couple of meditative cigarettes, he produced a pencil and commenced a metrical composition in the margins of the wine list.

He was still scribbling with unalloyed enthusiasm when Patricia got up and went for a walk down the train. She was away for several minutes, and when she returned, the Saint looked up and deliberately disregarded the confusion in her eyes.

"Give ear," he said. "This is the Ballad of the Bold Bad Man, another Precautionary Tale:

> *Daniel Dinwiddie Gigsworth-Glue*
> *Was warranted by those who knew*
> *To be a perfect paragon*
> *With or without his trousers on;*
> *An upright man (the Figworts are*
> *Peerlessly perpendicular)*

Staunch to the old morality,
Who would have rather died than be
Observed at Slumpton-under-Slop
In bathing drawers without the top.

"Simon," said the girl, "Perrigo isn't on the train." The Saint put down his pencil.

"He is, old darling. I saw him when we boarded it at Waterloo, and I think he saw me."

"But I've looked in every carriage—"

"Did you take everyone's finger-prints?"

"A man like Perrigo wouldn't find it easy to disguise himself."

Simon smiled.

"Disguises are tricky things," he said. "It isn't the false whiskers and the putty nose that get you down—it's the little details. Did I ever tell you about a friend of mine who thought he'd get the inside dope about Chelsea? He bought a pink shirt and a velvet coat, grew a large semicircular beard, rented a studio, and changed his name to Prinnlovcwz, and he had a great time until one day they caught him in an artist's colourman's trying to buy a tube of Golder's Green . . . Now you must hear some more about Daniel:

How lovely, oh, how luminous
His spotless virtue seemed to us
Who sat among the cherubim
Reserving Daniel's pew for him!
Impossible to indispose,
His honour, shining like his nose,
Blazed through an age of sin and strife
The beacon of a blameless life . . .
And then he fell . . .

The Tempter, who
Was mortified by Daniel Glue,
Played his last evil card, and Dan
Who like a perfect gentleman,
Had scorned strong drink and wicked oaths
And blondes with pink silk underclothes,
Bought (Oh, we saw the angels weep!)
A ticket in the Irish Sweep.

Patricia reached across the table and captured the Saint's hands.

"Simon, I won't be out of it! Where *is* Perrigo?"

"If you talk much louder, he'll hear you."

"He isn't in this coach!"

"He's in the next one."

The girl stared.

"What does he look like?"

Simon smiled, lighting a cigarette.

"He's chosen the simplest and nearly the most effective disguise there is. He's got himself up as a very fair imitation of our old pal the Negro Spiritual." The Saint looked at her with merry eyes. "He's done it well, too, but I spotted him at once. Hence my parable. Did you ever see a nigger with light yellow eyes? They may exist, but I've never met one. There used to be a blue-eyed Sikh in Hong Kong who became quite famous, but that's the only similar freak I've met. So when I got a glimpse of those eyes I took another peek at the face—and Perrigo it was. Remember him now?"

Patricia nodded breathlessly.

"Why couldn't I see it?" she exclaimed.

"You've got to have a brain for that sort of thing," said the Saint modestly.

"But—yes, I remember now—the carriage he's in is full—"

"And you're wondering how I'm going to get his trousers off him? Well, the problem certainly has its interesting angles. How does one steal a man's trousers on a crowded train? You mayn't believe it, but I see difficulties about that myself."

An official came down the train, checking up visas and issuing embarkation vouchers, Simon obtained a couple of passes, and smoked thoughtfully for some minutes. And then he laughed and stood up.

"Why worry?" he wanted to know. "I've thought of a much better thing to do. One of my really wonderful inspirations."

"What's that?"

Simon tapped her on the shoulder.

"I'm going to beguile the time by baiting Bertie," he said, with immense solemnity. "C'mon!"

He hurtled off in his volcanic way, with a long-striding swing of impetuous limbs, as if a gale of wind swept him on.

And Patricia Holm was smiling as she ran to catch him up—the unfathomable and infinitely tender smile of all the women who have been doomed to love romantic men. For she knew the Saint better than he knew himself. He could not grow old. Oh, yes, he would grow in years, would feel more deeply, would think more deeply, would endeavour with spasmodic soberness to fall in line with the common facts of life, but the mainsprings of his character could not change. He would deceive himself, but he would never deceive her. Even now, she knew what was in his mind. He was trying to brace himself to march down the road that all his friends had taken. He was daring himself to take up the glove that the High Gods had thrown at his feet, and to take it up as he would have taken up any other challenge—with a laugh and a flourish, and the sound of trumpets in his ears. And already she knew how she would answer him.

She came up behind him and caught his elbow.

"But is this going to help you, lad?"

"It will amuse me," said the Saint. "And it's an act of piety. It's our sacred duty to see that Bertie has a journey he'll never forget. I shall open the ball by trying to touch him for a subscription to the funds of the Society for Distributing Woollen Vests to the Patriarchs of the Upper Dogsboddi. Speaking emotionally and in a loud voice I shall wax eloquent on the work that has already been done among his black brothers, and invite him to make a contribution. If he does, we'll go and drink it and think up something else. If he doesn't, you'll barge in and ask him for his autograph. Address him as Al Jolson, and ask him to sing something. After that—"

"After that," said Patricia firmly, "he'll pull the communication cord, and we shall both be thrown off the train. Lead on, boy!"

Simon nodded, and went to the door of the compartment he had marked down.

And there he stopped, statuesquely, while the skyward-slanting cigarette between his lips sank slowly through the arc of a circle and ended up at a comically contrasting droop.

After a few seconds, Patricia stepped to his side and also looked into the compartment. And the Saint took the cigarette from his mouth and exhaled smoke in a long expiring whistle.

Perrigo was gone.

There wasn't a doubt about that. The corner seat that he had occupied was as innocent of human habitation as any corner seat has ever been since George Stephenson hitched up his wagons and went rioting down to Stockton-upon-Tees. If not more so. As for the other seats, they were occupied respectively by a portly matron with a wart on her chin, a small boy in a sailor suit, and a thin-flanked female with pimples and a camouflaged copy of *The Well of Loneliness*, into none of whom could Gunner Perrigo by any conceivable miracle of make-up have transformed himself . . . Those were the irrefutable facts about the scene, pithily and systematically recorded, and the longer one looked at them, the more gratuitously grisly they became.

Simon singed the inoffensive air with a line of oratory that would have scorched the hide of a salamander. He did it as if his heart was in the job, which it was. Carefully and comprehensively, he covered every aspect and detail of the situation with a calorific lavishness of imagery that would have warmed the cockles of a sergeant-major's heart. Nobody and nothing, however remotely connected with the incident, was left outside the wide embrace of his oration. He started with the paleolithic progenitors of the said George Stephenson, and worked steadily down to the back teeth of Isadore Elberman's grandchildren. At which point Patricia interrupted him.

"He might be having a wash or something," she said.

"Yeah!" The Saint was scathing. "Sure, he might be having a wash. And he took his bag with him in case the flies laid eggs on it. Did you notice that bag? I did. It was brand-new—hadn't a scratch on it. He'd been doing some early morning shopping before he caught the train, hustling up some kit for the voyage. All his own stuff was at Isadore's, and he wouldn't risk going back there. And his bag's gone!"

The embarkation officer passed them, and opened the door of the compartment.

"Miss Lovedew?" The pimply female acknowledged it. "Your papers are quite in order—"

Simon took Patricia's arm and steered her gently away.

"Her name is Lovedew," he said sepulchrally. "Let us go and find somewhere to die."

They tottered a few steps down the corridor, and then Patricia said, "He must be still on the train! We haven't slowed up once since we started, and he couldn't have jumped off without breaking his neck—"

The Saint gripped her hands.

"You're right!" he whooped. "Pat, you're damn right! I said you wanted a brain for this sort of thing. Bertie must be on the train still, and if he's on the train we'll find him—if we have to take the whole outfit to pieces. Now, you go that way and I'll go this way, and you keep your eyes peeled. And if you see a man with a huge tufted beard, you take hold of it and give it a good pull!"

"Right-o, Saint!"

"Then let's go!"

He went flying down the alley, lurching from side to side from the rocking of the train, and contriving to light another cigarette as he went.

He did his share thoroughly. In the space of ten minutes he reviewed a selection of passengers so variegated that his brain began to reel. Before his eyes passed an array of physiognomies that would have made Cesare Lombroso chirrup ecstatically and reach for his tape-measure. Americans of all shapes and sizes, Englishmen in plus fours, flannel bags, and natty suitings, male children, female children, ambiguous children, large women, small women, three cosmopolitan millionaires—one fat, one thin, one sozzled—three cosmopolitan millionaires' wives—ditto, but shuffled—a novelist, an actor, a politician, four Parsees, three Hindus, two Chinese, and a wild man from Borneo. Simon Templar inspected every one of them who could by any stretch of imagination have come within the frame of the picture, and acquired sufficient data to write three books or six hundred and eighty-seven modern novels. But he did not find Gunner Perrigo.

He came to the end of the last coach, and stood gazing moodily out of the window before starting back on the return journey.

And it was while he was there that he saw a strange sight.

The first manifestation of it did not impress him immediately. It was simply a scrap of white that went drifting past the window. His eyes followed it abstractedly, and then reverted to their gloomy concentration on the scenery. Then two more scraps of white flittered past his nose, and a second later he saw a spread of red stuff fluttering feebly on the wire fence beside the line.

The Saint frowned, and watched more attentively. And a perfect cataract of whatnots began to aviate past his eyes and distribute themselves about the route. Big whatnots and little whatnots, in divers formations and half the colours of the rainbow, went wafting by the window and scattered over the fields and hedges. A mass of green taffeta flapped past, looking like a bilious vulture after an argument with a steam hammer, and was closely followed by a jaundiced cotton seagull that seemed to have suffered a similar experience. A covey of miscellaneous bits and pieces drove by in hot pursuit. No less than eight palpitating banners of assorted hues curvetted down the breeze and perched on railings and telegraph poles by the wayside. It went on until the entire landscape seemed to be littered with the loot of all the emporia of Knightsbridge and the Brompton Road.

And suddenly the meaning of it flashed upon the Saint—so suddenly and lucidly that he threw back his head and bowed before a gust of helpless mirth.

He spun round to the door beside him. He had made sure that it was locked, but he must have been mistaken. He heaved his shoulder at it, and it burst open—it had been temporarily secured with a gimlet, as he discovered later. But at that moment he was not curious about that. He hadn't a doubt in his head that his latest and most sudden inspiration was right, and he knew exactly what he was going to do about it.

Five minutes later, after a brief interlude for wash and brush-up purposes, he was careering blissfully back along the corridor on one of the most supremely joyous journeys of his life.

At the compartment at which Perrigo had been, he stopped, and opened the door.

"Miss Lovedew," he said pensively, and again the impetiginous female looked up and acknowledged the charge. "Is your luggage insured?"

"Of course," said the woman. "Why?"

"You should begin making out your claim immediately," said the Saint.

The woman stared.

"I don't understand you. What's happened? Are you one of the company's servants?"

"I am the head cook and bottle-washer," said the Saint gravely, "and I did not like your red flannel nighties."

He closed the door again and passed on, carolling hilariously to himself, and leaving the lady to suffer from astounded fury as well as acne.

In the Pullman he found Patricia gazing disconsolately in front of her. Her face lighted up as he arrived.

"Did you find him?"

Simon sat down.

"What luck did you have?"

"Just sweet damn-all," said the girl wryly. "I've been over my part of the train four times, and I wouldn't have missed Perrigo if he'd disguised himself as a mosquito."

"I am inspired," said the Saint.

He took the wine list and his pencil, and wrote rapidly. Then he held up the sheet and read:

> The mountains shook, the thunders came,
> The very heavens wept for shame;
> A Gigsworth in a white chemise
> Visibly vortexed at the knees,
> While Dan's defection turned quite giddy

The ghost of Ancestor Dinwiddie.
If Dan had been a common cad
It wouldn't have been half so bad;
If he had merely robbed a bank,
Or floated companies that sank,
Or, with a piece of sharp bamboo,
Bashfully bumped off Mrs Glue;
They might have understood his whim
And, in the end, forgiven him:
Such things, though odd, have now and then
Been done by perfect gentlemen;
But Daniel's foul iniquity
Could hardly have been worse if he
Had bought (or so it seemed to them)
A chocolate after 9 p.m.

Patricia smiled.

"Will you always be mad?" she asked.

"Until the day I die, please God," said the Saint.

"But if you didn't find Perrigo—"

"But I did find him!"

The girl gasped.

"You found him?"

Simon nodded, and she saw then that his eyes were laughing.

"I did. He was in the luggage van at the end, heaving mentionables and unmentionables out of a wardrobe trunk. And just for the glory of it, Pat, the trunk was labelled with the immortal name of Lovedew—I found that out afterwards and tried to break the news to her, but I don't think she believed me. Anyway, I whaled into him, and there was a breezy exchange of pleasantries. And the long and the short of it is—"

"That Perrigo is locked up in that trunk, just where he wanted to be, but there's an entirely new set of labels on it that are going to cause no small stir on board the *Berengaria* if Claud Eustace arrives in time. Which I expect he will—Isadore is almost certain to have squealed. And all we've got to do is wait for the orchestra to tune up." Simon looked at his watch. "There's half an hour to go yet, old Pat, and I think we might stand ourselves a bottle!"

CHAPTER 10

A clock was booming the half-hour after twelve when Chief Inspector Teal climbed stiffly out of his special police car at the gates of the Ocean Dock. It had been half-past ten when he left Albany Street Police Station, and that single chime indicated that the Flying Squad driver had made a very creditable run of it from London to Southampton.

For Isadore Elberman had duly squealed, as the Saint had expected, and it had been no mean squeal. Considerably stewed down after a sleepless night in the cells, he had reiterated to the Divisional Inspector the story with which he had failed to gain Teal's ear the evening before, and the tale had come through with a wealth of embellishments in the way of circumstantial detail that had made the Inspector reach hastily for the telephone and call for Mr Teal to lend his personal patronage to the squeak.

Isadore Elberman was not the only member of the cast who had spent a sleepless night. Teal had been waiting on the doorstep of his bank when it opened in the morning. He asked casually for his balance, and in a few minutes the cashier passed a slip of paper across the counter. It showed exactly one thousand eight hundred pounds more to his credit than it should have done, and he had no need to make further inquiries. He took a taxi from the bank to Upper Berkeley Mews, but a prolonged assault on the front door elicited no response, and the relief watcher told him that Templar and the girl had gone out at nine-thirty and had not returned. Teal went back to New Scotland Yard, and it was there that the call from Albany Street found him.

And on the way down to Southampton the different fragments of the jigsaw in which he had involved himself had fitted themselves together in his head, dovetailing neatly into one another without a gap or a protuberance anywhere, and producing a shape with one coherent outline and a sickeningly simple picture lithographed upon it in three colours. So far as the raw stark facts of the case were concerned, there wasn't a leak or a loose end in the whole copper-bottomed consolidation of them. It was as puerile and patent as the most elementary exercise in kindergarten arithmetic. It sat up on its hind legs and leered at him.

Slowly and stolidly, with clenched fists buried deep in the pockets of his overcoat, Chief Inspector Teal went up the gangway of the *Berengaria* to see the story through.

And down in the well-deck aft, Simon Templar was sitting on a wardrobe trunk discoursing genially to two stewards, a porter, an irate lady with pimples, and a small group of fascinated passengers.

"I agree," the Saint was saying. "It is an outrage. But you must blame Bertie for that. I can only conclude that he doesn't like red flannel nighties either. So far as can be deduced from the circumstances, the sight of your eminently respectable robes filled him with such an uncontrollable frenzy that he began to empty the whole contents of your trunk out of the window. But am I to blame? Am I Bertie's keeper? At a moment when my back was turned—"

"I don't believe you!" stormed the irate lady. "You're a common thief, that's what you are! I should know that trunk anywhere. I can describe everything that's in it—"

"I'll bet you can't," said the Saint.

The lady appealed to the assembled spectators.

"This is unbearable!" she raved. "It's the most bare-faced imposture I ever heard of! This man has stolen my clothes and put his own labels on the trunk—"

"Madam," said the Saint, "I've never disputed that the trunk, as a trunk, was yours. The labels refer to the destination of the contents. As a strictly law-abiding citizen—"

"Where," demanded the pimply female hysterically, "is the Captain?"

And at that point Teal shouldered himself into the front rank of the crowd.

Just for a second he stood looking at the Saint, and Simon saw that there were shadows under his eyes and the faintest trace of flabbiness about his cheeks. But the eyes themselves were hard and expressionless, and the lips below them were pressed up into a dour line.

"I thought I should find you here," he said.

The last of the Lovedews whirled round.

"Do you know this man?"

"Yes," said Teal rigidly. "I know him."

The Saint crossed his legs and took out a cigarette-case. He indicated the detective with a wave of his hand.

"Ladies and gentlemen," he murmured, "allow me to introduce the *deus ex machina*, or whizzbang out of the works. This is Mr Claud Eustace Teal, who is going to tell us about his wanderings in Northern Euthanasia. Mr Teal, Miss Lovedew. Miss Lovedew—"

"*Teal?*" The infuriated lady leapt back as though she had been stung, "Are you Teal?"

"That is my name," said the slightly startled detective.

"You stand there and admit that to me?"

"Yes—of course."

The woman reeled back into the arms of one of the bystanders.

"Has everyone gone mad?" she wailed. "I'm being robbed in broad daylight! That is this man's accomplice—he hasn't denied it! Can nobody do anything to stop them?"

Teal blinked.

"I'm a police officer," he said.

"You're a liar!" screamed the woman.

"My good lady—"

"Don't you dare speak to me like that! You're a low, mean, impertinent thief—"

"But—"

"I want my trunk. I'm going to have my trunk! How can I go to New York without my trunk? That is my own trunk—"

"But, Claud," said the Saint earnestly, "have you seen the trunk of the butler of her uncle? That is a trunk of the most colossal."

Miss Lovedew gazed wildly about her.

"Will no one help me?" she moaned.

Simon removed the cigarette from his mouth and stood up. He placed one foot on the trunk, rested his right forearm on his knee, and raised a hand for silence.

"May I be allowed to explain?" he said.

The woman clutched her forehead.

"Is anyone going to listen to this . . . this . . . this . . ."

"Gentleman?" suggested the Saint, tentatively.

Teal stepped forward and took a grip of his belt.

"I am a police officer," he repeated trenchantly, "and I should certainly like to hear his explanation."

This time he made the statement of his identity with such a bald authoritativeness that the buzz of surrounding comment died down to a tense hush. Even the pimply protagonist gaped at him in silence, with her assurance momentarily shaken. The stillness piled up with almost theatrical effect.

"Well?" said Teal.

The Saint gestured airily with his cigarette.

"You arrive," he said, "in time to arbitrate over a serious misunderstanding. Let me give you the facts. I travelled down by the boat train from Waterloo this morning in order to keep an eye on a friend of ours whom we'll call Bertie. During the journey I lost sight of him. I tootled around to find out what was happening to him, and eventually located him in the luggage van and in the very act of throwing the last of Miss Lovedew's what's-its out of the window."

"It's a lie!" bleated the lady, faint but pursuing. "He stole my clothes, insulted me in my carriage—"

"We come to that in a minute," said the Saint imperturbably. "As I was saying, I found Bertie just crawling into the trunk he had so unceremoniously emptied. At great personal peril and inconvenience, Claud, I helped him towards his objective and locked him up for delivery to yourself. In order to do this, I was compelled to make a temporary alteration to the labels on the trunk, which I admit I borrowed for the good cause without Miss Lovedew's permission. I made one attempt to explain the circumstances to her, but was rejected with contumely. Then, while I was waiting for you to arrive, this argument about the rightful ownership of the property began. The trunk, as I've never denied, belongs to Miss Lovedew. The dispute seems to be about Bertie."

Miss Lovedew goggled at him.

"Do you mean to say that there's a man in that trunk?" she demanded hideously.

"Madam," said the Saint, "there is. Would you like him? Mr Teal has the first claim, but I'm open to competitive offers. The specimen is in full running order, suffering at the moment from a black eye and an aching jaw, but otherwise complete and ready for the road. He is highly-strung and sensitive, but extremely virile. Fed on a diet of rye whisky and caviare—"

Teal bent over the trunk and examined the labels. The name on them was his own. He straightened up and levelled his gaze inflexibly upon the Saint.

"I'll talk to you alone for a moment," he said.

"Pleasure," said the Saint briefly.

The detective looked round.

"That trunk is not to be touched without my permission," he said.

He walked over to the rail, and Simon Templar strolled along by his side. They passed out of earshot of the crowd, and stopped. For a few seconds they eyed each other steadily.

"Is that Perrigo you've got in that trunk?" Teal asked presently.

"None other."

"We've had a full confession from Elberman. Do you know what the penalty is for being in possession of illicit diamonds?"

"I know what the penalty is for being caught in possession of illicit diamonds," said the Saint circumspectly.

"Do you know where those diamonds are now?"

Simon nodded.

"They are sewn into the seat of Perrigo's pants," he said.

"Is that what you wanted Perrigo for?"

The Saint leaned on the rail.

"You know, Claud," he remarked, "you're the damnedest fool."

Teal's eyes hardened.

"Why?"

"Because you're playing the damnedest fool game with me. Have you ever known me be an accessory to wanton murder?"

"I've known you to be mixed up in some darned funny things."

"You've never known me to be mixed up in anything as darned funny as that. But you work yourself up to the point where you're ready to believe anything you want to believe. It's the racket. It's dog eating dog. I beat you to something, and you get mad. When you get mad, I have to bait you. The more I bait you, the madder you get. And the madder you get, the more I have to bait you. We get so's nothing's too bad for us to do to each other." The Saint smiled. "Well, Claud, I'm taking a little holiday, and before I go I'm giving you a break."

Teal shrugged mountainously, but for a moment he said nothing. And the Saint balanced his cigarette on his thumbnail and flipped it far and wide.

"Let me do some thinking for you," he said. "I'm great on doing other people's thinking for them these days . . . Overnight you thought over what I said to you last evening. This morning you verified that I hadn't been bluffing. And you knew there was only one thing for you to do. Your conscience wouldn't let you lie down under what I'd done. You'd got to take what was coming to you—arrest me, and face the music. You'd got to play square with yourself, even if it broke you. I know just how you felt. I admire you for it. But I'm not going to let you do it."

"No?"

"Not in these trousers," said the Saint. "Why should you? You've got Perrigo, and I'm ready for a short rest. And here's your surprise packet. Get busy on what it tells you, and you may be a superintendent before the end of the season."

Teal glanced at the book which the Saint had thrust into his hands, and turned it over thoughtfully.

Then he looked again at the Saint. His face was still as impassive as the face of a graven image, but a little of the chilled steel had gone out of his eyes. And, as he looked, he saw that the Saint was laughing again—the old, unchangeable, soundless, impudent Saintly laughter. And the blue imps in the Saint's eyes danced.

"I play the game by my own rules, Claud," said the Saint. "Don't you forget it. That profound philosophy covers the craziest things I do. It also makes me the only man in this bleary age who enjoys every minute of his life. And"—for the last time in that story, the Saintly forefinger drove gaily and debonairly to its mark—"if you take a leaf out of my book, Claud, one day . . . Claud, you will have fun and games for ever."

And then the Saint was gone.

He departed in the Saintly way, with a last Saintly smile and the clap of a hand on the detective's shoulder, and Teal watched him go without a word.

Patricia was waiting for him farther along the deck. He fell into step beside her, and they went down the gangway and crossed the quay. At the corner of a warehouse Simon stopped. Quite quietly he looked at her, propping up the building with one hand.

And the girl knew what his silence meant. For him, the die was cast, and, being the man he was, he was ready to pay cash. His hand was in his pocket, and the smile hadn't wavered on his lips. But just for that moment he was taking his unflinching farewell of the fair fields of irresponsible adventure, understanding just what it would mean to him to pay the score, scanning the road ahead with the steady eyes that had never feared anything in this life. And he was ready to start the journey there and then.

And Patricia smiled. She had never loved him more than she did at that moment, but she smiled with nothing but the smile behind her eyes. And she answered before he had spoken.

"Boy," she said, "I couldn't be happier than I am now."

He did not move. She went on, quickly:

"Don't say it, Simon! I don't want you to. Haven't we both got everything we want as it is? Isn't life splendid enough? Aren't we going to have more adventures, and—and—"

"Fun and games for ever?"

"Yes! Aren't we? Why spoil the magic? I won't listen to you. Even if we've missed out on this adventure—"

Suddenly he laughed. His hands went to his hips. She had been waiting for that laugh. She had put all she was into the task of winning it. And, with that laugh, the spell that had held his eyes so quiet and steady was broken. She saw the leap of the old mirth and glamour lighting them again. She was happy.

"Pat, is that really what you want?"

"It's everything I want."

"To go on with the fighting and the fun? To go on racketing around the world, doing everything that's utterly and gloriously mad— swaggering, swashbuckling, singing—showing all these dreary old dogs what can be done with life—not giving a damn for anyone—robbing the rich, helping the poor—plaguing the pompous—killing dragons, pulling policemen's legs—"

"I'm ready for it all!" He caught her hands.

"Are you sure?"

"Positive."

"Not one tiny little doubt about it?"

"Not one."

"Then we can start this minute."

She stared.

"What do you mean?" she asked.

The Saint loosened his belt and pointed downwards. Even then, she didn't understand.

"Remember how I found Bertie? He was halfway into the Lovedew's wardrobe trunk. We had a short but merry scrap. And then he went on in. Well, during the tumult and the shouting, and the general excitement, in the course of which Bertie soaked up one of the juiciest KOs I've ever distributed—"

He broke off and the girl turned round in amazed perplexity.

From somewhere on the *Berengaria* had periled out the wild and frantic shriek of an irreparably outraged camel collapsing under the last intolerable straw.

Patricia turned again, her face blank with bewilderment.

"What on earth was that?" she asked.

The Saint smiled seraphically.

"That was the death-cry of old Pimply-face. They've just opened her trunk and discovered Bertie. And he has no trousers on. We can begin our travels right now," said the Saint.

PUBLICATION

HISTORY

Like so many previous Saint books, this one has its origins in Charteris's work for *The Thriller* magazine.

"The Inland Revenue" started life as "The Masked Menace" in No. 116, published on 25 April 1931. "The Million Pound Day" was originally "Black Face" in issue No. 122 from 6 June that same year, and "The Melancholy Journey of Mr Teal" started life as "The Kidnapped Killer" in No. 131 from 8 August 1931.

These stories were combined under the title *The Holy Terror*, first published in May 1932 by Hodder & Stoughton. An American edition, under the much more mass market– friendly title of *The Saint Versus Scotland Yard*, was published by the Doubleday Crime Club in September 1932. The UK reverted to that title with the publication of the first Pan paperback in 1949.

Charteris dedicated the book to his first wife, Pauline, whom he'd married on 24 June 1931 in Nice, France. They'd met a few years earlier when both were living in South Kensington, London, and Pauline had accompanied Leslie throughout much of the early years of his career. Their daughter, Patricia, was born the following year. After her divorce from Charteris in 1937, Pauline went on to marry literary agent Innes

Rose, and for many years both worked at John Farquharson Ltd., which represented Charteris amongst many other authors. She passed away in June 1975.

This title wasn't translated quite so quickly as many previous Saint adventures; the Swedes called it *Helgonet contra Scotland Yard* in 1964 to coincide with the first Saint TV show, but it started life as *Helgonet på hemmaplan* in the 1940s.

The French opted for the bibliographically confusing *Le Saint à Londres* in 1939, whilst in 1933 the Spanish opted for *El Santo contra la policía*. The Portuguese meanwhile kept it straightforward and published *O Santo contra a Scotland Yard* in 1950. The Dutch christened it *De schrik der dieven* for the original translation in 1947.

A Hungarian translation, under the title of *Az Angyal a Scotland Yard ellen*, was combined with a translation of *The Saint Intervenes* (*Az Angyal beavatkozik* since you ask) and published in 1990.

A Braille version has been published in Australia by The Queensland Braille Writing Association.

"The Million Pound Day" formed the basis for the 1939 film *The Saint in London*, produced by RKO and starring George Sanders as Simon Templar.

Some commentators have suggested that the much derided 1997 film *The Saint* adapted the plot point from "The Melancholy Journey of Mr Teal" in which the Saint plans to retire once his bank account reaches a certain level, but such a deliberate homage to the original character seems wildly out of place for a film that deviated so far from the established character of the Saint.

"The Inland Revenue," which was adapted by screenwriter Paul Erickson and retitled "The Scorpion," aired as the forty third episode in the Roger Moore series *The Saint*, first broadcast on Sunday, 18 October 1964.

ABOUT THE AUTHOR

*I'm mad enough to believe in romance. And I'm sick and
tired of this age—tired of the miserable little mildewed
things that people racked their brains about, and wrote
books about, and called life. I wanted something more
elementary and honest—battle, murder, sudden death, with
plenty of good beer and damsels in distress, and a complete
callousness about blipping the ungodly over the beezer. It
mayn't be life as we know it, but it ought to be.*

—Leslie Charteris in a 1935 BBC radio interview

Leslie Charteris was born Leslie Charles Bowyer-Yin in Singapore on
12 May 1907.

He was the son of a Chinese doctor and his English wife, who'd
met in London a few years earlier. Young Leslie found friends hard to
come by in colonial Singapore. The English children had been told not
to play with Eurasians, and the Chinese children had been told not to
play with Europeans. Leslie was caught in between and took refuge in
reading.

"I read a great many good books and enjoyed them because
nobody had told me that they were classics. I also read a great many
bad books which nobody told me not to read . . . I read a great many

popular scientific articles and acquired from them an astonishing amount of general knowledge before I discovered that this acquisition was supposed to be a chore."[1]

One of his favourite things to read was a magazine called *Chums*. "The Best and Brightest Paper for Boys" (if you believe the adverts) was a monthly paper full of swashbuckling adventure stories aimed at boys, encouraging them to be honourable and moral and perhaps even "upright citizens with furled umbrellas."[2] Undoubtedly these types of stories would influence his later work.

When his parents split up shortly after the end of World War I, Charteris accompanied his mother and brother back to England, where he was sent to Rossall School in Fleetwood, Lancashire. Rossall was then a very stereotypical English public school, and it struggled to cope with this multilingual mixed-race boy just into his teens who'd already seen more of the world than many of his peers would see in their lifetimes. He was an outsider.

He left Rossall in 1924. Keen to pursue a creative career, he decided to study art in Paris—after all, that was where the great artists went— but soon found that the life of a literally starving artist didn't appeal. He continued writing, firing off speculative stories to magazines, and it was the sale of a short story to *Windsor Magazine* that saved him from penury.

He returned to London in 1925, as his parents—particularly his father—wanted him to become a lawyer, and he was sent to study law at Cambridge University. In the mid-1920s, Cambridge was full of Bright Young Things—aristocrats and bohemians somewhat typified in the Evelyn Waugh novel *Vile Bodies*—and again the mixed-race Bowyer-Yin found that he didn't fit in. He was an outsider who preferred to make his own way in the world and wasn't one of the privileged upper class. It didn't help that he found his studies boring and decided it was more fun contemplating ways to circumvent the law. This inspired him to write a novel, and when publishers Ward Lock & Co. offered him a three-book deal on the strength of it, he abandoned his studies to pursue a writing career.

When his father learnt of this, he was not impressed, as he considered writers to be "rogues and vagabonds." Charteris would later recall that "I wanted to be a writer, he wanted me to become a lawyer. I was stubborn, he said I would end up in the gutter. So I left home. Later on, when I had a little success, we were reconciled by letter, but I never saw him again."[3]

X Esquire, his first novel, appeared in April 1927. The lead character, X Esquire, is a mysterious hero, hunting down and killing the businessmen trying to wipe out Britain by distributing quantities of free poisoned cigarettes. His second novel, *The White Rider*, was published the following spring, and in one memorable scene shows the hero chasing after his damsel in distress, only for him to overtake the villains, leap into their car . . . and promptly faint.

These two plot highlights may go some way to explaining Charteris's comment on *Meet—the Tiger!*, published in September 1928, that "it was only the third book I'd written, and the best, I would say, for it was that the first two were even worse."[4]

Twenty-one-year-old authors are naturally self-critical. Despite reasonably good reviews, the Saint didn't set the world on fire, and Charteris moved on to a new hero for his next book. This was *The Bandit*, an adventure story featuring Ramon Francisco De Castilla y Espronceda Manrique, published in the summer of 1929 after its serialisation in the *Empire News*, a now long-forgotten Sunday newspaper. But sales of *The Bandit* were less than impressive, and Charteris began to question his choice of career. It was all very well writing—but if nobody wants to read what you write, what's the point?

"I had to succeed, because before me loomed the only alternative, the dreadful penalty of failure . . . the routine office hours, the five-day week . . . the lethal assimilation into the ranks of honest, hard-working, conformist, God-fearing pillars of the community."[5]

However his fortunes—and the Saint's—were about to change. In late 1928, Leslie had met Monty Haydon, a London-based editor who was looking for writers to pen stories for his new paper, *The Thriller*— "The Paper with a Thousand Thrills." Charteris later recalled that "he said he was starting a new magazine, had read one of my books and would like some stories from me. I couldn't have been more grateful, both from the point of view of vanity and finance!"[6]

The paper launched in early 1929, and Leslie's first work, "The Story of a Dead Man," featuring Jimmy Traill, appeared in issue 4 (published on 2 March 1929). That was followed just over a month later with "The Secret of Beacon Inn," starring Rameses "Pip" Smith. At the same time, Leslie finished writing another non-Saint novel, *Daredevil*, which would be published in late 1929. Storm Arden was the hero; more notably, the book saw the first introduction of a Scotland Yard inspector by the name of Claud Eustace Teal.

The Saint returned in the thirteenth issue of *The Thriller*. The byline proclaimed that the tale was "A Thrilling Complete Story of the Underworld"; the title was "The Five Kings," and it actually featured Four Kings and a Joker. Simon Templar, of course, was the Joker.

Charteris spent the rest of 1929 telling the adventures of the Five Kings in five subsequent *The Thriller* stories. "It was very hard work, for the pay was lousy, but Monty Haydon was a brilliant and stimulating editor, full of ideas. While he didn't actually help shape the Saint as a character, he did suggest story lines. He would take me out to lunch and say, 'What are you going to write about next?' I'd often say I was damned if I knew. And Monty would say, 'Well, I was reading something the other day . . .' He had a fund of ideas and we would talk them over, and then I would go away and write a story. He was a great creative editor."[7]

Charteris would have one more attempt at writing about a hero other than Simon Templar, in three novelettes published in *The Thriller* in early 1930, but he swiftly returned to the Saint. This was partly due to his self-confessed laziness—he wanted to write more stories for *The Thriller* and other magazines, and creating a new hero for every story was hard work—but mainly due to feedback from Monty Haydon. It seemed people wanted to read more adventures of the Saint . . .

Charteris would contribute over forty stories to *The Thriller* throughout the 1930s. Shortly after their debut, he persuaded publisher Hodder & Stoughton that if he collected some of these stories and rewrote them a little, they could publish them as a Saint book. *Enter the Saint* was first published in August 1930, and the reaction was good enough for the publishers to bring out another collection. And another . . .

Of the twenty Saint books published in the 1930s, almost all have their origins in those magazine stories.

Why was the Saint so popular throughout the decade? Aside from the charm and ability of Charteris's storytelling, the stories, particularly those published in the first half of the '30s, are full of energy and joie de vivre. With economic depression rampant throughout the period, the public at large seemed to want some escapism.

And Simon Templar's appeal was wide-ranging: he wasn't an upper-class hero like so many of the period. With no obvious background and no attachment to the Old School Tie, no friends in high places who could provide a get-out-of-jail-free card, the Saint was uniquely classless. Not unlike his creator.

Throughout Leslie's formative years, his heritage had been an issue. In his early days in Singapore, during his time at school, at Cambridge University or even just in everyday life, he couldn't avoid the fact that for many people his mixed parentage was a problem. He would later tell a story of how he was chased up the road by a stick-waving typical

English gent who took offence to his daughter being escorted around town by a foreigner.

Like the Saint, he was an outsider. And although he had spent a significant portion of his formative years in England, he couldn't settle.

As a young boy he had read of an America "peopled largely by Indians, and characters in fringed buckskin jackets who fought nobly against them. I spent a great deal of time day-dreaming about a visit to this prodigious and exciting country."[8]

It was time to realise this wish. Charteris and his first wife, Pauline, whom he'd met in London when they were both teenagers and married in 1931, set sail for the States in late 1932; the Saint had already made his debut in America courtesy of the publisher Doubleday. Charteris and his wife found a New York still experiencing the tail end of Prohibition, and times were tough at first. Despite sales to *The American Magazine* and others, it wasn't until a chance meeting with writer turned Hollywood executive Bartlett McCormack in their favourite speakeasy that Charteris's career stepped up a gear.

Soon Charteris was in Hollywood, working on what would become the 1933 movie *Midnight Club*. However, Hollywood's treatment of writers wasn't to Charteris's taste, and he began to yearn for home. Within a few months, he returned to the UK and began writing more Saint stories for Monty Haydon and Bill McElroy.

He also rewrote a story he'd sketched out whilst in the States, a version of which had been published in *The American Magazine* in September 1934. This new novel, *The Saint in New York*, published in 1935, was a significant advance for the Saint and Leslie Charteris. Gone were the high jinks and the badinage. The youthful exuberance evident in the Saint's early adventures had evolved into something a little darker, a little more hard-boiled. It was the next stage in development for the author and his creation, and readers loved it. It became a bestseller on both sides of the Atlantic.

Having spent his formative years in places as far apart as Singapore and England, with substantial travel in between, it should be no surprise that Leslie had a serious case of wanderlust. With a bestseller under his belt, he now had the means to see more of the world.

Nineteen thirty-six found him in Tenerife, researching another Saint adventure alongside translating the biography of Juan Belmonte, a well-known Spanish matador. Estranged for several months, Leslie and Pauline divorced in 1937. The following year, Leslie married an American, Barbara Meyer, who'd accompanied him to Tenerife. In early 1938, Charteris and his new bride set off in a trailer of his own design and spent eighteen months travelling round America and Canada.

The Saint in New York had reminded Hollywood of Charteris's talents, and film rights to the novel were sold prior to publication in 1935. Although the proposed 1935 film production was rejected by the Hays Office for its violent content, RKO's eventual 1938 production persuaded Charteris to try his luck once more in Hollywood.

New opportunities had opened up, and throughout the 1940s the Saint appeared not only in books and movies but in a newspaper strip, a comic-book series, and on radio.

Anyone wishing to adapt the character in any medium found a stern taskmaster in Charteris. He was never completely satisfied, nor was he shy of showing his displeasure. He did, however, ensure that copyright in any Saint adventure belonged to him, even if scripted by another writer—a contractual obligation that he was to insist on throughout his career.

Charteris was soon spread thin, overseeing movies, comics, newspapers, and radio versions of his creation, and this, along with his self-proclaimed laziness, meant that Saint books were becoming fewer and further between. However, he still enjoyed his creation: in 1941 he indulged himself in a spot of fun by playing the Saint—complete with monocle and moustache—in a photo story in *Life* magazine.

In July 1944, he started collaborating under a pseudonym on Sherlock Holmes radio scripts, subsequently writing more adventures for Holmes than Conan Doyle. Not all his ventures were successful—a screenplay he was hired to write for Deanna Durbin, "Lady on a Train," took him a year and ultimately bore little resemblance to the finished film. In the mid-1940s, Charteris successfully sued RKO Pictures for unfair competition after they launched a new series of films starring George Sanders as a debonair crime fighter known as the Falcon. But he kept faith with his original character, and the Saint novels continued to adapt to the times. The transatlantic Saint evolved into something of a private operator, working for the mysterious Hamilton and becoming, not unlike his creator, a world traveller, finding that adventure would seek him out.

"I have never been able to see why a fictional character should not grow up, mature, and develop, the same as anyone else. The same, if you like, as his biographer. The only adequate reason is that—so far as I know—no other fictional character in modern times has survived a sufficient number of years for these changes to be clearly observable. I must confess that a lot of my own selfish pleasure in the Saint has been in watching him grow up."[9]

Charteris maintained his love of travel and was soon to be found sailing round the West Indies with his good friend Gregory Peck. His forays abroad gave him even more material, and he began to write true-crime articles, as well as an occasional column in *Gourmet* magazine.

By the early '50s, Charteris himself was feeling strained. He'd divorced his second wife in 1943 and got together with a New York radio and nightclub singer called Betty Bryant Borst, whom he married in late 1943. That relationship had fallen apart acrimoniously towards the end of the decade, and he roamed the globe restlessly, rarely in one place for longer than a couple of months. He continued to maintain a firm grip on the exploitation of the Saint in various media but was writing little himself. The Saint had become an industry, and Charteris couldn't keep up. He began thinking seriously about an early retirement.

Then in 1951 he met a young actress called Audrey Long when they became next-door neighbours in Hollywood. Within a year they had married, a union that was to last the rest of Leslie's life.

He attacked life with a new vitality. They travelled—Nassau was a favoured escape spot—and he wrote. He struck an agreement with *The New York Herald Tribune* for a Saint comic strip, which would appear daily and be written by Charteris himself. The strip ran for thirteen years, with Charteris sending in his handwritten story lines from wherever he happened to be, relying on mail services around the world to continue the Saint's adventures. New Saint books began to appear, and Charteris reached a height of productivity not seen since his days as a struggling author trying to establish himself. As Leslie and Audrey travelled, so did the Saint, visiting locations just after his creator had been there.

By 1953 the Saint had already enjoyed twenty-five years of success, and *The Saint Detective Magazine* was launched. Charteris had become adept at exploiting his creation to the full, mixing new stories with repackaged older stories, sometimes rewritten, sometimes mixed up in "new" anthologies, sometimes adapted from radio scripts previously written by other writers.

Charteris had been approached several times over the years for television rights in the Saint and had expended much time and effort during the 1950s trying to get the Saint on TV, even going so far as to write sample scripts himself, but it wasn't to be. He finally agreed a deal in autumn 1961 with English film producers Robert S. Baker and Monty Berman. The first episode of *The Saint* television series, starring Roger Moore, went into production in June 1962. The series was an immediate success, though Charteris himself had his reservations. It reached second place in the ratings, but he commented that "in that distinction it was topped by wrestling, which only suggested to me that the competition may not have been so hot; but producers are generally cast in a less modest mould." He resented the implication that the TV series had finally made a success of the Saint after twenty-five years of literary obscurity.

As long as the series lasted, Charteris was not shy about voicing his criticisms both in public and in a constant stream of memos to the producers. "Regular followers of the Saint saga . . . must have noticed that I am almost incapable of simply writing a story and shutting up."[10] Nor was he shy about exploiting this new market by agreeing to a series of tie-in novelisations ghosted by other writers, which he would then rewrite before publication.

Charteris mellowed as the series developed and found elements to praise too. He developed a close friendship with producer Robert S. Baker, which would last until Charteris's death.

In the early '60s, on one of their frequent trips to England, Leslie and Audrey bought a house in Surrey, which became their permanent base. He explored the possibility of a Saint musical and began writing some of it himself.

Charteris no longer needed to work. Now in his sixties, he supervised the Saint from a distance whilst continuing to travel and indulge himself. He and Audrey made seasonal excursions to Ireland and the south of France, where they had residences. He began to write poetry and devised a new universal sign language, Paleneo, based on notes and symbols he used in his diaries. Once Paleneo was released, he decided enough was enough and announced, again, his retirement. This time he meant it.

The Saint continued regardless—there was a long-running Swedish comic strip, and new novels with other writers doing the bulk of the work were complemented in the 1970s with Bob Baker's revival of the TV series, *Return of the Saint.*

Ill-health began to take its toll. By the early 1980s, although he continued a healthy correspondence with the outside world, Charteris felt unable to keep up with the collaborative Saint books and pulled the plug on them.

To entertain himself, Leslie took to "trying to beat the bookies in predicting the relative speed of horses," a hobby which resulted in several of his local betting shops refusing to take "predictions" from him, as he was too successful for their liking.

He still received requests to publish his work abroad but had become completely cynical about further attempts to revive the Saint. A new Saint magazine only lasted three issues, and two TV productions—*The Saint in Manhattan*, with Tom Selleck look-alike Andrew Clarke, and *The Saint*, with Simon Dutton—left him bitterly disappointed. "I fully expect this series to lay eggs everywhere . . . the only satisfaction I have is in looking at my bank balance."[11]

In the early 1990s, Hollywood producers Robert Evans and William J. Macdonald approached him and made a deal for the Saint to return to cinema screens. Charteris still took great care of the Saint's reputation and wrote an outline entitled *The Return of the Saint* in which an older Saint would meet the son he didn't know he had.

Much of his time in his last few years was taken up with the movie. Several scripts were submitted to him—each moving further and further away from his original concept—but the screenwriter from 1940s Hollywood was thoroughly disheartened by the Hollywood of the '90s: "There is still no plot, no real story, no characterisations, no personal interaction, nothing but endless frantic violence . . ." Besides, with producer Bill Macdonald hitting the headlines for the most un-Saintly reasons, he was to add, "How can Bill Macdonald concentrate on my Saint movie when he has Sharon Stone in his bed?"

The Crime Writers' Association of Great Britain presented Leslie with a Lifetime Achievement award in 1992 in a special ceremony at the

House of Lords. Never one for associations and awards, and although visibly unwell, Leslie accepted the award with grace and humour ("I am now only waiting to be carbon-dated," he joked). He suffered a slight stroke in his final weeks, which did not prevent him from dining out locally with family and friends, before he finally passed away at the age of eighty-five on 15 April 1993.

His death severed one of the final links with the classic thriller genre of the 1930s and 1940s, but he left behind a legacy of nearly one hundred books, countless short stories, and TV, film, radio, and comic-strip adaptations of his work which will endure for generations to come.

> *I was always sure that there was a solid place in escape literature for a rambunctious adventurer such as I dreamed up in my youth, who really believed in the old-fashioned romantic ideals and was prepared to lay everything on the line to bring them to life. A joyous exuberance that could not find its fulfilment in pinball machines and pot. I had what may now seem a mad desire to spread the belief that there were worse, and wickeder, nut cases than Don Quixote.*
>
> *Even now, half a century later, when I should be old enough to know better, I still cling to that belief. That there will always be a public for the old-style hero, who had a clear idea of justice, and a more than technical approach to love, and the ability to have some fun with his crusades.*[12]

---

1 *A Letter from the Saint*, 30 August 1946
2 "The Last Word," *The First Saint Omnibus*, Doubleday Crime Club, 1939
3 *The Straits Times*, 29 June 1958, page 9

4 Introduction by Charteris to the September 1980 paperback reprint of *Meet—the Tiger!* (Charter), the last ever print edition.
5 *The Saint: A Complete History*, by Burl Barer (McFarland, 1993)
6 PR material from the 1970s series *Return of the Saint*
7 From "Return of the Saint: Comprehensive Information" issued to help publicise the 1970s TV show
8 *A Letter from the Saint*, 26 July 1946
9 Introduction to "The Million Pound Day," in *The First Saint Omnibus*
10 *A Letter from the Saint*, 12 April 1946
11 Letter from LC to sometime Saint collaborator Peter Bloxsom, 2 August 1989
12 Introduction by Charteris to the September 1980 paperback reprint of *Meet—the Tiger!* (Charter).

WATCH FOR THE SIGN

OF THE SAINT!

THE SAINT CLUB

*And so, my friends, dear bookworms, most noble fellow
drinkers, frustrated burglars, affronted policemen, upright
citizens with furled umbrellas and secret buccaneering
dreams that seems to be very nearly all for now. It has been
nice having you with us, and we hope you will come again,
not once, but many times.*

*Only because of our great love for you, we would like
to take this parting opportunity of mentioning one small
matter which we have very much at heart . . .*

—*Leslie Charteris,* The First Saint Omnibus *(1939)*

Leslie Charteris founded The Saint Club in 1936 with the aim of
providing a constructive fanbase for Saint devotees. Before the War, it
donated profits to a London hospital where, for several years, a Saint
ward was maintained. With the nationalisation of hospitals, profits
were, for many years, donated to the Arbour Youth Centre in Stepney,
London.

In the twenty-first century, we've carried on this tradition but have
also donated to the Red Cross and a number of different children's
charities.

The club acts as a focal point for anyone interested in the adventures of Leslie Charteris and the work of Simon Templar, and offers merchandise that includes DVDs of the old TV series and various Saint-related publications, through to its own exclusive range of notepaper, pin badges, and polo shirts. All profits are donated to charity. The club also maintains two popular websites and supports many more Saint-related sites.

After Leslie Charteris's death, the club recruited three new vice-presidents—Roger Moore, Ian Ogilvy, and Simon Dutton have all pledged their support, whilst Audrey and Patricia Charteris have been retained as Saints-in-Chief. But some things do not change, for the back of the membership card still mischievously proclaims that . . .

The bearer of this card is probably a person of hideous antecedents and low moral character, and upon apprehension for any cause should be immediately released in order to save other prisoners from contamination.

To join . . .

Membership costs £3.50 (or US$7) per year, or £30 (US$60) for life. Find us online at www.lesliecharteris.com for full details.